Yellow Birds

Yellow Birds

KAREN GREEN

TORONTO, 2024

RE:BOOKS

www.rebooks.ca

Published in Canada by RE:BOOKS

RE:BOOKS
Brookfield Place
181 Bay Street, Suite 1800
Toronto, Ontario
M5J 2T9
Canada
www.rebooks.ca

First RE:BOOKS Edition: March 2024
ISBN: 978-1-998206-14-8
eBook ISBN: 978-1-998206-15-5

Printed and bound in Canada.
1 3 5 7 9 10 8 6 4 2

Cover design by Chloe Faith Robinson and Jordan Lunn
Typeset by Karl Hunt

To Jen, for letting me tag along
when the bus came by.

ON A REMOTE hillside in a mountainous region of Denmark, a herd of 300 reindeer was struck by a lightning bolt. They died instantly. Up through the hooves of one animal and straight into the next, the lightning didn't discriminate; the greatest of the bucks and the slightest of the yearlings fell where they stood. This remarkable event, the scientists said, as they stood among the carcasses, occurred when the electric current hit the plateau the pack was standing on, then traveled up the many routes provided by 300 animals, each with four feet planted firmly on the ground, clustered together for warmth and safety. The official cause of the beasts' death was cardiac arrest. Their only hope, the scientists said, would have been to scatter when the storm hit; to have found refuge in separate rocky coves, away from their pack. But that, they agreed, is not the usual behaviour for most animals. The usual behaviour is to huddle together: to look for warmth and protection in each other.

To take our chances when the thunder rolls in, and hope that the lightning will simply strike elsewhere.

PART I

THE YELLOW BIRDS

1

IN THE END, I chose Kait. The important thing was that it was spelled with an "i," not that it would matter, since we never had much of a reason to write our names down. And if anybody was going to write to me, they would no doubt spell it "Kate," the conventional way, with an e. But every time I told somebody that my name was Kait, I could picture the word in a pretty scroll just above my head; feminine and lilting and original, with an i; not hard and squared off and ordinary. Kait.

I could have gone with anything: Aura or Aurora or something even more rainbow, like Pixie or Atlas or Love or Sunshine. Or Rainbow. Most people's rainbow name sounded like it was inspired by an acid trip or a weather report, but I didn't want a crazy hippie name. Just a name. A new name. And really, I didn't even know I wanted a new name until I said it. I was in Eugene, Oregon, which is probably the rainbow name capital of the world.

I had made it to Eugene after a four-day stretch of travel with a couple from North Carolina named, remarkably, Nick and Nicole, and who each seemed wonderful on their own and did nothing but argue and harp at each other when they were together. And there was nowhere to be but together as we drove through the vast Midwest and over the Rockies for four days, in a white Honda Civic covered in Open Road stickers and dead bugs. My only reprieve was when we stopped at night to camp and I could unroll my sleeping bag as far from the unhappy couple as possible.

My first show that summer had been with schoolmates a couple of weeks earlier. We were only going to be gone five days but I had overstuffed my backpack, unsure of what I should wear, what I would need or with whom I might end up. Getting out of the car in Pine Knob, Michigan and walking through the Field, which is what the parking lots were called when the Yellow Birds took over, I was instantly happy. And overwhelmed. Trying to get my bearings, I stood and watched as the most interesting and vibrant looking people I had ever seen rolled by in a constant technicolor stream of tie dye and patchwork. A parade of people with long skirts, long hair, rainbow dreads falling out of crocheted tams, bare feet, and scraggly dogs on leashes. There were normal looking people too, in jeans and crisp t-shirts, but I barely glanced at them, enthralled by the freaks and hippies that seemed so grounded and comfortable they must have grown straight out of the earth they were standing on. I looked down at the band t-shirt, jean shorts, and Birkenstocks I had on, and felt like I was wearing someone else's clothes. I rubbed the scar that marked the back of my left arm; a habit since I had acquired it in a car accident the year before. My hair, in a neat and practical ponytail to keep the heat of it off my neck, made me feel juvenile and unstylish. I pulled the elastic and shook out my waves, heat be damned.

I explored the Field before the show and I tried to take it all in, this impossible spectacle of sights and sounds and smells. We made it to Main Street, which is what the thoroughfare of vendors that set up in the Field was called. Main Street was where you went to buy food and all the things people were selling—t-shirts and jewellery and clothing and art and purses and lyric books and posters and kites and—it was like the heart of a farmer's market or international bazaar, and it radiated out in makeshift arteries from there. You could find some of the goods in the rows further back, but Main Street was where the most serious set up remained.

Music came from everywhere; from guitars, from speakers, from people singing. Every vehicle or stand or shop set up in the Field has its own micro-environment, with goods and people and smells and a unique soundtrack of activity, but linked together they created a harmonious ecosystem. It was a hive of constant sensory engagment but it avoided being chaotic, as each person here seemed to understand exactly where the thin boundary between order and anarchy existed. One could sustain this unconventional community; make it flourish, and one could make it disappear quickly under the nearby hand of authority.

In modern philosophy, there's an idea that temporary autonomous zones can exist in society; that likeminded people can establish a community void of conventional control or structure but that remains intentional nonetheless. It's a place where the rules we're used to don't apply; where thousands of freaks can land all at once, move in, take over, set up shops, set up homes, drink and smoke and dance and fuck and live anywhere within the confines of that space and the agreed upon parameters of that micro society. It's a place where freedom is limited only by imagination and creativity and the complete lack of permanence, because as soon as you try to coax it into something solid, something immovable, it can't exist. And it's where I wanted to be for as long as it could last.

That first night, the audience seemed to know the music was about to begin even before the bright lights of the concert bowl went down. There was a tiny, brief silence; a wave of anticipation that rippled through the stands—and then everything changed. Lights out, plunging 26,000 screaming Yellow Birds into a momentary darkness somehow made even more impenetratable by the roar of the audience. Soon, spotlights brightened the stage, illuminating the drumkit, the guitar stands, the keyboard, moving across the stadium over hands raised above heads. And then the lights returned to the front as the five members of the Open Road walked onto the stage, walked to their instruments, and paused.

"Welcome home," said lead singer Ernest, strumming the first notes on his guitar. I threw my arms in the air as the crowd erupted again.

I wanted the perfect impermanence of Open Road Tour for as long as I could have it. When the trip to see three shows in five days was over, I said goodbye to my school chums and went on to Eugene with the North Carolinian squabblers.

Birds weren't just fans of the Open Road; they were the ambassadors, the insiders. I was just beginning to learn the secret language, the hidden code the Yellow Birds all seemed to share, but it didn't take long to figure out that getting to shows, and helping other Birds get to the shows, was part of that code. I would not have considered myself a Yellow Bird only weeks earlier but in my desire to stay on Open Road Tour, to only move forward, I learned enough of the language to pass for one. And the longer I stayed on Tour, the more fluent I became.

Pulling into Eugene, Oregon, as Nick and Nicole argued over whether or not there was time for a Target grocery run, the only words I could say were *Get me out of here.*

The West Coast leg of summer Tour was about to begin and I was thousands of miles from where I began without a plan, a ride, or even a place to drop my small bundle of belongings. I was starting to think I should have just gone home, while home still seemed like an option for me.

And then I crossed paths with Skate and Easy and Vivi and I hoped they were my answer, and then I met Eartha, and that was that.

"Aren't you new and shiny," said Eartha, in the way that I would come to know as affectionate. "I'm Eartha."

"I'm Kait," I said. And then I was.

This crew called their van Big Blue Bertha, and as far as I could tell, the five people in it had been friends for a long time and travelling together the entirety of summer Tour, criss-crossing the country as I had. And like me, they were Canadian, though all five of them were from the West Coast; British Colombia and Alberta. They had road-tripped out to Vermont to start Tour for the very first Open Road shows of the season, but according to Easy, the van's tall, lanky owner and seemingly defacto leader of the crew, Bertha had just made her last cross-country trek.

"She won't be doing that again," he said, tucking his long blond hair behind his ear, as I sat outside the van that afternoon for the first time. "She's a good Bird, but she's an old Bird." Vivi, his girlfriend, was the van's resident goddess: tall, slim, and graceful, with gorgeous long ringletted locks the colour of Swiss chocolate, and eyes to match. It would be easy to hate Vivi for her perfection if she hadn't also been such a sweet, welcoming person. Vivi sat atop the blankets on the ground, leaning against Easy's chair. Her eyes were closed as she angled her head against his leg, up towards the sun. Easy twirled a ringlet lazily around his finger.

"She's a shitbird who's falling apart," said Skate.

"Why don't you hop right on that board of yours and freeload your way into someone else's van," said Easy, pointing to what I gathered was the four-wheeled source of Skate's nickname.

"Nah, he can't," said a girl who was introduced to me with the unexpected moniker of JuJube. "There's nobody left on Tour that he hasn't slept with, owes money to, or both. Except her." JuJube motioned towards me.

"Don't bother, Skate," I said, "I need a ride too."

Everybody sitting around the circle laughed and I expected that these barbs were well-rehearsed and trod out often.

Skate had a baby face anchored by a slightly crooked smile and eyes that were dark shining pools made even darker under the shade of the baseball cap he wore. He was flirtatious and quick-witted and I got the feeling these traits were a definite asset on Tour. Skate had been the one to invite me into the company of Bertha's crew; he had been sitting in one of the folding chairs outside the van and I had stopped to ask him if he had a line on a ticket to the show that night. He said he didn't, but that he thought a friend of his would; she'd be back soon, I was welcome to wait. I sat in another of the folding chairs, Skate passed me a beer, and we started chatting.

Easy and Vivi showed up next, then JuJube, then Eartha, who did in fact, have a line on a ticket. She was the line, and the extra ticket was hers, a fluke, a mistake in an order she had placed months earlier. I was welcome to it at face value. I loved Eartha immediately, I couldn't help it. She was familiar and a bit gruff and funny and I just wanted to be around her.

"There's just one condition to the sale of this ticket," she said, holding it out, but not releasing it to me.

"What?" I asked, wondering if I had misjudged her and she was going make some sketchy request like procuring mushrooms for her or something.

"I can't let you go into the show alone. You gotta come with me."

"How do you know I'm alone?"

Eartha made a face and pressed the ticket into my hand.

"You'd have to be alone or desperate to spend all afternoon with these fools."

I didn't tell her that for the first time in a long time, I finally felt neither of those things.

"We've got room if you need a place to crash," Skate said, "It's supposed to rain tonight." He was back from the show already, comfortably sprawled in a camping chair outside of Bertha, drinking a beer as throngs of people walked by. Eartha was inside the van, rummaging for something or perhaps swapping sweaty show clothes for less sweaty after-show clothes. Our breezy comeraderie had continued throughout the concert and the walk back through the Field. I had been hoping for the invitation Skate extended, hoping I wouldn't have to go find Nick and Nicole and put up with one more night of their bickering before sleeping in a leaky tent, but I didn't want to seem like an interloper angling for a place to stay.

"Um," I said, shifting the patchwork satchel I had bought in Indiana from one shoulder to the other, "That's okay, I might I have a place I can go."

"Yep," said Eartha, emerging from the van, "You do. I just made you one." I peeked inside and counted six bedrolls spread out in the open area behind the two bench seats; pillows and blankets and sleeping bags were piled to the side of the makeshift mattress.

When the evening's laughter, drinking, and talking finally died down and the Field drifted into hushed tones, we retreated into the van for the night. The space in Bertha was tight but not cramped; there was just enough room for all six of us, arranged like matchsticks in a great steel box. I was laying between Eartha and Skate. Skate leaned over and kissed me on my cheek.

"Goodnight, Kaity-cat," he said, and I wondered if he was going try to put the moves on me, but his breath changed almost immediately into the deep, quiet intake of sleep.

I woke up some time later. A misty rain was blowing into Bertha and I was freezing. In the ambient light from the cloud-filled sky, I looked around me. Eartha was turned towards the back of the van, the top of her head and all that glorious hair the only part of her I could make out. On the other side of me, Skate lay on his back, an arm slung over his eyes. He had my blanket pulled over him as well, one of the reasons I must have woken up so cold. JuJube wasn't next to Skate, but I saw a shape laying on the bench that ran along the driver's side of the van and assumed she had found another perch for the night. Easy was curled around Vivi towards the front of the van. She shifted slightly and Easy adjusted his arm around her. Vivi murmered something and settled further into him.

I carefully got up from my nest and crawled to the open side door. The Field was calm and I guessed we were a couple of hours away from sunrise. Tents rippled in the breeze that was carrying the mist right into Bertha. I closed my eyes and inhaled. Then quietly as I could, I pulled the side door closed on the deep, cool night.

2

AS SOON AS we opened Bertha's doors, the Arizona heat pummeled us. There would be no relief from the stifling air inside the vehicle, though at the very least, now that we were parked we could all spread out and stop transferring our heat to one another as we had in the close quarters of the van.

We had been travelling together for a month and I had quickly and comfortably established a natural place within the family. I made coffee on the Coleman stove in the mornings, helped set up camp each time we stopped, and rolled the best cigarettes, according to Easy. Eartha had brought me on as partner in her travelling hair wrap business, and Skate was trying to teach me how to do an Ollie, the result of which was a number of bruises and an endless supply of laughter. Vivi and Easy mostly did their own thing, coming and going from Bertha during the shows, meeting up with friends everywhere we went. JuJube was a trip. She believed in fairies, carried crystals for strength and healing (*and spells,* I once suggested to Eartha), and was a habitual thief.

I surveyed our surroundings in the Field, where we would stay for the two nights of the Tempe shows. We were in a distant corner of a secondary lot, as far as we could possibly have been from the heat's repreive of the river or the shade. The ground was hard packed and dusty, marked by the occasional patch of scrub grass, and I began to grumble about the temperature as soon as we opened Bertha's doors.

Travelling in Bertha was fun and I loved my crew, but I was annoyed by the steep incline, or lack of privacy, or whatever other inconvenience came along with the cheap real estate we always seemed to inhabit, thanks to constantly making it to the Field so much later than other Birds. Easy seemed never to care about any of this. At least, I never heard him complain. I believed he was too dumb or careless to be bothered by our parking situation, but as soon as I voiced my criticism, JuJube snapped at me.

"Do you think that's what any of us want to hear after being in this van for eight hours? Do you think that's what Easy wants to hear after driving for eight hours? Why don't you fucking contribute something besides negativity, *Kait.*" She practically sneered my name, and it shot a pang of uneasiness through me.

"I would contribute, *JuJube,*" I sneered back, "but you'll have to open your backpack first so I can get all my shit back." I don't know what had set me off so much that made me challenge her, but I normally wouldn't have said anything. I was a little afraid of JuJube.

Surprisingly, it was Easy who stepped between us.

"Ladies," he said, putting a lanky arm around each of us, "No fighting in the family van. Jube's right, I definitely don't want to hear it after driving for eight hours, and Kait's right—it's as hot as hell's tits here. But you know what, my sweet soul sisters? You guys all seem pretty content to let me handle every aspect of transportation, and I get you everywhere you want to be, safe and sound. So why don't both of you shut up and start unpacking the van—I want to take a nap in here with my girl. And," he added, with a wry smile, "if you can't get along, you can walk to the next show." He kissed JuJube on the cheek, then he did the same to me, unwrapped his arms from around our shoulders and gave us a push away from him. JuJube glared at me, but I silently vowed to keep my mouth shut about our accommodations for the entire rest of the time I travelled in Bertha. I felt a little sheepish that I had underestimated Easy's sense of self-awareness and his concern for us.

Later that night, I noticed that the jar of homemade chamomile moisturizer I had bought from a vendor at the Ann Arbor show was missing from my bag. And JuJube smelled like a freshly brewed cup of tea.

People connected quickly on Road tour, partly out of need and partly out of adventure. The travelling community relied on itself, and the people within the community, for everything. Each stop on Tour became a mini city with trade and commerce, housing, healthcare, camaraderie, and entertainment. We had a common goal, and I guess, a common religion: the music. It meant that we also had a necessary and almost instant belief in each other. But make the mistake of allowing blind trust and the curtain would be pulled back quickly. An easy mark was an easy mark, no matter where you were, but especially somewhere the conventional rules seemed to not apply. I had lost my innocence—along with several pieces of my scant wardrobe and an inflated portion of gas money from my purse—early enough to be open-minded, but careful.

The community was also, for almost everybody that stayed on Tour for more than a stop or two, a means of escape from something.

One night in Utah, after the Compton Terrace shows in Tempe, me and Eartha lay on the grass on the top of a hill outside the stadium, looking up at the stars and talking about Road Tour as refuge. We had gotten in to the show that night; scored tickets for cheap after the first set had already begun, and afterwards had climbed away from the exuberant, frenetic energy of the Field to bask in the vibe of the what we had just seen for a little while longer.

It was hot and the Pilgrims, a non-sanctioned but ubiquitous group led by a fairly enigmatic, long-haired dude named Steve, were out in full force. I had only seen Steve a few times, standing next to the school bus they based their camp around on Tour. The Pilgrims offered first aid to the injured, and born-again prayer services to the desperate (or just really high) masses, and they had been busy in the heat. We saw lots of people walking around with "Holy Water," bottles that Pilgrims handed out that had their own labels printed on them. On one side of the label was always a bible verse:

For false messiahs and false prophets will appear and perform great signs and wonders to deceive, if possible, even the elect. – Matthew 24:24

And on the other, a line from an Open Road song.

Sweet mama, sweet mama, where'd you go?
Sweet mama, sweet mama don't you know?
You can't run from the devil or the sun,
Or the pain of the long, long ago. – Help Comes Along, The Open Road

The two passages seemed random and disconnected to me, sometimes in total opposition of one another, and I could never tell if the Pilgrims thought of the Open Road as allies or enemies, or if the Yellow Birds were the sinners or the saved.

Although I never sought out Pilgrims for water or prayer, I always picked up any discarded bottles I found, just to read the passages.

"You'd think they could find a more sustainable way to spread their message," Eartha said as I deposited a bottle into a garbage bin. It had said that the "lord washed the filth from the daughters of Jerusalem" (*Isaiah 4:4*), and that "the love you gave made me cry for a god I had never met" (*Looking Up, The Open Road*). Sometimes I would read the passages and think that a member of the uninitiated (in gospel and/or The Open Road) might not be able to tell which was which.

That night in Utah, the Road had closed the show with "Looking Up," a song both Eartha and I loved. It was a beautiful, sad love song that opened quietly and calmly and built to a crescendo of lead singer Ernest Winter's warbling vocals and vibrating guitar chords until it felt like the words and music crashed straight into my heart and there was nothing left to do but allow the longing and despair wash over us. There was no redemption to be found in the song, and for that, we were besotted, grateful. That particular brand of celebrated misery felt so good. So we headed to the hill, wanting to bask in it alone, the only two people out of the tens of thousands gathered below who understood just how important that feeling, that truth, was.

As we lay in reverie, we allowed what we liked to refer to as "The Existential Dread" to seep into our conversation, which felt perfectly self-indulgent for the occasion.

"This is the Island of Misfit Toys, Kait," Eartha said, stretching an arm out above her head on the grass. "How much did you truly relate to the people back home? How fucked up was your home life? Did you enjoy high school?" she said.

Her armpit, with its forest of hair growth, was nearly in my face. I shifted delicately, but Eartha didn't seem to care about my slight retreat if she had even noticed it. Shaving wasn't a priority on tour. It was too hard to keep up with, and forgoing the effort was easily justified as a relic of a beauty myth propagated by a patriarchal society that we didn't agree with. Freedom and rebellion symbolized in every hairy pit.

"Nobody enjoys high school, Eartha."

Eartha turned onto her side, rested her head on her arm as I continued gazing up at the stars.

"No, dude, seriously, some people truly love high school. It's the best time of their life. They get to be young and golden and either have no worries or are just too stupid to realize what they are," Eartha said. "They go home to perfect families, and hey, yippee for them, but they have no clue, or don't want to know, that there is more to life than the right jeans, the right car, the right friends, the right address. We're here, dude. Those people are now working at the same exclusive summer camp they attended every year since they were seven and their parents got rid of them for July so they could go to Europe. We can't be that. That's not us."

Well, that wasn't me, anyway. The years I had just left behind had been marked by growing chaos. At home, I had to eventually accept that my sister and I wouldn't be able to depend on our mother to take care of things like buying groceries, let alone sign us up for some exclusive extra-curricular activity. And then came the accident and that became my identity. The girl in the car. I took trips to the physiotherapist, not to Europe.

But Eartha, she was as upper-middle class as a girl could get. She had the right jeans, the right car, the right address—but the right friends had always eluded her. The golden girls at her high school rejected her outright; wanted nothing to do with her. Eartha was not delicate, and she was fiercely smart: two things that were not necessarily celebrated in the exclusive neighbourhood she grew up in. Eartha's father had been a doctor, but died suddenly when she was fourteen. Her mother came from old money, and along with her husband's estate, managed a very comfortable life for Eartha as a young widow. Eartha made it through high school and was about to go off on an all-expenses paid four-year sojourn at university, when a boy walked into a poetry reading Eartha was attending, and blew her mind with his words and his face.

Turned out he was a Yellow Bird, and he introduced Eartha to the world of the Open Road. She deferred university, suffered through her mother's wailing disappointment, and hit Tour with her new boyfriend. Eartha quickly came to realize that the boyfriend was a pretentious dick, but Tour stuck. She had found her people, her place. She missed her deferral window for university, then missed it again the next year. She had her own apartment in Vancouver now that I suspected her mother paid the rent for, since Eartha only worked occasionally at a used bookstore called Dog Eared when she was in town. I can always apply again, Eartha had told me. But I wondered if Eartha realized that she benefitted from her privileged background. She had way more choices and opportunities—not to mention money—than most people did. But we all see the world through our own little windows, even in a place like this, I thought. Still, I loved Eartha fiercely, and felt mostly like an equal out here.

"Except, it's kind of us," I said.

"Well—no, it's . . . what do you mean?"

Eartha had looked at me, and though I hoped that she had acknowledged a sliver of that truth in herself, I also didn't really feel like challenging someone who was fast becoming a person I needed—and wanted—to depend on.

"Isn't this just a bit like our own exclusive summer camp that we keep coming back to?" I asked. "It's just, we sing different campfire songs, and we're allowed to swim naked in the lake. And sleeping with the counsellors is encouraged."

We burst out laughing.

"No, no, it totally is, I guess," Eartha said, once we had calmed down and were back to stargazing. "And I suppose everybody has trauma or hardship in their life, but you have to admit, there is a special blend out here. Why can't any of us just deal with society?" We were both leaning back on our arms now, raising our bodies as the conversation went on.

"Why would we want to? And besides, this *is* society. A better society," I insisted. "We may be nomadic and seem a little lost to people, but we've stripped away all the nonsense here. What's the rush to get back to a conventional life? What's the rush to go back and become good little corporate citizens, and lose our opportunity to truly pursue the things that matter to us without worrying about 'the game?'"

Fragmented thoughts stacked on top of each other jumped through my head at that moment: home, my mother, the accident, real life. I swallowed hard. *Please don't take this away from me yet.*

"Yes, Kait, let's keep pursuing things that matter, like perfecting our recipe for the very best veggie burrito one can possibly make on a Coleman stove."

"Eartha, that's a very important goal for me right now, and I think it's unkind of you to belittle my endeavours." Eartha stared at me hard for a second, and then we had both collapsed back on the grass, unable to control ourselves.

The next day, Skate and I were walking through the Field when we passed a girl handing a flyer to some Birds waiting in line at a food stall.

"Everybody's welcome," she said, before she reached into the bag she was carrying and handed them water bottles. Ah, she was a Pilgrim. I hadn't seen her around before. Maybe a new recruit.

"Shalom," she said with a little bow before she walked away from the grilled cheese vendors. She looked right at Skate and started her approach.

"Yeah no thanks," he said, heading her off. She gave a little dip of her head and changed course slightly, confident, I was sure, that she would find someone else to try to convert soon enough.

"Shalom," she said again as she passed by us.

"Clowns," said Skate. We walked a little bit more and then he asked if it bothered me that the Pilgrims pillaged so much from Judaism to do their own weird thing.

"Should it? Just because I'm Jewish?" I asked. Maybe it was the proximity to Mexico, but the vendors on Main Street seemed overpopulated with imports from across the border. Bags and clothing embroidered with traditional patterns; woven sarapes and blankets—all beautiful, all emblematic of somebody else's customs.

"If a Pilgrim calling himself Levi bothers me, then this should too, right?" I gestured at the colourful prayer flags hanging from a tented stall. They were similar to a string of flags hanging in Big Blue Bertha. Vivi had hung them long before I was travelling in the van, and they were pretty. Part decoration, part totem to guard against trouble on the road, which, I greatly suspected, was not their intended use.

"Yeah, yeah, for sure," said Skate, "but like, doesn't it bother you to see people running around with red string on their wrist, as though they have a right to an ancient practice just because a singer told them about it?"

"Nope. I'm a not a Kabbalist. I'm barely a Jew as far as practicing a religion goes. As long as the people wearing the red strings aren't making fun of my 'Jew nose,' or telling somebody they got a good deal on Main Street because they 'Jewed her down,' have at it. I don't need to police everybody."

I stopped and touched one of the pretty turquoise necklaces hanging in the vendor's stall in front of us. I turned to Skate. "You know who made my life in elementary school hell? The people that made fun of me on the bus ride to school every day, called me Beaker, told me I was ugly? It was these two brothers, Jonah and Elliot Winkler. They were Jewish. Eventually, I tried to hide from the bus and walk all the way to school so they couldn't do it. So no, I don't care if somebody wears a red string or calls himself Moses and says he can part the sea. A good person is a good person and a shit person is a shit person."

"Ain't that the truth," said Skate, stepping on the toe of his board so it flipped up into his hand. "And Kait?"

"Yeah?"

"You have the nose of a goddam Greek goddess."

"Skate," I warned, "I can't steal a face from a culture I don't belong to. I have the nose of a goddam Jewish princess. And a proud one at that."

"Fuck those Winkler brothers."

I scrunched up my big royal Jewish nose. "Never."

I had a great-aunt that everybody called Bunny, sometimes Bun for short. Aunt Bunny was really Aunt Betty, but the only people who called her that were people who didn't know her. The story goes that her youngest sister, my Aunt Trix, couldn't pronounce Betty's name and it was so cute hearing her call her sister, Bunny, in that little baby voice. Soon, everyone called her Bunny. They were the two youngest of five sisters. Going up the ladder was Aunt Rachel next, but everybody called her Wittie, or Wit. Even her nickname had a nickname. Aunt Wittie was my favourite; everybody's favourite. She had a deep, gruff, and generous laugh and she always carried paper rolls dotted with candy buttons in her purse for all of us kids when we were little. Wittie used to tease her sisters all the time, but had a knack for not being mean about it. When Aunt Trix divorced Uncle Rob and dated one man after another, Aunt Wittie used to tell her to put flypaper on her coat, and maybe this one would stick. If anybody else had said something like that to Aunt Trix, she would have left the room in a huff, but Aunt Wit's good nature shone through and allowed people to laugh at themselves. Maybe that's where she got her nickname from, though I had never heard anybody say that.

My grandmother, Ellie, short for Eleanor, was next, then the oldest sister, Aunt Evelyn. She was always Evelyn, no diminutives—never Eve or Evie or Lyn. It didn't make any sense to me, given her sisters' pet names, but she was always Evelyn. Aunt Evelyn was married to Uncle Pricey. It took me years to figure out that that wasn't his real name, that Price was their last name. I didn't know what his real first name was until he was referred to by it at his funeral. Samuel. My great aunts and great uncles all seemed to have had friends with crazy nicknames, too: Dinty (after a comic book character he resembled), Peach (after the coloring of her complexion or the shape of her derriere, depending on who was telling the story), Net (short for Annette), Shank (a butcher), Gimmie (for Gimlet, his drink of choice), and his wife, Shook (no idea where that one came from).

"Your family sounds insane," Eartha said when I told her the story of the nicknames among my people. She was wrapping my hair in embroidery thread, so I had little rainbow snake growing longer as Eartha worked, from the top of my head to the middle of my back. The easiest way for us to make money on Tour was to set up a quilt and two stools in front of the van and offer hair wraps to people walking through the Field. First we would make a thin braid starting at the crown of the head, then we would wind different colors of embroidery thread around the braid, leaving a little rope hanging down. Kind of the Yellow Bird equivalent of getting cornrows at a resort in the Caribbean.

We charged a dollar per inch of hair, with a five dollar minimum, but most of the Birds and even the Twinkies had really long hair. On a good day, we could make about two hundred dollars each. Eartha was better at it than me, and fast, fast, fast, but what she did in volume, I compensated for in up-selling. People didn't know how long their hair was. "So, your hair is about eighteen inches long, don't you think?" Even if it wasn't, lots of girls took my estimate as a high source of flattery. "Maybe even twenty inches," they would counter, proudly, stupidly. "Ok, so twenty then—two dollars more if you want beads or little bells on the end." They always wanted the beads or bells on the end.

"Sure," I said, gesturing to the line of people passing by us, "Bunny and Wittie are insane, but Moondance and Guidance are top-ten normal, huh?" Eartha gave a little snort of acknowledgement.

"People have had nicknames as long as they've had names, but at least Gimmie and Shank got their nicknames organically, to commemorate something at least a little bit significant to somebody." I continued, "Their nicknames are like a bookmark in a story. They didn't just show up on some scene and decide they needed a new name to go with their new life."

"Harsh," said Eartha, searching through her little tackle box of threads for the next colour.

"My point is," I said, keeping my head straight while Eartha tugged on it, fingers flying as she incorporated the next cotton thread, "It feels like so many people on Tour are just playing a part. Jackson from middle-class suburban Toronto is playing Marley, the dirty guitar-player who always has good dope so people will hang out with him. Julia, the rich girl from Grosse Point, dropped out of ballet school, let her hair dread, and is playing AuraLee, a girl who, after spending one night with Marley, now has total enlightenment. And crabs."

"Harsh!" Eartha cried again, pulling on my hair deliberately.

"Ow!" I said.

"Kait," Eartha said, a little sternly, "Since when are you the cynic? Come on, that's my job. Anyway, lots of people here are totally genuine. Maybe they've been liberated from something that never felt right, never fit. Maybe Marley survived childhood cancer and spent so much time being told that life is a gift that he forgot he was allowed to live it on his own terms, the way he wanted to. And maybe AuraLee actually hates ballet and decided that she didn't want to spend her entire youth with bloody toes, bitchy girls, and bulimia. The crabs are unfortunate. They should really look into that." Eartha gave my hair another tug.

"The thing is," she said, more gently than before, "No matter how much we make fun of them, this place is for everybody. It's a place to be whoever, whatever, whenever. If that means trying on some stuff to see what fits, then so be it. And sometimes a name is just a name that somebody thinks sounds nice. Why shouldn't we have nice things like a name that feels right in this place, at this time?"

"Easy for you to say, *Eartha*."

My friend laughed, the best sound in the world.

"Yes," she said, "For this time and this place, my name is the right name. But dude, do you know how fucking miserable my name made me back home in bourgeois normal land? My parents liked jazz. They called me Eartha. My classmates liked being dicks. They called me Eartha-worm. So here I'm in style, big deal. When this ends, I'll either find a place to live with the rest of the freaks, or I'll go back to being Eartha-worm, a freak among the normals. Or maybe I'll cut my hair and wear normal clothes myself and play the role of a girl called Brittany who has to deal with meaningless bullshit I don't believe in and hate supporting. But hey, I'll fit in at the mall."

We were quiet for a few minutes as Eartha tied off my hair wrap. No bells or beads for us, an unspoken understanding.

"Eartha," I said.

"Yes, buddy."

"I don't want this to end." I sounded dumb, and young, but I couldn't help it.

"Oh Kait," she sighed, "It will end. Everything does. Let's just enjoy it while it lasts."

A sting in the corner of my eyes came swiftly, but I wiped the unformed tears away as a pretty girl with long blonde hair approached us. She was squeaky clean. A tourist; a Twinkie.

"You guys do hair wraps?" she asked.

"We sure do," said Eartha, patting the quilt beside me. "Sit." I shifted out of the way and the blonde girl sat down cross-legged in front of Eartha's stool.

"What's your name?" I asked. The girl smiled big, her shiny, straight white teeth gleaming.

"Everybody calls me Ocean."

3

WHEN WE WERE back in Eugene again for the second leg of the West Coast Tour, I had been Kait for almost two months. There was a show going on, the last of three nights at Autzen arena, but we didn't see it. We rarely ever got into the concerts anymore, even though that was supposed to be the point of what we were doing. Instead of seeing the show, we were hanging out in the Field where the van was parked, with everybody else who was there, but also not seeing the show. A party inside, a party outside. A few guys that everyone but me seemed to know had come by and were standing around with us, and before long, a joint was being communally smoked.

On its second pass, I looked more closely at the boy I transferred it to. He was spectacularly hot, and nothing like the boys I thought I was attracted to. He had short wavy hair the colour of dry sand, and was more clean-cut than most of the guys on Tour, certainly more clean-cut than any of the guys I had been spending time with. His jeans were loose on his hips and when I handed him the joint, a quick little well-practiced dance of our fingers, I saw his bicep flex beneath the sleeve of his t-shirt. A flicker of electricity seemed to move from his hand to mine even though we hadn't actually touched.

"Hi," I said, trying to pack as much sexy casualness as I could into one syllable. "And what's your name?"

"Horizon. Horizon Evans."

Of course.

He pulled long on the joint, passed it next to him. His cheekbones and jaw were insane, even if his name was ridiculous. He raised his eyebrows in question, exhaled smoke.

"Kait," I said.

"Kait," he said, and something forgotten inside of me sparked to life.

Later, when he was on top of me, he said it again. "Kait. That's as pretty as you are."

"Thank you," I whispered, and rose to meet his hips.

"Are you like a full-time Bird, Kait?" Horizon took a drag of his cigarette and passed it to me.

"Well, I'm not . . . I'm not hardcore."

"So where do you live?"

"In that van over there."

"Dude, that's hardcore." He adjusted the blanket over us, but I wasn't cold and I still had my dress on so nothing was really showing. And anyway, we had just made out behind a van on the weedy ground in a stadium parking lot with people walking past us in the dark. Now was not really the time to be modest.

"Obviously that's not really my home, just while we're on Tour, I guess."

"Ok, so where do you actually live?"

"I don't really know anymore."

Horizon Evans looked at me, and by the faint glow of the cigarette's tip, I realized again just how nice his face was. His eyes were hazel, almost topaz, wide-set, and his cheeks were broad though the structure was angular. His lips were full. I had already discovered how nice his body was. I sat up and passed the cigarette back. He pointed at my arm.

"What's that from?" He meant the three-inch scar that ran from the back of my elbow partway to my shoulder, a fault line permanently drawn across my skin.

"I broke my arm in a car accident a little while ago. Needed surgery. It's fine now." I tugged on the short sleeve of my dress, knowing it wouldn't cover the scar and turned away from Horizon slightly, hoping not to invite any further discussion. For a second, neither of us talked and I wondered if I had unintentionally ruined the moment.

"You could come with me if you want, Kait."

I looked over at Horizon and then at the van I had been travelling in. That van was gross. I was tired of being in the cramped, uncomfortable space; tired of listening to Easy and Vivi have sex, of listening to JuJube argue with Skate about where his smokes went. I wouldn't miss any of it. Well, I would miss Eartha, but she would understand. I would still see her at the next show. They were my family out here, but Horizon was clean, and cute, and sexy as hell. I wanted to be his girl.

That felt like enough.

After the densely packed darkness of Easy's van, where we slept on makeshift beds and pallets of foam, cloistered together like disgusting, sweaty castaways on a raft, or outside in tents if we bothered to put them up, Horizon's sparse camper felt like a luxury condo.

It was later that night, just the two of us, and being in his space with the pop-up top that let the air and the moonlight in felt like being in a lung expanded. Horizon turned on a lamp and I gazed around the small, but surprisingly open space. The cupboards that ran the length of one side of the camper were pear green-painted rough wood, speckled with band insignias and bumper stickers that said things like, *I believe in whirled peas*, and *Try Love*, with a peace sign where the O should be. The counters were butcher's block and had nothing on them, which made sense in a kitchen that was regularly rolling at a hundred kilometers an hour down a highway.

At the back of the van, under the pop-up was a loft bed, big enough for two, piled with woolen blankets bearing turquoise and coral Navajo patterns, old quilts, and embroidered pillows. Right under the bed was a deep bench, like a lower bunk, laden with the kind of cushions you usually see on patio furniture, and knitted afghans draping over the cushions onto the floor. The floor itself was old linoleum, maybe once yellow?—whose pattern had been scuffed away by twenty-five years of sneakered feet. The two small windows opposite the kitchen, flanking the camper door, were strung with canvas dyed dark blue and spattered with gold paint, a thousand pin-point stars. The camper was remarkably clean and uncluttered compared to Bertha or the house I grew up in or really any place I had ever stayed besides maybe a hotel room, but it was also unlike any space I had been in because it was a work of art.

Every inch of wall and ceiling space was painted—blue, green, white and gold whirls and swirls—not frenetic, hippie shit like tie-dye, or something you get when you give your friends mushrooms and a can of spray paint. This was gorgeous: an ocean of colours, each spiral set deeper at the centre and expanding into a fine mist of watery spray. It was a topographical chart of a magical sea, but rather than making the camper feel like a boat, adrift, it made the space feel calm, grounded, safe.

"Did you do this?" I asked, head up, around, behind me, trying to take it all in.

"I did."

"It's amazing. You're an artist?"

Horizon gave a modest half-shrug, while I traced the sea with my fingers.

"Do you like it?" he asked.

"Are you kidding? It's gorgeous; I love it." Horizon stood behind me, putting his arms around me. He kissed my neck and I bent my head into him. "Good, because maybe you'd like to stay here with me. Do you want to do that?"

Turning in his arms, I nodded. We were all on the same trip, right? Heading to the same shows, on the same roads. What difference did it make which van I travelled in? And if it didn't make a difference, I may as well be in the clean, quiet one with the clean, quiet boy.

Could Horizon be the partner in crime I was searching for, or at least lead me to the place I was meant to be? I knew why I would want to be here with him. Why he would want me to be there was something I didn't feel like puzzling over tonight.

Horizon's face was calm, serene, smooth, golden. He kissed me and I let him lead me to the loft, a dock on the ocean where he crested me like a wave rolling gently onto the shore.

"Do you need to go get your stuff?" Horizon pulled on a new t-shirt from a stack hidden in a drawer under the bench. Sunlight streamed through the open top of the camper, and snuck in from around the edges of the curtained windows. In the bright of day, the camper was not as empty as I had first thought; everything was merely stored carefully, safe from shifting movement while the camper was in motion. But Horizon was methodical, his stuff was not thrown haphazard like my things had been at home, where cleaning up meant shoving books and pens and bottles of Advil into the nearest drawer, detritus I would forget about, lose, ignore.

"You're so neat!" He buttoned up his jeans. God, those hip bones. "I don't think I've ever met a guy that's so neat. What's wrong with you?"

"That's just because most people are lazy, and on Tour, Birds think that being a slob means you're more authentic."

He was right. Dirt seemed to be a point of pride on Tour, representing hours on the highway, weeks away from a real shower or a washing machine. I had spent the past few months trying to stay clean, but when home is a tent you assemble every night, or a van you share with five other people, your shower becomes whatever rest station sink—or hose—you can stick your head under, and your wardrobe consists of whatever you can carry in a backpack. Staying clean becomes, for some, a losing battle, and for others, an unnecessary distraction. Hardcore Birds that stay on the road following the entire tour don't go back to their parents' suburban homes in between shows like the tourists, the Twinkies, to shower and shave. And nothing makes you look more like a Twinkie than being scrubbed and clean. But I was the worst tourist of all, of course, because I was pretending I didn't have a choice. Even though the house that was supposedly my actual home was more chaotic than any Field dumping ground.

Except Horizon was scrubbed and clean, and seemed to live in a camper that was scrubbed and clean, and as far as I could tell, had been on Tour just as long as any of us Birds. He certainly knew all the hardcore Birds by name. He must be mainly West Coast, I thought, which was why I hadn't met him before. But Horizon was legit. He was amazing. I would enjoy getting to know more of what his deal was.

"We gotta hit the road soon if we want to get a good spot on the beach in Cougar Rock. Let's go get your stuff out of Easy's van."

"You're going to come with me?" I asked.

"Of course," he said.

Casually. Like we were a couple, which I guess we were. A hookup wouldn't be making plans with me, right? If this were just a hookup, he wouldn't care about how I was getting to the next show, or if I was getting to the next show at all, or where my things were—or about getting them so I could bring them back here, where he was. And a hookup certainly wouldn't escort me back to my former dwelling in a disgusting van to get said things at the break of day. I had had enough hookups to know that was not how they worked.

In the early morning light, the Field after an Open Road show usually looks like a cross between a summer camp and a refugee camp. RVs, vans, cars, and tents are scattered everywhere, sometimes in strict and even lines, sometimes in random groupings depending on whether the venue staff had attempted to be organized or not. Here in Eugene, it was clear the venue staff knew not to bother. We made our way down along makeshift, meandering rows to the southwest corner of the Field, where Big Blue Bertha was parked. Last in, as usual. Beer cans ringed campfires smouldering in pits and portable stoves; blankets, sleeping bags, and folding chairs lay abandoned around the sites, and there were people everywhere—sleeping on the ground, poking still feet out of the open hatchbacks of cars, reluctantly unzipping the doorways of tents, pissing in the alleyways created by vans parked side-by-side.

But even with the haphazard remains of last night's party strewn about, morning in the Field was quiet and peaceful. If you weren't suffering from any kind of brutal hangover, it was lovely, always my favourite time of day on Tour. With Easy's crew, I always got up early, usually before anybody else, and extricated myself from the pack of bodies around me to get outside, get some air. In the early sun I felt new and light, part of something special. *Morning, sister. Morning, brother*, I would say in greeting to the other early risers who passed by as I lit the camping stove to get a pot of coffee on.

Today I felt the joy of the Field in the morning even more because I was not just by myself. I was one of the couples walking by the other early risers. After a second's hesitation, I reached for Horizon's hand. I held it easily in my own. They fit together well. We walked past a guy strumming a guitar and singing quietly. It was beautiful; soft and gentle and welcoming, like a lullaby, but a song for waking up instead of falling asleep, and I wondered why we didn't have more of those.

It took us about fifteen minutes to walk to Easy's van, and by time we got there the sun over Eugene was warming up, though there was still time before the heat would begin to make tents and vans feel like ovens, the air dense and dank with bodies. Big Blue Bertha was standing with all doors ajar, airing out, and its regular inhabitants were in various stages of undress around it. JuJube was sitting on the van's running board in a sundress, braiding Vivi's hair.

She was so beautiful, and for a beat I felt scared that Horizon would see her and realize that he had made a mistake asking me to stay with him. With dark wavy hair, grey-green eyes, and features that were glaringly imperfect but somehow cohesive, I always considered myself more cute than pretty, but I was a mutt compared to Vivi. JuJube raked her fingers through Vivi's curls, then saw us approaching.

"Hey girl," she said, voice made hoarse by a night of smoking and laughing. Vivi opened one eye and distorted her perfect face to see who had arrived through the bright light.

"Morning, sunshine," she said, then closed her eyes again. She didn't even acknowledge Horizon, completely vanishing my worries of being abandoned. *Oh Vivi,* I thought, *This is why everybody loves you.* I felt a pang. These people, especially JuJube, drove me crazy, and—I suspected, glancing at JuJube—stole from me, but they were my people for the last few months. Could I leave them?

"Yo, yo, yo, Zion, what is up?" Easy said, using the nickname I had heard a few times the night before. He came around the van and gave Horizon a thumping one-armed hug. He was shirtless, wearing the shorts he slept in on the nights that he didn't just pass out in his sweaty clothes. Or in no clothes at all. He didn't bother to acknowledge me because I was not new and cool, and Easy often ignored me. Horizon was treated with a sort of deference and I guessed that Easy felt it upped his game to be around Horizon. I wondered if Horizon registered the slight towards me. The pang of affection that I had felt for this crew just a second before instantly dissolved.

"Easy, what's up? Keeping your operation classy, I see," Horizon nodded at the mess still strewn about the campsite, proof of the major partying that had gone on long after we had left. Horizon's small cruelty would only endear him to Easy, a bro-joke worth being the butt of if it meant calling Horizon a friend. The social capitol of hardcore Birds went undiscussed but not unnoticed on Tour. I wasn't sure if I was more relieved to be with Horizon, so therefore protected by—and by some measure of proxy, equal to—his weird social status, or embarrassed that merely one night ago, my social alignment had been with Easy and this messy campsite. A moment of shame burned in me, for thinking of the people that had been my family for months that way, but I hadn't done anything, I reminded myself. I didn't forsake anybody. Horizon picked me.

Before I could involuntarily delve any further into the question of my allegiances, both new and possibly crumbling, I felt an arm drape heavily around my shoulders.

"Looks like you had a good night," Eartha rumbled into my ear, and gave me a big kiss on the cheek.

I looked over to where Horizon was chatting with Easy and tried unsuccessfully not to blush. Eartha's blond hair was hanging wildly from her head, big and out of control, always looking like it was one sweaty night away from finally becoming a head full of dreads, but never quite succumbing. I respected her for that. The Field didn't need one more white girl with dreads walking around. Nevertheless, I had never actually seen Eartha brush her hair, so I had to believe that her look was one cultivated over years of scaring her hair into submission; some sort of purgatory between the soft, Cinderella locks they probably once were, and the wild orgy of knots they could so easily become.

She threw a tangled tress out of the way, pushed her glasses back up her nose, and we walked back behind the van together, where she picked up a blanket from a jumble on the ground. I always made the coffee, but Eartha was the den mom, forever trying to keep things decently hygienic in the van, even if that sometimes only meant sweeping it free of dried mud and airing out the blankets, flicking them in the soft wind to rid them of the dirt and detritus that gathered on them each night. Grass and fluff flew off the blanket as she waved it into the breeze, travelling all together in a line like punctuation marks in a sentence, before floating away.

"So," she said, "Horizon, huh?"

"I guess," I said. " What do you know about him?"

Eartha turned, considering me intently for a second. Why would I care to know what she thought about someone I was about to discard, someone who was just going to be a Field hookup? Was she deciding what she should tell me? For a second, my heart dropped. I trusted Eartha, and she had always been protective of me, like a big sister. Of course, I was protective of her too, not that Eartha ever seemed to need protecting.

"He's cool," she said, and went back to flicking blankets.

"Ok, good, because I think I'm going to go to Olympia with him."

"Be careful Kait. Horizon's had a rough time."

Her words surprised me. Maybe it wasn't me that Eartha was being protective of.

"Rough time? How? What am I missing, Eartha?"

Eartha put down the blanket and rolled up a Scooby-Doo sleeping bag that belonged to Skate. If Skate wasn't in it this early in the morning, he had no doubt found another sleeping bag to spend the night in. Eartha turned to me, still holding Scooby-Doo.

"Horizon was with this girl Larissa for ages, like before Tour even. They're both from Vancouver, I kinda knew their friend group there. Maybe they even went to high school together, I'm not sure. Anyway, they hit East Coast Tour a few years ago, and got sucked up into some hardcore shit—dealing, but not just weed. E, coke, and then I heard it was heroin. You didn't know them on the East Coast? Larissa is fucking gorgeous; they were like the golden couple. I thought everybody knew them."

Fantastic. A beautiful junkie with a beautiful junkie ex-girlfriend. *What the fuck, I can handle it!* I thought, and tried not to laugh out loud. I walked over to help Eartha fold up the rest of the blankets while she told me what she knew of Horizon's story. Apparently, things got really sketchy once Tour ended, and Horizon and Larissa were squatting somewhere in Boston, just wrecked and hopeless. Somehow, Larissa's family tracked them down, and took her back to Vancouver, but Horizon got busted. Maybe Larissa's parents even called the cops on him. Eartha was unsure of details, but Horizon was able to go to rehab instead of jail, and after that, he went back to BC to finish college. But that didn't work out either for some reason, so here he was, back on Open Road Tour, apparently without a girlfriend or a drug problem.

"Seems a bit weird, don't you think?" Eartha asked me.

"What's weird?" I asked back.

"Going back on Tour where all of his problems started. It's not like this is a chaste and clean place."

I thought of our night last night; it had most decidedly not been either chaste or clean. But this had all gone down a few years ago. People got over stuff like that, and Horizon seemed seriously in control of his situation.

"I think he's okay now," I said to Eartha. I could handle this.

"I'm sure he is. Though I hear his ex goes to school in Olympia now."

My heart sank. I could handle this.

PART II

HORIZON

4

"THAT'S ALL YOU'VE got?" Horizon pointed at my bag, a patchwork satchel that I slung across my body.

"It's all I can find," I said, and glanced at JuJube.

She was actually wearing a pair of my jeans under her sundress, but she had taken them out of my bag so many months ago, without asking or acknowledging, that they were now more hers than mine. JuJube was a habitual thief, without self-control or shame. Sometimes she would deny taking things, other times, like with the jeans, she would just shrug when confronted, like, *Oh well, I guess I have them now*. I didn't even know what I was missing anymore.

"It's all right," I assured him, "I didn't really start out with a lot more than this anyway. I don't need much."

Everybody from Bertha had gathered to see me off. JuJube gave me a perfunctory hug, more because she was not a hugger than out of any malice between us. I didn't trust her, but I liked her. Vivi hugged me close and long and rubbed both my arms and quoted a song from the Road. *Be well, my sweet one, may we meet when we're both done.* I laughed and kissed her cheek. That line was often quoted by Birds, but more for a dead friend than a travelling one. Vivi. Next came Easy, who wrapped his long, lanky arms around me. "See you in Olympia, Kaity-cat, be good."

"You too, Ease," I said. He hugged me tighter, and I felt my affection for him bubble back to the surface. He nodded to Horizon. "Good luck with her."

"Easy!" I cried, "Are you going to miss me?"

"Nah," he said, "You can still make me coffee when we get to Olympia."

Eartha was next, burying me in her substantial bosom and squeezing tight.

"You be careful, and if we don't see you on the highway, come find me in the Field as soon as you get to Olympia." I nodded.

Eartha meant when *they* got to Olympia, which would probably be an entire day after we did. Easy liked to wring the last drop out of every party, never hitting the highway until venue security finally told him and the other stragglers it was time to roll out. Horizon was obviously not somebody who cared to dally when there were places to go. I was excited to travel with someone who had a plan. I bet we wouldn't ever run out of gas—or gas money—either.

"Seriously, though," said Eartha, leading me by the hand slightly away from the group, "If anything starts to seem sketchy, you're coming back to us. I know he's a great guy and he seems to have his shit together. But if things don't work out the way you want them to in Olympia, don't you dare space on us."

I nodded, but I was a bit annoyed. I didn't really want to be reminded of a possible ex-girlfriend situation again, and besides, I had no clue if I really even wanted to stay with Horizon. It just felt like the right move, right now.

"Be smart, girl, I love you." Eartha squeezed me hard again.

"I know, Eartha, love you too."

Me and Horizon were just about to leave when I heard the unmistakable sound of Skate riding back towards the van. He flipped the board up into his hand and looked around at the gathering. I pulled him into a hug.

"Hey," I said, "you're just in time to say goodbye."

"What's up, Kaity? Where you going? Hey man," he nodded to Horizon.

"I'm going to head to Olympia with Horizon, so you'll have room to bring a new girl into the van every night." I tousled Skate's already very-tousled hair.

"Are you serious?" He stepped back from me, a look of concern on his face I had never really seen before. It was disconcerting.

"Yeah, Skate, I'm going to Olympia with Horizon. No biggie. What's wrong?" Skate squinted at Horizon, then back at me. He shook his head. "Nah, nothing man, it's cool."

"Don't worry, I'll come bug you in Olympia. See you soon."

Skate hugged me again, then kissed me on the lips. It was a bit longer than just a goodbye kiss between friends, and I blushed just a bit, wondering what Horizon might be thinking. Had that been Skate's intention? But if anything did pass through Horizon's mind about me and Skate, it didn't seem to show. Or rather, I admitted, I didn't know him well enough to know if it did.

"Ready, Freddy?" Horizon smiled at me and put the camper in gear. It felt strange being up front next to him in the girlfriend seat. In Easy's van, that was always Vivi, unless she was sleeping, and then it was Skate. The only time I ever sat in the front seat was when Easy asked me to roll him up a cigarette. But here with Horizon, everything was different. The whole thing felt a bit like an absurd scene in a movie—Horizon at the wheel, me in the passenger seat, trying like hell to find a natural, non-self-conscious way to look relaxed and like I belonged there; the entire cab and the camper space behind kind of glowing from the sun and the paint and the joy. It was such a random, unthinkable place for me to end up, but it wasn't difficult to banish any second thoughts. *It's karma that I ended up here*, I thought, and then laughed, because even though I had dealt with some unconventional situations in my life, I didn't think anybody was saintly enough to deserve this.

"What's so funny," asked my driver, smiling with me.

"I just—I'm happy to be here," I said.

"I'm happy you're here too."

Horizon turned the wide steering wheel in revolutions that brought us out of the Field and on to the road that led to the interstate. I was holding the map book he had taken out of the glove compartment in my lap. Girlfriend seat. Co-pilot. Partner. But this made me think of Skate again, sitting in the front seat in Easy's van. I found my sunglasses in my patchwork satchel and put them on. They were cheap, with white plastic frames and large dark round lenses. I loved them.

"You look like Sonny *and* Cher in those," Horizon said. "But you know—way cuter."

"Well thank you," I said in a deep melodic voice imitating the 70s icon. "So hey," I asked, "how do you know Skate?"

"From Tour," Horizon said. "East Coast."

My heart sank. Skate knew Horizon from Back Then. He must have known Larissa too, and all about whatever had happened.

"Were you guys friends?"

"Not exactly, but we had some friends in common. You know how it is. We weren't really into the same things."

No, because Skate had never been a junkie. The thought came to me before I could stop it. I didn't really want to know this story right now, I decided. Not so soon. I didn't want the crazy glow to fade yet; to discover that I had made a mistake in being here, in trusting him enough to go along with him. And I certainly didn't want to flirt with the possibility that he felt he had made a similar mistake.

We had been driving northeast from Eugene for nearly two hours, en route to Cougar Rock, where we would camp for a few days before the shows in Olympia. Going to Cougar Rock, with it's pretty beach and nearby hot springs, was a good plan, better than just hanging out in Olympia watching the freaks roll in. It would give us a few days of just the two of us, to get to know each other. There's no way we would be alone on the beach—this was the same route all the other Birds were taking to get to Olympia, and no doubt some others would have the same detour idea we did—but we had no plans to meet up with anybody, so the trip felt deliciously private.

"You hungry, my girl?"

My heart flipped. *His girl.* Could this guy make me fall for him any harder, any faster? I almost laughed at the ridiculousness of it. "I am, how about you?"

"Totally. Starving. Let's hit the Benny's."

Benny's! Tour food. The 24-hour diners were fluorescent-lit beacons of consistency in the always-changing landscape and relative uncertainty of the road, and incredibly popular with Yellow Birds, or anybody on a long trip really. The food was cheap, plentiful, and familiar, and the restaurants were just dingy enough that nobody judged the ratty throngs of kids ordering stacks of comforting pancakes. Not that Horizon was ratty. At all. And I was glad that I had never succumbed to the pull of total hygiene inertia, managing to stay clean, and preferring to wear cute little handmade dresses I bought in the Field, or jeans with tank tops rather than the raggedy costume some of my compatriots (like JuJube, unless she was in my stolen clothes) sported daily.

We snaked past several small groups of Birds standing around in the Benny's front vestibule. They were waiting to be seated, or waiting for a friend to get out of the bathroom, or waiting for a coffee-to-go.

I smiled warmly or said "hey," to just about everybody, some who were familiar, all who seemed familiar. That's how it was on Tour. Seeing the other Birds up and down the highway, no matter where you stopped, was one of my favourite things. We were Yellow Birds; a pack. A herd. A flock. I slid past some ragamuffins to follow the host to our table. There were people from Tour lining both sides of the entryway to the dining room. A jam. A jam of Yellow Birds.

"If we were flamingos, our collective noun would be called a flamboyance," I said to Horizon.

"Ha," he answered, "some of us certainly are."

We were seated at a round booth big enough for eight, and though I could have spent days wondering exactly where I should sit in relation to where Horizon may or may not end up perched, he simply followed me right in to the depths of the deep vinyl bench, until I scooched to a stop smack dab in the centre, and there he was, right next to me.

A bespectacled waitress who looked like she had walked straight out of a Gary Larson cartoon stepped up to the table. "Coffee?" she asked.

"Yes, please."I answered for both of us, and skimmed the menu. Under the table, Horizon took my hand, casual as can be. *I need to learn to just fucking relax*. I willed myself not to think about literally every single move my body was making, and accept that what we were doing was real; that we belonged here, together. Fake it 'til you make it, my mother liked to say, which is not actually reassuring advice at all.

"So you're a Benny's, guy, huh?" I asked Horizon, sipping the coffee that had just been set down before us.

"My parents stopped at Bob Evans when we went on road trips when I was a kid," Horizon said. "They joked that we were related and would be getting our inheritance any day now. Turns out I'm a Benny's man, myself. They have cuter waitresses." I laughed, and our blue-haired server turned back to take a quick look at us, a little disapprovingly. Horizon winked at her. "You take your coffee black." Horizon nodded at my chipped mug.

"Yeah," I said. "You just never know if you're going to have cream and sugar around, so it's smarter just to learn to like it as-is."

"That is very pragmatic. And just a little sad," Horizon said, as he poured cream from the plastic cup into his own mug, also chipped. "I don't think I want to live in a world where I have to take my coffee black out of desperation. There's usually a gas station, or you know, a store to be found. And also—"

Horizon picked up a few of the remaining half-dozen accordioned plastic cream containers and held them towards me like an offering. "As long as we stop at Benny's every now and then, we'll always have cream for our coffee." He tipped his hand over my bag, and the containers fell in.

"Very pragmatic. And illegal." I said to him.

"Illegal! No way. They know these are to-go creamers. They build it into the price of the food." The waitress came back and we ordered while she refilled our coffee mugs.

"Excuse me," Horizon said to her, "can we please have some more cream?"

I stifled a laugh worried I was going to do a spit-take of hot coffee all over the table, and when I looked over at Horizon, his eyes were goddam sparkling in the dusty light of the Benny's dining room.

5

WE SPENT OUR first days at Cougar Rock walking back and forth for miles across the vast white sand beaches; swimming in the cool waves of the ocean; talking. Every new discovery we made about each other seemed like one note following another, building towards a melody that became the prettiest song I ever heard. Any awkwardness I felt in being with him went away as soon as I let it, like petals falling from a cut flower.

My worry that I was an intruder in this person's space seemed to exist in my mind only: Horizon did not seem capable of operating with a hint of unsuredness or self-consciousness around me. His space in the camper became mine, and we moved with an easy rhythm in that tiny home. We had made a decision to be together. What a simple decision it was. But the real refuge, for me, was in his arms. They were strong and sure, and when my body was next to his, it knew what to do. We had sex often, as new couples do, and there was a definite abandon in it. No doubting if what I was doing was right; no being embarrassed by, or trying to control, any of my responses to his hands, his mouth. There was no act, no role I was trying to play. The learning curve between our bodies was short and easily navigated beneath the rumpled blankets.

"So what's your deal, kid?" We were sitting on the warm beach and Horizon was pushing the sand with his toe, up and over the bridge of my foot. The sun was setting over the ocean, and the shoulder that I was leaning against still radiated with the heat of the day.

"Like, what's my favourite flavour of Ben and Jerry's," I teased.

"Yes, definitely. Please don't say Chunky Monkey."

"What's wrong with Chunky Monkey? But obviously it's Coffee Coffee Buzz Buzz." Horizon scrunched his eyes at me for a second. "Really? How revealing. Girls don't usually pick flavours like that."

"Are you insane? There's no such thing as feminine ice cream flavours, and until they make wonton soup ice cream, that will always be the best flavour of any ice cream, anywhere, period."

"Wonton soup ice cream? That's doesn't sound good."

"Dude, you just found out so much about me. That's my deal. There it is, right there."

"Well, I'm glad I know all about your deranged taste in flavour combinations, and I'm sorry that I made a generalization regarding the frozen dessert preferences of women. But I want to know, Kait. I do." Horizon nudged my foot gently with his. "What's your story? I want to know everything. Where'd you come from, and more importantly, how the hell did you end up here?"

"Well, Easy never really liked me very much, and I'm pretty sure JuJube was stealing all my shit, and then you asked me—"

"Okay, okay, I get that part. Why are you being so evasive?"

"I'm not, I'm sorry. It's just—it's not that interesting."

Horizon shook his head. "I don't believe that for a second, because you, Kait, are an interesting Bird. You grew up in Toronto, right? I know that part."

"Yep, suburbs, really. The best house on the worst street, worst street in the best neighbourhood. You know. It was okay. It was crowded."

"Your street?"

"My house."

"Lots of kids? I thought you said you just had one sister."

"Yep, one younger sister. Still crowded. My mother is a . . . collector."

"A collector? What does she collect? Like porcelain owls or commemorative plates or something?"

I sighed and grabbed a handful of sand and let the grains spill out of my fist like an hourglass turning. The pile accumulated on the edge of my skirt; a little hill building up to a perfect tiny peak before spilling over.

"Mostly shoeboxes and empty coffee cans," I said. "But magazines and office supplies, too. Printer cartridges, empty. Batteries, dead. And hey, if you ever need flashlights or a broken radio, I'm your gal."

"I'm sorry. I get it." He paused. "That's fucked up." He tried to take my hand but I pulled it away and the sand flew all over my skirt.

"You don't have to be sorry. It's fine. Everybody's life is fucked up." We were silent for a minute.

"So, like was it everywhere? Is that why you left?"

I softened. He wasn't the bad guy here. Besides, he had no idea. "No. No that's not why I left. Her stuff is mostly in the basement, out of sight. If you saw the rest of my house, yeah, it's cluttered, because she didn't care if anything was ever put away, but you wouldn't necessarily know what was going on.. I mean, it's shabby but you don't see all that stuff until you go downstairs. The thing is—she's just so preoccupied with it all, so it feels like it's everywhere. It's become her job. She's always gathering, rearranging, bringing home more. She's not—she's not a terrible mother. She's just busy with this crazy stuff that she thinks we'll need or we won't be—I don't know. Safe? Prepared?"

"Prepared for what?"

"Whatever you'd need 400 empty coffee canisters and 60 broken radios for."

"Jesus," said Horizon, looking out towards the water. We were quiet for a bit.

"So, when did your dad die?"

I cocked my head. "My dad's not dead." I saw the surprise in his eyes. "I'm sorry," he said, "I thought—I don't know why I thought that. I'm sorry. But where's your dad, then?"

"He's gone," I answered. "My mom got worse, my dad left. When my dad left, my mom got even worse than she had been. Tale as old as time."

"Is it?"

I didn't say anything for a minute. I didn't blame my dad. I didn't blame my mother either. People can't really help who they are, and life should be more than something you just tolerate.

"He's a biologist; worked at the university. He got a job offer for a position in Thunder Bay, way up north, and he took it. It has something to do with bacteria that gets trapped in icy water. Apparently his specialty. My mother wouldn't, or maybe couldn't, go with him. My father wouldn't, or maybe couldn't, stay. I'm glad he went. I'm glad she didn't. People only go up there to escape something."

"You think?"

"Why else would you go up there?"

"Why are we here?"

"For the view, of course," I said, gesturing to water. I blinked away the brightness. "Did you know that a group of gnus together is called an implausibility?"

"No," said Horizon, "I did not."

"My father taught us all of these names for the collective nouns of animals. Some of them are great. I love an implausibility of gnus."

A giggle of girls, he used to call my sister and I, pulling us on to his lap and tickling us. *You are my giggle of girls.* We would quiz him on our favourites, over and over again. What are elephants? *A memory.* What are crows? *A murder.* We'd say *More! More!* as he went through the comically absurd group names. A tower of giraffes. A wake of buzzards. A prickle of porcupines. A flamboyance of flamingos. A giggle of girls.

"So you don't see him at all," Horizon asked?

I shook my head. "Not really, maybe a couple of times a year. We talk on the phone. We write." The sun was partly shrouded behind low, bench-like clouds, throwing alternate lines of shadow and glinting light on the ripples of small waves being softly pulled to and from the shore. It reminded me of a song by the Road called Constellations. I hummed.

And it shines from above on those searching below
An explosion set free in the long, long ago
Maybe it's the light of the world-weary, the wise,
But maybe it's just the sun in my eyes.

I loved their sad songs the best; Ernest's wavering voice that seemed to be begging for someone to tell him everything would be okay while at the same time somehow offering us reassurance. I had a t-shirt with the last line of the song silk-screened on it, and an illustration of two people in silhouette, a boy and a girl, walking, maybe skipping, down a road, their backs to us, holding hands. The sun is bright and shining just above their heads. It's a bit more cartoony of a t-shirt, from the band or otherwise, than I normally wear, but I liked it. I liked the fact that we couldn't see where the cartoon couple was headed, what was next for them, only that the sun felt good and they were together, even if the hope is unfounded, not real; even if it's just the sun in their eyes, tricking them into thinking it's a beautiful day, that everything is fine.

"Hey, you guys got a light?" A skinny guy with long hair and frayed shorts approached us. Horizon stood up and brushed the sand off of his pants.

"Yeah dude, sure."

He pulled the Zippo he always carried out of his pocket and lit it while the shirtless guy leaned in so Horizon could touch the flame to the tip of his joint. He was pretty road-worn; his long hair was greasy and his complexion was greyish, not the healthy, bronzed appearance most guys sported on Tour from too much hacky-sack in the sun.

"Thanks," he said and exhaled a stream of pot smoke. He nodded at Horizon. "Hey man, long time."

He sat down in the sand and took another haul. I peeked at Horizon who raised his eyebrows and after a second's hesitation, sat back down. I had to shift to make room, since our visitor had made himself comfortable in the space Horizon had just occupied. Horizon sat decidedly between us and put his hand on my crisscrossed knee.

"Jimmy," he introduced himself, then held out the joint to me.

"Hi. Kait," I said, taking a puff and immediately coughing. Ack. Not smooth. I took another small pull. Better that time. I offered Horizon the joint but he shook his head, so I reached across him and passed it back to Jimmy.

"Pretty sweet place to waste time, huh?" Jimmy asked. He had a bit of an affected west coast accent, a bit surfer-like. I couldn't figure out if this guy was twenty-five or forty-five. "Heading to Olympia?"

"Yep," said Horizon. I waited for him to ask the reciprocal question, but it didn't come. I wasn't in the mood for strangers either, but Horizon knew the drill. No such thing as a stranger on Tour, everybody welcome, everybody friends, blah blah blah. But I guess this wasn't exactly Tour; this was our break. I supposed Horizon just wasn't in the mood for company. I understood, but still felt like I had to offer some hospitality to this guy, even if he had the annoying Bird habit of completely ignoring boundaries and was a bit rougher than most of the people we encountered.

"You?" I asked Jimmy. Horizon and I both declined another hit of the joint, but Jimmy seemed happy to just sit right next to us on the beach and smoke it himself.

"Yeah. No. Maybe. Not sure yet. Depends on if we can get some cash together. The city shows are expensive, right. You guys looking for anything?"

Ah. So this wasn't just a random friendly Yellow Bird drop-in on the beach at dusk. This guy was a Shaker, which is how we referred to the drug dealers on Tour. (Also from a Road song: *There's movers, there's makers/get high with the shakers.*) Jimmy didn't mean weed, either. Nobody, even the most boundary-ignorant Bird needed to approach total strangers to buy or sell weed. He meant pills, powders, maybe psychedelics. Maybe other stuff. I swallowed hard.

"Nope, we're good," Horizon said decisively.

That should have been it. There was a code of conduct. Jimmy should have said, Cool, no worries, and walked away. Only he didn't.

"Dude," said Jimmy, "If ever there was a beach to sit and get high on, this is the one. And with your lovely lady beside you, this is an opportunity you shouldn't waste." What a salesman.

Horizon stared right through Jimmy. "I said we're good, man."

"You sure about that, Horizon?" My stomach dropped and I wished that I hadn't even had those two small pulls on the joint. Horizon stood up and held his hand to me. "Let's go, Kait." I got up quickly, feeling alarmed even though Horizon still remained calm and decisive.

"Dude, I fucking know you," Jimmy said. I watched him as I scrambled to grab my sandals out of the sand. Jimmy was standing now as well. "You fucking never said no to anything. Fucking goody two-shoes poser." I almost stumbled as Horizon walked faster, my hand still in his. I ran a little to keep pace with him, and peeked back again to make sure Jimmy wasn't following us. He wasn't, but I was rattled. My heart was beating quickly and there was a weird ringing in my ears. I didn't say anything until we were off the beach, and back at the camper, relieved that Horizon had parked down a bit from the other Yellow Birds, in a more secluded area with a thicket of trees between us and the beach. I was a little out of breath from jogging through the sand. Horizon opened the door on the side of the van and sat on the lip. He lit a cigarette. I waited a second for him to say something, but he just pulled hard on his smoke.

"What the hell was that?" I asked.

My tongue felt thick and dry in my mouth. I got two glasses out of the green cupboard and filled them both with water from the jug on the counter. I handed Horizon one of the full glasses. I saw his eyes flash anger, but then soften. He exhaled the smoke for a long time.

"I don't know, I don't remember that guy," he said, a bit aggressively.

"He sure seemed to know who you were." I didn't want to sound accusatory, but my adrenaline was pumping, and I was still higher than I wanted to be from the pot, so the least Horizon could do was offer a bit of an explanation. I was sure this wasn't just post-smoke paranoia. But Horizon hadn't said a word to me about that part of his past yet. Would we just have to keep dodging Shakers and junkies while he evaded questions about why these people kept ending up in his orbit? My orbit? No fucking thanks. Maybe I wasn't ready to be with a guy like Horizon.

Maybe I wasn't ready to be with anyone. Maybe I wasn't safe here. The heat of paranoia and panic started to rise in me, flushing through my entire body and I sat down in the open side doorway next to Horizon, afraid I was going to pass out.

"Kait, I seriously don't remember that guy. But if he did know me, it wasn't from a good time." Horizon's voice was back to its normal calm tenor, and my panic subsided, just a bit.

"Is he going to come looking for you?" This stupid camper was all we had right now, and I hated the thought of its veneer of sanctuary, however temporary, being punctured. Horizon regarded me.

"What? No. No, of course not. He's not ever going to bother doing something like that. He'll go bug somebody else or find a party to get wasted at. Is that what you're worried about?"

"I don't know. I thought you said you didn't know him. How do you know he won't come back?" Horizon stubbed his cigarette out under his foot.

"Because even if I don't think I know him, I know lots of assholes like him. He's a dirt-bag Shaker, but he's not dangerous. We just don't need to be around people like that."

My heart was beating quickly again. "But you used to."

Horizon turned to me. The expression on his face was pure neutrality, but his eyes were intent. "Used to what?" he asked.

"Spend time around people like that." I swallowed. My mouth had become dry again. Horizon searched my face with his eyes for a second then turned away towards the dark trees beyond the path the van was parked on. He took a drink of the water I had placed next to him.

"I don't know what you heard, but it was probably wrong," he said. He got up and climbed into the camper; put his glass on the counter. After a minute, I followed him into the small, dim space. The sun had completely set, but the dark was not yet impenetrable.

"Then tell me what's right," I said.

Horizon turned from the counter and faced me. My legs still felt wobbly, but now I wasn't sure if it was from the pot and the adrenaline or from Horizon's presence so close to me. So I leaned against the counter next to him.

"I will, Kait," he said, "But I don't want all this to ruin our night. I don't have anything to do with that shit, with guys like that. *We* don't have anything to do with guys like that. I'm sorry if you got scared on the beach. I promise, everything is fine." I stood motionless for a moment.

"All right."

"Are you sure," he asked. "Do you want us to go somewhere else tonight? Or," Horizon paused for a second. "Do you want to go somewhere else without me tonight?"

"No," I said, finding my voice again, and he moved so that now he was standing in front on me. He put his hands on the counter on either side of me, and leaned in even closer. I lifted my head a bit to see him. Was my stomach ever going to stop flipping when I was near this guy? Fuck. He brushed his lips against my neck, moving up to my cheek, my ear.

"I promise you can trust me, Kait. I'm sorry." He whispered.

His lips reached mine and I put my hands on his hips, bringing them in closer. He kept his hands on the counter and I let his body enclose me there. He kissed me more intently and I pushed myself away from the counter as much as I could, into him. Then he stopped kissing me. "Hey," I said, dizzy. He turned and walked a step to the door of the camper. He pulled it closed and when my eyes dilated, adjusted to the light, I saw his hand, outstretched towards me.

"Come," he said, and I knew I would.

6

WE SPENT THE rest of the week in a fog of harmony, wanting to erase the bad vibes of that night, where the discoveries of a new relationship got to unfold on a vacation from any other real-life interferences. After the encounter with the Shaker, we opened up to each other more, trading stories about our upbringing, family, experiences on Tour. We talked about the groups of people you see on Tour: the Birds that followed Tour, the Birds that showed up to local shows when they could; the Twinkies with their brand-new concert T-shirts, and the frat boys trying to find a party.

"Those are the kinds of fans you might see at shows for any big band. But then," I said to Horizon, peeling an orange and handing each of us a section, "then there are the types of people that for some reason only exist on Road Tour—" Juice from the orange dripped down my hand and I swiped it across my jeans. "No other band gets Tapers. Or Pilgrims. Or Shakers." Horizon squeezed my leg. "Or Spinners," he said.

"Definitely not!" I responded. "But to be fair, they are the most consistent and pure in their motivation. They go, they spin, they—what? See God? If we ever go to an Open Road show that the Spinners don't show up to, we truly will know the end of the world is nigh and we should seek shelter." Horizon chuckled and popped another segment of orange into his mouth. "We'll keep an eye on them, then," he said. "Open Road's own harbingers of doom—or maybe just a great encore."

He told me about his parents, well-meaning but rigid: Dad, a manager at a shipping company in Vancouver; Mom, a homemaker who busied herself with charity work and entertaining.

"When I was in middle school, I used to skip class to go to the skate park, but my mother would literally show up there after the school called to see where I was, and she would grab me by the arm and make me leave. You should have seen this woman—five feet tall, striding in on heels in a fancy skirt, her hair and nails done, and everybody—I mean everybody—at the skate park would just stop what they were doing and look down guiltily while my tiny mother dragged me to the car. Once she noticed my friend Tye was with me as well, and she dragged him out of there too. His own mother wasn't even searching for him yet. When we got back to the school, she pushed us into the office and banged on the principal's door. When he opened it, my mother told him, 'You missed one,' and turned and walked out."

"Oh my god, Kait, Tye was shitting himself because he had told his mother we were on a field trip that day, and she had even given him twenty bucks for lunch. Now he was in trouble with my mother, his mother, and the principal. I don't know which one he was more scared of."

These morsels of information gave me insight into the person I was with, but more importantly, it felt conspiratorial, like I was trusted. Every anecdote, every answer to my questions, brought this person further from the realm of stranger, and gave me something besides a physical attraction and superficial magnetism to connect us together. I cared about Horizon and could see the depth of my caring continue to build if things continued this way.

He had still not gotten to the part of his life the Shaker had alluded to, but we were leaving Cougar Rock for Olympia soon, and if I was thinking about a possible encounter with gorgeous Larissa, the ex-girlfriend, then Horizon had to be as well.

The day before we left Cougar Rock, the sky was grey, threatening rain, so we eschewed the beach for a walk in the woods to the hot springs a few kilometers away. They were a popular destination in the area, a series of six geothermal pools that sat like steps in an ancient rock face and drained into each other, before continuing to follow a small river all the way back to the ocean. We had avoided them so far, expecting the natural cascading pools to be overrun and possibly a little gross, as hundreds of Yellow Birds crowded into them, enjoying their first bath in weeks. Waiting a few days, we reasoned, would increase our chances of sharing them with fewer people.

"We're still only going to sit in the pool at the very top," Horizon said.

Towels slung over our shoulders, we followed an easy flat trail through the woods, holding hands, talking and pointing out the occasional stone or root to be aware of on the path.

"I could get lost in here," I said, looking up at the massive trunks that made up the mature stand of sitka spruce, hemlock, and fir trees. "I'd like to get lost in here."

"I'd like to get lost with you," said Horizon, coming up from behind and putting his arms around me.

"I'd like it too," I said, and moved my head to kiss him. "I got lost once when I was kid," I told him.

"You did? What happened? You're here so I guess they found you."

"Yes, Horizon, I wasn't abducted, I just got lost. Actually, I didn't even get lost; I got left."

I hadn't thought of that incident in a long time. I had never told anyone about it until I told him.

When I was little, maybe six or seven, a few years before he left, I lost my dad at the grocery store. We were there to get the things we needed for a barbeque we were hosting for his birthday. That's how things worked in my house, even when my dad was still around. It might be your birthday, but don't think it means you're off the hook to do the work for it.

My aunt and uncle and cousins were coming over, as well as the Shapiros who lived down the street. We needed burgers, buns, a few bags of chips, a couple of bottles of pop, which my dad said I could pick out. I gleefully left my dad in the bakery section where he was searching for the right sized hamburger buns, and ran to the aisle with all the bottles of soda. It was a bright, gleaming oasis, bottles and cans of every size and colour, and I was allowed to decide with complete impunity which of those bottles would be coming home with us. (*A fantasy of pop bottles*, I decided to tell my dad.) I went straight to the Diet Coke, which my mother drank, glasses and glasses of it every day, the ice clinking and then melting into the fizz, but I stopped before my hand touched the bottle. Why should I waste my choices on what my mother wanted? This little thought of rebellion sent my stomach flipping momentarily, but I pursued my own unchecked desires. Lemon-Lime . . . Cream Soda . . . Orange Fanta . . . Grape Crush . . . had my dad said one or two bottles? I studied each bottle thoroughly, thinking about which flavours would go best together if the kids decided to drink a half-and-half, and also which bottles the adults would most definitely not want to drink so there would be more for us. After considering each bottle carefully, I grabbed the Root Beer and the Cream Soda. Not as exotic as the choices I could have made, but these were my favourites. With a sticky, two-litre bottle tucked into each arm, I proudly made my way back to where I had left my dad in the bakery section. Except my dad was no longer there.

I peeked behind displays of mini-cupcakes topped with electric blue icing, sweating under their domed plastic containers, and around bins of loose bagels and Kaisers. No big deal, I thought, Dad's already got the buns and he will be on his way for the lettuce and tomatoes, or maybe the bags of chips. I hoisted the heavy bottles back, one each into the crook of my elbow and walked along the bottom of the aisles, scanning each row as I went past. It was busy at the grocery store, not surprising for a summer Saturday afternoon, and the aisles were crowded with people and their carts. When I made it all the way to the other end of the store, the frozen-food section, without spotting my dad, I stared up the row, winding my way through the shoppers opening the doors to the freezers. Halfway up the aisle, I bumped into a large lady who had unexpectedly moved from a standing position to a half-folded stance so she could reach way into the back of a freezer. Her giant butt was sticking out into the aisle, which delighted me, and I laughed as my tiny hip caught her half-moon and spun me into the middle of the crowded row.

I would tell my dad when I found him, and he would laugh his honking laugh with me. We could turn anything into an adventure. At the top of the aisle, I walked the length back across the store, turning my head right and left to glimpse first down the rows from this side, and then into the long lines of shoppers emptying the contents of their carts onto the conveyors of the check-outs. I couldn't see my dad anywhere.

The bottles of pop were getting really heavy, and I was tired of stopping every few feet to hike them back up into my arms, so I made my way back to the bakery section, and stood the bottles on a table filled with packaged cinnamon buns. I'll come back and get them after I find dad, I promised myself. Unencumbered by the pop, I quickly ran through the store again, looking. This time, I went up one aisle and back down the next, tamping down the momentary panic that struck each time I turned a corner and did not see my father's tall, slightly stooped body among the crowds.

He was no longer in the grocery store. That was the only explanation. I must have taken so long choosing the pop that my dad had finished getting the groceries, checked out, and gone home. Convincing myself of this brought me a good deal of relief, as I no longer had to try to find him. There was no point; he was not here anymore. I just shouldn't have taken so long, that was all. Dad left, he had a barbeque to get ready for, and mum would definitely yell at him when he got home. "Where the hell have you been?" She would holler. "I have too many goddam things to do here and you spend the whole afternoon at the store? Goddam it!" Dad just didn't want to get in trouble, so he left. It made sense.

Anyway, I knew how to get home. The grocery store was attached to the mall like an afterthought, and the mall was just down the street from our townhouse complex. I could walk home. We almost always walked to the mall anyway, unless we were only going to get groceries. But if me and mum were going to the bank, or to Sears or just to get a coffee (for her) and a cookie (for both of us) and waste some time browsing the stores, we always just walked.

The trickiest part was deciding which direction to cross the road first. The street I lived on was kitty-corner from the mall and then down the road a little way, so I would have to cross twice; wait for two traffic lights to flash the "walk" sign. With my mum, we just crossed whichever way was green at our approach, and sometimes we would have to start running halfway through the intersection, mum pulling me by my hand, because the light had suddenly turned orange on us. But this time I didn't have mum's hand to hold, and I wasn't sure I could keep track of staying in a straight line and whether or not the light was about to turn, so when I got to the corner of the intersection, I decided not to cross on the side where the light was already green, but to stand facing the red, and wait for it to change so that I would have the full length of the next green light to cross with. I felt triumphant when I had crossed both corners safely and was on the side that would lead to my street. Almost home already, all by myself. I felt very grown-up, like I had accomplished way more than just choosing which flavours of pop we should have at the barbeque.

But my sense of pride and triumph at having returned myself safely home dissolved the second I walked through the door to our house. My mother roared over to me, grabbed my arm, raising it high and turning me away from her, and spanked me, hard on the behind. "Where the hell did you go?" she yelled while hitting me, "Why aren't you with your father? He has the whole store looking for you!"

"Daddy left me there! I walked home! I walked home!"

I was crying and trying to shield myself from my mother's blows with my free arm, while working through my shock at what exactly had gone wrong. My mother abruptly let go of me and turned briskly down the hall. "I have to call the store back and tell them you're alive. Jesus Christ!" I ran upstairs to my room and slammed the door, throwing myself on my bed. I was mad and humiliated. At the grocery store, I had chosen the pop myself, searched all over for my dad without crying like a baby, got myself all the way home including crossing two lights by myself, and then I got in trouble. My mother didn't even care about all the things I had done right. I cried into my pillow and eventually fell asleep on the wet, snotty sheets.

My dad woke me up when he came in a little while later. I knew he wouldn't be mad because he wasn't like that. He patted my back and I tried not to start crying again. "Why did you leave the store, honey?" he asked. "Because I looked for you everywhere, and you were gone." I tried not to sound accusing. It wasn't my dad's fault, and I'm sure my mum had already yelled at him plenty, too.

"I would never, ever leave you anywhere. Never. You should have gone to the store manager or another adult, and told them you couldn't find me. They would have helped you if you were lost."

"But dad," I said, "I wasn't the one that was lost. You were. I was just getting pop."

My dad pulled me close, hugging me, and said, "Oy, yoy, yoy." He sat on the bed and kind of rocked me for a while, even though I knew he had to go start the barbeque. But sitting here was nice and calm.

"Anyway, dad," I said after a little bit, "Why would I stay lost when I knew the way home?"

Horizon squeezed my hand tighter as we picked our way up the slope toward the highest pool. "I'm glad you didn't stay lost, so I could find you," he said, then raised my hand to his lips and kissed it softly.

7

"ARE YOU GOING to know lots of people in Olympia?" We were laying in the loft, studying our hands as our fingers moved over the other's, lacing, unlacing, tracing lines, as if studying an object for clues of its meaning. We were tired after our outing to the hot springs. Our timing had paid off and there were only a few people there when we arrived. They soon left and we had the top pool to ourselves for the majority of the time we stayed. Between the heat of the water and the hike to and from Cougar Rock, we were too beat to do much of anything else.

Horizon's hand was bigger than mine, the skin soft but worn for someone our age. There was a bit of light hair between the knuckles on each finger. The camper's pop top was open above us, as it usually was, letting in moonlight and the sound of cicadas chirping in the tree canopy above us. A guitar, people singing out of tune, was audible beyond the insects, and their sounds were not competing, but neither were they particularly harmonious. Still, it wasn't unpleasant.

"What do you mean, *know people*?" Horizon asked, stroking the back of my hand with his index finger. Up, down. Slowly. "You know it'll be the same clowns we just saw in Eugene. You'll know as many people as I will, Kait."

"Will I?"

"Won't you?" He didn't get my inference. Or if he did, he wasn't taking the bait. I changed course.

"You know everybody. I know Easy and Eartha and them."

"You know me."

"Do I?" Horizon's hand stopped moving, and he turned to me.

"Why did you say that? What's going on, Kait?" It wasn't a challenge, how he said it, and I regretted the implied drama. Everything I did know about Horizon supported his disdain for dramatics.

"I just mean . . . come on, it's not like we've been together for very long." Still looking at our hands, still not moving. He took his away.

"Kait, yeah, I get that, but I'm right here. We know each other as much as two people could by now, and I like it. I like getting to know you. It's awesome Kait, it's so good getting to know you. We're exactly where we should be by now. I like unravelling you."

I covered my eyes with both of my hands, trying to figure out how he could be so honest with me and it still didn't feel like enough. Why didn't it feel like enough? Or was it just that I didn't know the one thing I felt the most insecure about, so how could we not still be strangers? But I couldn't ask him outright about Larissa if he wasn't ready to talk about her. I knew that. So I deflected.

"Yeah, but." I uncovered my eyes and turned to him. "Dude, I don't even know your name!"

"What?" Horizon laughed. "Of course you do! What do you think my name is?"

"I'm sure it's Horizon. Just like Easy's name is Easy and JuJube's mother named her after a candy, and that guy we met at the campfire the other day, I'm sure there were lots of babies named Umber the year he was born."

"Maybe if he was born in Hollywood."

"It's not funny! I'm serious."

"Kait, I'm serious, too." But there was a playful lilt in his voice. "Honestly, my name is Horizon James Evans. I swear to god." I furrowed my brow at him.

"I may not know much about you, but I know that your parents weren't hippies, so how the hell did you end up with that name? Are you sure you didn't just change it yourself? Your name is really Alan, or Michael, or, or Fergus, isn't it?"

"Fergus is a great name, but no. Listen," He grabbed my hand again, but just held it this time. "My parents were going to name me Harrison, after my grandfather who died way before I was born. But apparently, my birth was seriously rough on my mother, and she puked through the entire labour—something like ten hours of puking. So my dad, who was clueless, but you know, was trying to help, kept talking to her about their honeymoon, which was a cruise to Mexico. There had been a storm right before the ship left the port in California, and the ocean was still pretty rocky. My mother spent the entire first day of the cruise totally seasick. She couldn't walk, she couldn't eat, and she definitely couldn't just lie in their tiny room—it didn't really have a window, just one of those little round portholes, you know? So the only thing that would make my mother feel even the slightest bit better was sitting on one of those deck chairs outside. My dad kept telling her to find the horizon, because it was always there, always a straight line, always still. They even spent the first night in the deck chairs outside, my mother watching the horizon the entire time, even when it was way too dark to actually see it, until she finally fell asleep. By morning, the ocean had calmed down, and my mother felt perfect again. They had a great trip.

"So anyway, when my mother was in labour and she couldn't stop puking, my dad led her to the window of the hospital room, and he rubbed her back and just kept telling her, look at the horizon, just look outside at the horizon—which, since they were on the fourth floor of a hospital, and not on a cruise ship—was apparently the roofline of the top of another building directly across from them. So my mom focused on that 'horizon' until she finally got me out of her. And a little bit later, when the nurse came in with all the forms and birth certificate and stuff, and asked my parents what my name was, my dad said 'Harrison,' but my mom said, 'Horizon.' And the nurse listened to my mom. So that's what my name is. That's the story."

I lay on my back staring up at the stars. The singing and guitar playing had stopped. It was just the cicadas now. How many times would I underestimate this guy?

"That's a really good story," I said quietly.

"So do you feel like you know me enough for now, Kait?"

Kait. I almost laughed out loud.

"Please, can we just stay here for a bit longer?"

I meant lying here next to Horizon, tracing my finger up and down his arm as we lay facing each other on the blanket. But I also meant Cougar Rock, at our little campsite, just the two of us. A second blanket was pushed in a heap by our feet, cast off after having done its job of providing additional cover as we had sex under it. I had insisted on its use.

"Who's going to see us?" Horizon had whispered in my ear, as he eased my sundress up my legs and over my hips.

He had licked my neck slowly, from my shoulder to my ear, and it had felt like my skin was dissolving under his tongue. He was right, nobody would see us here, on our little plateau at the end of the path few others had walked beyond the entire time we had been here, above and away from most of the campers. But I still felt exposed, like I needed a shield, a cocoon for our intimacy at that moment. I was still feeling insecure about the Shaker and Olympia, I guess.

So we were both sweaty and flushed as we lay there afterwards, and I knew it was more from the extra blanket than from the sex. It had been so hot under there that Horizon moved fast, much faster than usual, and although I enjoyed the intensity, it would have been better without the blanket. Well, cooler anyway. I would have just been rushing him out of fear of being seen. It probably wouldn't have been great either way, which was why I wanted to prolong our time in each other's close company afterwards; to not just bolt up after clumsy sex and pack all of it away except the awkwardness.

Horizon turned onto his back and closed his eyes, raising an arm above his head.

"It's supposed to rain tonight. We should load everything up." His sleepy, honey-smooth voice made even the most practical of sentences sound sexy, and I rolled over on to him.

"I don't want to pack up. I want to stay out here all night. I want to stay here forever." I kissed his neck and he put his hands on my sides, my back, my ass. His eyes were still closed, and I could feel him hard again, pushing into my leg. I shifted my hips ever so slightly back and forth over his.

"You can stay out here if you want, but you're going to get wet."

"I already am," I whispered to him. He opened his eyes, and this time I left the blanket crumpled at our feet.

The rain began overnight. I woke up to its steady drumming on the roof of the camper. The popup was angled just right, or maybe the wind was blowing just right, that we got the breeze without being dripped on and I lay there in the loft bed beside Horizon, not wanting to disturb him, just listening to the rain and appreciating from here how insistent he was about packing up earlier, while it was still warm and dry. We had originally planned on leaving Cougar Rock mid-morning some time after breakfast, but with the gloomy weather report, we had agreed that a better plan would be to load up and out early and hit the road as soon as we woke up, treating ourselves to breakfast at whichever cheap roadside joint we saw signs for first. "Ooh, Benny's," I said, rubbing my hands together as we talked through the plan, "you sure know how to treat a girl!"

"Hey," he said, waggling his eyebrows, "could be Bob Evans, yeah?" I smiled and shook my head reverently. "A girl can dream."

As we got ready to leave Cougar Rock for Olympia the next morning, the rain showed no signs of stopping. It was the kind of persistent, cold, miserable rain the coast seems to kick up to remind you that it is stronger than you think; that you don't really belong there. Or at least, that's how it felt to me. You're just visitors—no not even visitors; trespassers. Trespassers sneaking through, and it's time to go now. Sure, you just had a week of gorgeous, summer sun; the sand and the ocean and the rocks and the hot springs making you contemplate staying in paradise for good. But no, the party is over, it's time to get out. You will not settle here. This place isn't for you. Go.

Horizon stood on the running board at the side of the van, checking that the bungee cords pulled tight over the soft-sided cargo bag he stored some extra gear in on the roof were secured. He was getting soaked, but he didn't rush the job. In solidarity, I was also outside of the van, circling the space to make sure we hadn't left anything behind. We hadn't; Horizon was tidy and careful, and we had packed everything up before bed, under darkening clouds. Camping chairs were folded and stored; the Coleman stove and cooking implements we used were cleaned and housed in their interior compartments, and the blankets we had we had been laying on outside had been shaken clean of pine needles and sand, folded and placed in the box below the window seat.

Knowing that I wouldn't find anything left behind in the rain to scavenge or salvage, I stood next to the van where Horizon was working the bungees, hurried but efficient. He regularly flicked his head to get the wet, falling hair out of his eyes, but otherwise, he seemed mostly unbothered by the rain. I tried to adopt the same nonchalance, but I was there only out of a sense of duty and support. I hated being cold and uncomfortable, and hopped back and forth from one foot to the other, as though I could dodge the cool falling drops. I blinked quickly and shielded my eyes from the deluge as I tilted my head up at Horizon. Fuck, did he ever have sexy arms, toned and strong as they flexed with the effort of his movements. Even in the pouring rain, he was gorgeous.

Horizon's was the most beautiful body mine had ever come in contact with. It was perfection, as far as I would ascribe that word to anything.

He jumped down from the running board, smacking his wet hands against his jeans, interrupting my reverie.

"Kait, what are you doing! Why are you standing there?" I was starting to shiver.

"Solidarity!" I said, teeth chattering.

"Why? Oh my god dummy, let's go inside." He ushered me back into the van, securing the door behind us. I stood on the mat in middle of the little space while Horizon got towels out of the seat box. He tossed one to me, then turned the camper on to warm us up, since the little generator and heater we sometimes used at night were also secured in their cubbies for travel. Horizon quickly peeled his wet clothing off, and towelled himself dry. He moved without any sense of inhibition, so sure of his body, his place, his space, even with me in it. I tried to act with the same surety, but undressed a little less casually, pulling my sopping dress off over my head once my towel was already tucked in around my body.

"You warming up?" he asked, rubbing the towel over his head, then walking to the front of the van to put a hand out in front of a small, round heating vent.

"Yes," I said, hoping to sound casually perky, despite the deep, damp cold I was sure I wasn't going to shed for ages, "I'm good."

Horizon put on a dry pair of jeans and a t-shirt, then zipped a gray hoodie over top. He would fit in anywhere. On Tour, on a university campus, in a mall, on a city street. He had such an ease about him, a confidence that seemed like it could only come with total acceptance of yourself and the people around you. I was jealous of it, and I misunderstood it.

I put on a similar outfit to Horizon's, soft bell-bottom jeans I had bought at a second-hand store at home, a handmade, patchwork dress that someone had given me on Tour, and a blue hoodie with a kangaroo pocket over the dress. The wool socks I had made me feel instantly warmer, and I slipped my feet into the brown leather clogs I refused to get rid of, even if they were heavy to carry in a satchel, which I often had to do. I rubbed my hair a bit with the towel, then left it to air dry into the messy waves I knew would form. I plopped into the passenger seat beside Horizon, who was folding up some papers to put into the glove box in front of me. He studied me appraisingly. "Cute," he said, with a smile. "Ready?" He put the van in gear. It clunked into first with a bit of a lurch as the camper shook off its days of unuse, and slowly proceeded down the wet, muddy little road out of the woods. A few other vehicles were in front of us, making their way out of Cougar Rock, but most were still parked as their occupants scrambled to pack up. Some people were running around gathering sopping wet blankets, chairs, and coolers, and a few were shedding their shirts or raising their arms in the air, doing a little rain dance as they surveyed their soaked and ruined campsites. "Idiots," Horizon muttered, but his tone was good-natured. Some tents were yet pitched and still, as if the occupants inside did not even realize that the ground swelled around them, their discarded items getting pummeled by the rain outside. And they probably didn't know, or didn't want to know, as they slept off whatever they had drank, ingested, or smoked the night before. Why worry, right? I preferred the cozy warmth of the camper, our things all packed and dry, me the co-pilot and my captain at the hub, guiding us out of one adventure, and into the next.

8

JUST BEFORE THE turn off that would take us to Olympia, we decided to stop for gas and some groceries. We had left the rain behind in Oregon, and as we crossed into Washington, the day warmed up. For the past hour we had shed layers of the extra clothing we had put on that morning. I was down to my jeans and homemade patchwork dress. Horizon was in jeans and an Open Road t-shirt that had an illustrated picture of the band's second album, Pandora, re-imagined as the eponymous box that opened to release not doom and disaster, but rainbows, birds, and shooting stars.

Exiting the northbound highway, Horizon pulled into a Target parking lot. He dropped me at the entrance with a quick kiss. "Meet you inside when I'm done," he said, then drove in the direction of the gas bar at the far end of the plaza. The blast of cold air inside the store made me shiver after just warming up again, and I rubbed my arms as I veered left into the washrooms, which was always the first stop in a clean, reliable place like Target. *In any almost place, really*, I corrected myself, *as long as it's not an outhouse.*

After using the toilet, I washed my hands thoroughly and surveyed myself in the mirror. My hair, after the rain, was big, parted haphazardly to the side and falling in unbrushed waves over my right eye. I had lost a little weight on Tour and I could see it in my sunkissed face. It had lost a little bit of its usual roundness and my cheekbones were more defined. I didn't mind that but I wondered if it made my nose look even bigger than I thought it already was. My eyes were the clear, deep, sage-flecked grey they always were and my lips looked a little chapped. I grabbed some Burts Bees from my bag and swiped it over my mouth, admiring the raspberry tint it left as I smacked my lips together. My favourite patchwork dress could have used a wash, but I loved how comfy and softly worn it now was. One of the thick straps slipped off my shoulder and I left it there. All in all, I liked what I saw. I liked who I saw. My jeans flared over my feet, but as I walked, my clogs peeked out. Trusty satchel slung over the shoulder where the dress strap still held and I felt cute and unconventional. Self-assured.

I was walking confidently towards the produce when a beckoning behind me made me turn around.

"Oh my god, it is you!"

My heart sunk. Holly Janes, one of the school mates I had started Tour with months ago, was standing in front of me. *How . . .*

"Holy shit girl, I almost didn't recognize you! Look at you!"

Almost involuntarily, I did—I looked at myself and everything I had seen in the mirror just a moment ago, dissolved. I saw a worn-out dress, giant ripped bag, fraying jeans and old clogs. I self-consiously put my hands to my head, twisting my dissheveled hair into a bun that released and fell back over my eye the second I let go.

Holly, however, looked exactly the same as she had the last time I saw her in Indiana, right before she turned around and went home and I changed my entire life.

"Holly," I said, unable to hide my shock, "What are you doing here?"

"Same as you, I'm guessing. I'm seeing the Olympia shows with a couple of my cousins who live out here, and figured if I'm going to be in the States, I may as well do a Target run—we definitely needed some of this!" Holly pulled a bottle of Boone's strawberry wine out of the basket she was holding and shook it in my direction.

"But what are you doing *here*," I asked again, "on the West Coast." I didn't remember any conversation about my schoolmates coming to shows all the way out west. If they had been planning to travel that far, I probably would have just gone with them.

"I'm going to uni in Victoria, remember? Creative Writing."

As soon as she said it, I did remember, and told her so, with an apology. I began to ask her some dumb follow-up question about student housing because I felt bad for not recalling her life plan, but she interrupted.

"Dude, you look like you've been sleeping in a forest. Who are you here with?"

Panic flared in my chest with her question. Horizon. I quickly scanned the store in the direction of the entrance to see if he was approaching. The last thing I wanted was for Holly to meet Horizon. My old life to meet my new life. Before Kait and After Kait.

"Just some friends." I tried to think of a way to end this interaction, this random, coincidental imposition of the world I had left on the world I had so carefully composed.

"When are you going home?" she demanded.

"I—not yet," I stammered, but she was unrelenting.

"Have you been on Open Road Tour this entire time? Don't you start school soon?"

"No, not yet." I couldn't remember what I had told her my plans were for the fall.

Holly peppered me with questions that I deflected until she moved on to try to tell me some of the gossip regarding people back home. I could hardly recall who she was talking about.

"Holly, I'm so sorry, I think I see the people I'm with leaving the store. I've got to go catch up with them."

"I better go too, my cousin's waiting for me. I can't believe I ran into you! Are you heading East after this? Call me when you're home!"

"Not yet," I shook my head and walked quickly away. "Have a good show!" I called over my shoulder.

Sweating despite the air conditioning still blasting throughout the store, I walked straight back into the washrooms. I threw my satchel onto the wet counter and turned on the tap, splashing cold water on my face. It had been months since I had seen anybody from home and had expected it to be much longer still. I looked in the mirror. Water dripped onto my neck and I swiped it away quickly. I surveyed myself once again as I tried to calm my breathing. I didn't see somebody sunkissed and cute and confident. I saw somebody dissheveled and dirty.

Holly had come here to start university, start her life. I was doing everything I could to keep mine on hold. If Horizon had found me in the store, interrupted us, Holly would have told him how different I looked, revealed me for the fraud I was. Playing dress-up in clothes that weren't mine four months ago, with a boy I just met. But at that thought, I swallowed my panic and looked at myself in the mirror again. No, if there was one thing in this world that was real, it was Horizon, and how I felt about him. There was nothing about that I needed to conceal to anyone.

As I was making my way out of the store, Horizon approached the entrance. For a second, I believed he was going to walk right past me, wouldn't recognize me.

"Done already? Where are the bags?"

"I'm sorry," I said, "I didn't feel well. I had to get some air." His look of concern sent a wave of affection through me. He took my hand.

"What is it? What can I do for you?"

"I'm okay, really. I got a little lightheaded. I think I'm just tired." None of this, at least, was a lie.

"Why don't you go lay down and I'll get what we need." I nodded in agreement and Horizon handed me the keys to the van. He always parked far from the crowd towards the back of most lots, and I hurried away from the store, worried that Holly would once more spot me and call out to me. Call my name. Once inside the camper, fatigue overwhelmed me and I really did feel the need to lay down. The bed, arranged for travel, was a welcoming relief. *This is no forest floor,* I thought, then drifted away.

The whine of the side door opening up woke me, leaving me momentarily disoriented as Horizon stepped into the van, set down two grocery bags and climbed up beside me. I blinked against the light filtering in, dislodging the torpor. I draped my arm across Horizon's lap and he rubbed it gently.

"Hi," I said.

"Hi," he said. "You feeling better, my girl?"

"Mmm-hmm." I was. I was feeling grounded again, still a little tired, but better. Horizon got off the bed and reached into one of the grocery bags. He pulled out a small bottle of ginger ale.

"Here, I thought this might help." He unscrewed the top and handed it to me.

"Thank you," I said, touched by the thoughtful gesture. "You really are the sweetest."

"I just want you to feel better," he said.

"I do," I said, "I feel much better. But will you stay here with me for a minute?" His presence next to me seemed like the only thing I needed.

"Of course," he said, kissing me on the temple, then my cheek. I squeezed his leg and he kissed me on the neck just under my jaw, sending a surge of desire through me. Turning my head towards him, ensuring our lips met, my hands urged him on top of me. He brushed my hair away from my face as I undid his jeans, reaching for him, already hard, pushing against the denim. He lifted his hips and I slid his jeans down, then his boxers. He kicked them off then sat up, crossed his arms around the band of his shirt and pulled it up, over his head. I ran my hands over his smooth, muscular back as he pushed my dress up and put his mouth on one nipple then the other, biting, sucking lightly. I pulled off my dress and quickly stepped out of my jeans. He was laying back, reaching into the little drawer beside the bed for a condom, but I stopped him.

"Not yet," I said and got back onto the bed, kneeling beside him. Horizon groaned as I put my mouth on him. He raked his fingers through my hair, tugging gently but without command. When his breathing became shallow and his hips rose urgently, I sat up. "Not yet," I said again, reaching into the drawer myself. Horizon laid me on my back and pushed my arms above my head. He ran his hands down the length of them, then down the sides of my body to my hips. I kissed him greedily and pulled him into me.

"Now, " I whispered.

"What the hell is this?" Horizon was staring intently out the windshield as he slowed the camper to a crawl. In front of us, a line of vehicles snaked around a bend in the road, the cause of the delay as yet unknowable. We had turned off the main highway about half an hour ago, and when we had, a noticeable change had moved through the air like a current. It was the feeling of getting closer, of being Nearly There, of arriving to a promised land.

"This is my favourite part," I said to Horizon, when the excitement of what was to come was nearly on top of us, like a layer of ozone had been replaced with this freak show energy.

"You're just getting a contact high from the exhaust from all these broken-down cars," Horizon joked, then leaned over across the gearbox and stroked my cheek affectionately. The disorientation that had overcome me after running into Holly had mostly dissolved but I still felt a little rattled and was glad I was back in a world I recognized. It would be even better when we finally got to the Field, and out of this limbic state. It was hot in the van, and without movement, even hotter.

The traffic on the secondary road had been thick with cars all headed to the same destination but until now we had been moving at a decent clip, and it was still much too early to be stop and go already. There was a good twenty miles until the next junction would take us to the fair grounds in Olympia where the shows were being held, which were yet another twenty or so miles farther after that. The curve in the road allowed us to see only a dozen or so car lengths ahead of us, and the vehicles we had been travelling beside, behind, around, for miles now, offered no clues as to the hold-up ahead. Still, when we regarded the neighbouring vehicles, people seemed happy. Music and limbs, long tanned legs and braceleted arms, drifted out of nearly every open window. Passengers were talking and laughing to each other, and a few had stuck their heads out the window and were singing along with their music to people in other cars. Open Road songs, of course, and sometimes all the people in a collection of two or three cars in close proximity would turn the delay into a spontaneous sing-along, holding out their arms and serenading each other until one of the cars finally inched ahead of the other. One thing about Birds; they could turn any situation into a party.

I was happy to watch the party from my perch in the camper next to Horizon. It was enough just to be in the midst of it all.

It would take a while for this merry crew to become antsy, but with barely any movement for half an hour, a strange impatience replaced the former crackling, anticipatory energy. Legs that had previously been stretched out of windows or onto dashboards were now planted on the highway, as more and more Birds got out of their cars. Some walked over to other cars, and leaned in with arms folded on window ledges, to compare theories regarding the delay or to have cigarettes lit. Others were just walking down the highway between the two lanes of cars because they could no longer sit still. One shirtless guy with long, stringy brown hair was juggling devil sticks, and he tottered between cars trying not to drop his toys. Some other cars had ditched the highway altogether and were parked on the grass beyond the gravel shoulder, choosing to wait out the traffic jam sitting on the hood of their car or roof of their van, or standing around smoking cigarettes. A group of people were playing hacky sack, hopping and dancing as they tossed the little bean bag from foot to elbow to ankle back to foot. To some of the people on Tour, everything was a game; there was no time to waste being sullen in traffic jams.

The two lanes heading east were now at a standstill, while barely any cars were passing this merry caravan heading west.

"What do you think the problem is," I asked as a little parade of people streamed past the van banging bongo drums and tambourines.

"Who knows? An accident? A hold-up with parking?" Horizon said.

"Already? You think this huge back up is people trying to get into the Field?"

The venue in Olympia was a fairgrounds owned by and adjacent to the university, and tickets to the show could be bought with either a day pass for parking or an overnight camping pass. There were three shows scheduled, with a one-night break between the second and third show. Horizon had tickets for us for all three shows, plus a camping pass for each night. He had tickets for almost every show that Tour.

"Who would you be taking to the shows if I wasn't with you," I asked.

"I definitely would have found another girl by now," said Horizon, and I gave him a playful punch on the arm. "Ow! Easy there, Rocky." He rubbed the spot where I had made contact in exaggerated circles, and peered around the steering wheel at the line of traffic ahead.

"I guess I always get two tickets as a matter of habit," Horizon said. "I knew I'd always find a friend to go in with—though I'm also perfectly fine to go in by myself and get rid of the other one. But I really was starting out on my own, so I wanted to be organized for this Tour and know I could get into the shows I really wanted to see. And since I was doing mail order anyway, the tickets come in pairs. But I'm glad it's you who gets the second seat."

Mail ordering was the best way to ensure getting tickets to the shows, especially when they could be attached to special vouchers like the camping pass, but only the first 5000 most organized Birds would score these tickets. The other advantage to the mail advance was that each order was hand-processed by Open Road's own sales and distribution team. That meant no scalpers, shysters, or illegitimate businesses could scoop up the tickets. They were for fans only; those who were committed enough to spend the time filling out the order forms by hand and mailing in each request separately. In addition to the guarantee of seeing the show, lucky recipients were rewarded with special edition stubs, often embossed with illustrations and logos symbolic of the band's vast repertoire. Keepsakes. The majority of the people attending the shows in Olympia would likely have a combination of tickets and parking or camping passes, but probably not both for all three nights. Or they might be empty-handed, expecting to get tickets on the Field, or just to show up and party with the rest of the Yellow Birds, attendance to shows not being mandatory to life on Tour for many. Everybody, including us, assumed we would stay on the Field for the entire duration of the shows. That was usually how it went; local authority bending to the will of the huge, unruly group, knowing it was easier, cleaner, safer, and frankly, a losing battle, to have the kids stay anywhere but where they were already parked and established for that empty space of time. But we also knew from experience that sometimes, once in a while, the local authorities didn't see it that way.

As much as an influx of ten, twenty, or even fifty-thousand Yellow Birds could swing a local economy from red to black in one weekend, there were some people who just did not appreciate us being in their town. It was like a big, freaky circus had arrived on their nicely manicured lawn. A mostly peaceful circus, but still a circus. And these circus freaks could scare some of the locals, especially in the rural, out of the way venues the Open Road tended to book, knowing that they'd have to accommodate a circus of fans at every show.

But while Farmer Jed in Buckeye, Ohio might rent out his land and his farm and welcome the troops with open arms (and open wallets), his neighbours at the county general might not appreciate the Birds in the same way. When I was with Easy and his crew, we had a routine to help things go as smoothly as possible.

"We'll get the gas, you girls get the provisions." Easy knew that the girls, even the ratty, tattooed, dreaded girls, were seen as less of a threat than the guys, so we were the ones that dealt with the store owners, the service station clerks, or the motel managers in the smaller towns. Vivi always entered a store first, beautiful and clean as she was. Men and women both reacted well to her, as one would to a pretty bauble. She distracted people from the less pretty. In the bigger cities, we didn't usually have issues; business owners in urban centres were less concerned with people who dressed and acted differently than they did, but bigger cities weren't really on the schedule anymore; not since the number of touring Birds had swollen to the size of a travelling city itself. The last big city on a Tour had been about a year earlier in Philadelphia. I hadn't been there, but I had heard about it from other people, who either had been there, or wanted others to think they had been there. Curious now, I turned to Horizon, who was adjusting the large sun visor hanging in front of him.

"Hey, were you in Philly for that show last year?" It wasn't necessary to go into more detail about *what* show, exactly; the stop, the story, was notorious enough.

"I was," he answered, "but it's not like I saw anything; I wasn't in the vicinity when it happened. Word spread pretty quickly though. It was a mess." *It* was the death of a seventeen-year old girl. She overdosed after snorting what she thought was coke, but was really a speedball—a mix of cocaine and heroin. The official story, told to the media, was that when the police found the girl, she was already in the throes of an overdose, and that she died en route to the hospital. But that's not the story that the rest of us heard.

"The cops were trolling for anybody breaking the rules," he said. "They busted kids for having an open beer on the lot, for pissing behind a van, for selling grilled cheese—anything. You know that some cops bashed a couple of kids trying to sneak into the show? Hit them with their billy clubs, cracked some kid's head open."

"That's so awful," I said, shaking my head.

"Right? I was told was that they busted into this van because they smelled weed, and grabbed all the kids in there. There were like four or five of them, but they weren't just smoking weed, they were also doing lines. When the cops saw the coke, they threw all the kids in the back of the wagon. Then they made them sit there, not going anywhere. Meanwhile, this girl starts having a really bad reaction to the dope, which, it turns out wasn't actually just your yuppie-grade coke like they thought it was, and the others are, like, screaming and pounding on the walls of the van to come help this girl, and nobody came." Horizon paused, took a drag of the cigarette he had lit, then passed it to me.

"Nobody came," he said quietly. I just held the cigarette, watching Horizon. He shook his head, remembering, and adusted the visor again before going on. "These guys, they sat there in the back of this police wagon, holding their friend and screaming as she died. And nobody came, not for ages. And by then, it was way too late anyway." The long ash of the cigarette fell on my leg and I brushed it away quickly. I didn't want to interrupt.

"The cops eventually made their way back, checked in and saw what happened, then finally called an ambulance. Then told everybody that she was fine when they packed her in the van, and that they had only been gone five minutes. But I heard it was like half an hour. Want to know the best part?"

"What?" I whispered.

"They still busted all the rest of the kids; charged them with possession, use, whatever."

"Were you—" I thought about the words I should use. "Were you ok when this all happened?"

Horizon flinched. I had scratched an old wound. He looked right at me.

"Of course I was."

"Okay," I said.

"Okay." He said. He took the cigarette back from me and inhaled, a long drag.

The Open Road didn't know about it all until later I guess, so they issued a statement to the family and to the public, the Birds, and this Tour, stopped playing in big cities where the cops were dicks. Road Tour was now playing mostly out-of-the-way areas where the numbers of Yellow Birds could be accommodated and police had no need to act the militarized force that became the norm in urban centres.

Generally, the people and the police in the rural venues were more chilled out about the whole thing. We were a spectacle to some and a menace to others—though when it came to police and security, it was still hard to guess which way the wind was going to blow. The Road had played in Olympia before—many times before, and there had never been a problem with the locals or security as far as I knew.

"Maybe it is just an accident or something," I said turning back to the hold up on the highway.

"Maybe," said Horizon. He didn't sound convinced as he looked out the front window of the camper again, as if an answer would come floating around the bend in the road. He sighed and relaxed back into the seat, adjusting the vents even though the camper didn't have air conditioning and without movement, there was no air was flowing in from outside, either. He took a swig from the water bottle lying in the console beside us.

"We might as well get comfortable," he said, shifting into park and turning off the engine. I was fine with that, fine with an extension of this trip, even if we were stuck sitting in a hot vehicle going nowhere fast. Prolonging our arrival in Olympia, and whatever—whoever—might be there, was okay with me.

For a little while we didn't talk, and I nearly dozed off as I rested my head on the seat back, the music and the chatter of the people around us creating a comforting, ambient soundtrack. It reminded me of lying in my bed at home on hot summer afternoons when I was little, when it was too hot to do much else but nap, and the hydro lines outside buzzed like insects in the heat. That memory sent my mind on a quick, silent journey leaping from one momentary thought of past summers to another. The long, lazy days when my sister and I would play "farm" in the backyard, digging for potatoes that were really just rocks we would pile up on the concrete pavers outside the back door until we got too hot and ran inside for the refreshment of a freeze pop and the tiled relief of the basement playroom.

A few years later, Janine and I reading teen magazines while sitting on a blanet under the shade of the big sugar maple in front of the house, trying to distract ourselves from what was happening inside. My father was packing to leave us that summer, to take the temporary position up north that would soon become permanent. And the permanence with which I had always thought of my family that would soon be revealed as temporary. Another summer, just the three of us; my mother by then unable to resist the pull of her illness into her own obsessions and away from us. My thoughts jumped again a few years in time until they landed with a heart-sinking thud where they often did. I thought about everything that had happened that morning, running into Holly, about my life before now. I opened my eyes.

"I was in an accident, you know."

Horizon cocked his head a bit, questioningly.

"What kind of an accident," he asked.

"A bad one. A little while ago. With my boyfriend."

"I didn't know that."

"I know. I don't really like to talk about it much."

"It's ok then."

"No, I mean, I want to talk about it now, with you. I just, I just don't really like to talk about it much in general. You know?"

Horizon nodded. "Of course. What happened, Kait?"

I tried to sound casual, but my voice came out reedier than usual.

"My mother had been in one of her moods. A mean mood. She had been kind of high, manic, I mean, for days, and then—we always called it the drop. When she dropped, it wasn't into a total sad depression, just this super frustrated, exhausted meanness."

Janine and I knew that would also last days, and it was worse than the manic crazy energy. There were some cycles of just nothing, peace, our closest version of normal, but we never knew how long that might last. Then the moods would start again. Chaotic or catastrophic. So high she couldn't deal with us, or so tired and frustrated she couldn't deal with us. For weeks at a time, there was no in-between. Both were awful.

"So, I don't know," I continued the story. "One day I moved a ceramic owl I wasn't supposed to, or maybe I tripped over a pile of her magazines and woke her up from a nap when I fell. I don't know. Anyway, she was on a rampage, and I didn't want to be there anymore. So I called Alex. My boyfriend," I looked quickly at Horizon. He had turned his body towards me in the seat. His hand was on the knob of the gearshift but he was careful not to extend any part of his body over it, into my space. Giving me room.

"I called my boyfriend to come get me, and I was upset of course, but he knew. Alex knew how my mother was, he understood about her issues and her . . . her *collections* and all of it, so he said he'd come right over. But he'd had a few beers, they were at his friend Manny's, playing poker or something. They got Manny's brother to drive. Manny was in the front, and when they got me, I sat in the back with Alex. I was behind Manny's brother, on the driver's side. Alex was behind Manny, on the passenger side." I paused, biting at a cuticle on my finger. I gazed out my window, away from Horizon. Two guys hanging out at the side of the road were trying to get something—ice?—down the front of a girl's sundress. She had long brown hair streaming down from under a floppy hat and wore huge sunglasses. Horizon followed my gaze.

"That girl looks like Janis Joplin," I said. She was laughing and digging between her breasts for the melting lump. The guys were high-fiving each other.

"The real Janis Joplin would kick their asses if they tried something like that," he said. We didn't say anything for a minute as we watched them all walk towards a car parked on the side of the road.

"Did you know that the back seat on the passenger side is the most dangerous place to sit in a car?" I kept looking out the window as I continued.

The driver, I learned, will always try to protect himself by steering away from whatever he thinks the danger is, leaving the passenger side vulnerable to impact. It's instinct. I pulled hard on the cuticle between my teeth and tasted blood.

"It's almost always the back passenger seat that gets hit first. Takes the brunt of the crash." I looked at Horizon who seemed calm but intent, just listening to me.

"Anyway, as we were driving, the car next to us drifted into our lane, and Manny's brother swerved away from it. But when he swerved, he ended up going over the line into the oncoming traffic lane. Instead of going back into our lane, he went hard to the left when he saw the car heading towards us, and it T-boned the passenger side. Slammed right into us."

The driver, Manny's brother, was fine. Manny's pelvis was crushed, and even now he can barely walk. I got a concussion and broke my arm and my shoulder when I was thrown into the door beside me. I needed surgery twice.

"That's what this scar is," I pointed to the back of my arm above the elbow, ran my finger over the raised seam as Horizon had done countless times over the past weeks.

"What happened to Alex?" Horizon asked gently.

"He was in the bad luck seat," I said simply. Horizon was quiet for a minute. Then he took my hands in his and kissed one then the other.

"Kait. I'm so sorry. Seriously, Kait." I gently pulled my hands back, no longer allowing him to comfort me.

"It's okay; it's just a thing that happened." It was my standard response. I don't know why. To keep it away, I guess. To keep it from being the only thing that I thought about, now that finally, it wasn't.

"You know that that's huge, though, right?"

"No, I know. But, it's—it's just something that happened."

"That doesn't just happen to someone."

"It happened to me."

"I'm sorry it did. It shouldn't have." We were quiet again for a moment. Sitting together in the camper, surrounded by noisy strangers, talking about the things that shame you, shape you—it's more intimate than having sex. But that thread between us, the one that was coiling itself tighter every day, lashing us together with stronger and stronger fibres, I could almost see it and I could certainly feel it.

I took a cigarette out of the pack lying in little box between our seats, but as soon as I put it between my lips to light it, I felt nauseous. My mouth was dry and my head hurt. I put the cigarette back in its pack. I swallowed hard and it hurt my throat

"Is that when you decided to run away and join this circus?" Horizon asked.

"I didn't *decide*," I said, a bit sharply. "It just kind of happened."

I explained how I was out of school for a couple of months, recovering mostly from the concussion, but I was able to graduate anyway because my grades had been really good. But like, university? No way. I just couldn't wrap my head around sorting out student loans and housing or figuring out my courses or even a food plan.

And it's not like I had much help. Alex's parents had made a couple of brief visits while I was in the hospital, and we had tried to stay in touch, but Alex's mother cried when we were on the phone and his father didn't seem to have anything to say at all. I understood of course—they were shattered and I was only connected to them through the son they had lost. By the time I went back to school, the stilted phone calls had ended and we weren't checking in with each other at all. My classmates at my large north Toronto high school didn't seem to know what to say to me either. Some girls I was closer with, Holly among them, tried to act like a protective ring around me, deflecting stares and whispers aimed my way with a pointed glare or slammed locker door, but I had become an object of morbid curiosity. Manny was still recovering and hadn't returned to school, so it was just me, the tragic girlfriend—and Alex of course. In death, Alex became the most popular kid to have ever walked the halls of Baylea Ave. Secondary School. The makeshift memorials that had been erected around the building after the accident had been taken down by time I returned, but I was shown photos: his locker door plastered with yearbook pages, posters, flowers, and trinkets; the trophy case that housed awards he had helped win for the track team festooned with blown up photos of Alex and printed copies of articles out of our school's newsletter or from local papers that had mentioned his sporting accomplishments. Shrines had also grown in front of my and Manny's locker—fake flowers and unlit pillar candles for me, unopened cans of energy drinks and CD cases for him. I tried not to roll my eyes at the images and was glad that the detritus had been swept up and taken away before my return.

But I couldn't avoid the other students and like it or not, I was a novelty. If humans in general have a propensity for rubbernecking, then teenagers in particular have perfected the art. Maybe it was natural to want to be close to tragedy. Maybe doing so felt like it offered some insulation from future bad luck, like a talisman worn to ward off the evil eye. *If it already happened to you, it can't possibly happen to me.* I didn't leave the hospital to go to Alex's funeral as my arm was so messed up, and while I held that fact with equal measures of relief and regret, six hundred people did attend. There's no way everybody there knew Alex personally, but I'm glad his parents would have seen an overflowing chapel and I hope they felt nothing but love and support. At school, even if the initial shock and grief had passed, my return to classes also resurrected the spectre of what had happened and I endured a burst of popularity I hated. Kids I didn't know would come up to me and tell me how beautiful the funeral had been; how they were so sorry for my loss; how much they had loved Alex or thought Alex was funny or what a great runner Alex had been, *and oh my gosh, how are you?* Eventually, this also waned and although I still lived with the notoriety of being the girl whose boyfriend had died, I could fade back into the crowds of students just trying to get to class, just trying to get through the day. Trying to forget about what happened.

Because I didn't tell Horizon that I had planned to break up with Alex several weeks before the accident; that I had felt smothered by him for months, that the last thing I needed was something else taking up what little mental and physical free space I still had in my life at that time. We were young. Things were not great and we both felt it. But I called him that day, and he came to get me.

"The accident, it triggered more of my mother's anxiety, her obsessions, but of course it wasn't about me. The accident had just proven to her that the world could be as out-of-control as she always feared it was, and that she had to do all these things to keep her space safe. But it was hard for her to focus on me.

"I mean, she was good to me while I was recovering from my surgeries, and she kept food in the house and did the laundry and whatever, but she just . . . my needs are pretty abstract to her." I knew my mother wouldn't be able to help me plan my future—just like she wouldn't stop me from putting it on hold.

"So when some people I knew said they were going to see a few Open Road shows right after grad because ours is early, in May, before they went back home to summer jobs and responsibilities and then university and stuff, I asked if I could go too."

"And here you are?"

I looked out the window again. None of the cars had moved; nobody had come walking down the highway to tell us what was going on—nobody seemed to care. I felt a flush of relief: for the boys playing hacky-sack and the girls blowing bubbles and the couples chasing each other around a guy playing a guitar and the people encircling him, singing a Bob Marley song, and the sun shining down on us, and my place in the van with a boy who right now, this moment at least, understood.

"And here we are."

9

A LITTLE WHILE later, cars began to head away from us, on the side of the highway that had previously been nearly empty of traffic. It was definitely a caravan of Birds going by; you could tell by the band stickers on the outside of the cars, and the freaks on the inside. Some of the drivers honked and threw a peace sign as they went, but most just drove. It was weird and disorienting to see so many of us heading in the wrong direction. Soon a guy on a motorbike, no helmet, long ebony dreads flying like a flag behind him, came riding up the centre line of the highway before stopping about a half-dozen cars down the road from our camper. He leaned in towards one of the cars, talking to the people inside. He shook his head, and pointed behind him, gesturing towards the direction he had come. I sat up in my seat.

"I bet that guy has news; we should go see." I reached for the door handle.

"He'll come this way, just stay here," said Horizon. He was always so calm; so patient. I usually jumped at any news, any information, always over-eager to know what was going on and to share what I knew. The funny thing was, I seemed to never know what was going on, and people like Horizon, with no visible sense of urgency to compel them on, they always knew. "Who says he's going to come and talk to us?" I asked. "I should just go walk over, like those guys." I nodded towards a crowd of people who had gathered around the Bird on the motorbike, talking to him and to each other, gesturing and pointing.

"Kait," said Horizon, with a shortness to his tone that I wasn't used to, "Relax. It's not like we're going anywhere."

Annoyingly, Horizon was right. Eventually, the crowd dispersed and motorbike guy made his way up the road. People were talking, and they sounded irritated, but I couldn't glean exactly what information they were sharing. Snippets of frustrated conversation floated past our window.

There were several versions of, "Man, that sucks," and one particularly vehement, "Fuck this shit, dude!" The shirtless guy with the devil sticks was mimicking Cheech, or maybe it was Chong. "Hey, c'mon man, let's just get high and go to Mexico."

Great, I thought, the shows are cancelled. They shut it down! I was just about to vocalize my worries to Horizon when he leaned out the window. The motorbike had made its way to us and stopped right at Horizon's door. I could just see the top of the rider's head out the window. Horizon crossed his arms against the window frame and leaned down.

"Hey man, good to see you, Matteus." He hailed our visitor casually and I shook my head, amused. Of course Horizon knew the guy. Was there anybody he didn't fucking know? That's why he told me to stay put; he knew Matteus would recognize his camper and stop to give Horizon whatever news he was bearing.

"Zion, bro," said Matteus, calling Horizon by the nickname I had heard people use on Tour. They clutched each other's fists in greeting. Matteus stood up and peeked into the camper, nodding at me. "Kait," said Horizon, "This is Matteus. Matteus, Kait."

I smiled at Matteus, and tried not to stutter my hello as Matteus's almond-shaped, almond-colored eyes flashed at me.

"Kait, hello," he said, and thankfully turned back to Horizon before I said something dumb. The good-looking guys always knew each other, didn't they? I tucked my legs under me, waited for news.

"So what's up, Matty," Horizon asked him, "have you been to the Field?"

"Yeah, man, that's what I've been telling these clowns," he gestured behind him with a nod of his head, dreads swinging. "They're being hardcore. No tickets, no camping passes, no dice. You set?" Horizon nodded calmly at this news.

"Yeah, I had heard that they were cracking down this year, so I made sure I was sorted. Tickets and passes for all three shows. We're good. They just turning everybody else away?" It was Matteus's turn to nod calmly. What an agreeable pair, I thought, a little miffed that Horizon hadn't shared his previously held intelligence with me. How had he known that they'd be cracking down? Who, exactly had he heard it from? Even though the more I got to know of Horizon, the more I got to know of his vast and far-reaching network of friends and acquaintances, I couldn't help but fixate on the one person that I knew for sure he was connected to in Olympia. And I had no right to be concerned that he had talked to her, and definitely no right to be jealous if he had. But still.

Matteus and Horizon talked for a few minutes more then clutched hands warmly once again before the motorbike revved back to life and Matteus drove off. The steady stream of cars heading back east towards the interstate was filled with the people who hadn't worried about tickets or passes, just figured they'd pay at the gate or, as was the case at so many other Open Road venues, that the sheer volume of attendants would force the hand of organizers to open the Field to all, for free, understanding that it was much safer to corral the disorganized Birds than to send them packing. But Olympia had a different plan for feckless freeloaders this year: Get off my lawn.

"How did you know they were going to be hardcore about tickets here," I asked Horizon once Matteus had driven away. Horizon got out of his seat and stepped over the console to the space behind us and reached into one of the overhead cupboards in the back of the van. He fished out the little brown case that he kept all the show tickets in. Crouching down, he flipped through the contents of the case like he was sorting through files in a cabinet. I knew the tickets were organized by show and date, meticulous and neat like all of Horizon's things.

"An email went out to all students at the college. Last year, the grounds were almost completely ruined by so many cars on the lawns when it rained. Just chopped up all the grass and cost a fortune for the college to fix." He didn't raise his head up from his task. "So they wanted to avoid another lawn disaster and warned everybody that they were limiting entrance to only the cars that had passes, and put a pretty strict cap on how many passes they'd sell." He brought the case back to the front seat with him, satisfied that all its contents were safe, and keeping them close in anticipation of needing the passes soon. There was no way Horizon had ever received an email from the college directly, but he didn't mention whom exactly he had received the warning from. He leaned over and kissed me, smiling. "Lucky for you, I am prepared."

"You didn't even know I would be here with you for this, " I said. He leaned over and kissed me again.

"Lucky for me, you are."

Ahead of us, horns beeped and people on the side of the highway scrambled to their rides, whooping and shouting. Horizon turned the key in the camper's ignition and eased the gearshift into drive. We were moving again.

Moving approximately five miles an hour. Horizon showed no signs of impatience, singing quietly along to the CD he had pushed into the slot, matching the lead singer's tenor and drumming his fingers on the steering wheel to the erratic beat of what Horizon jokingly called his "favourite peasant music."

"Sure," I said, "If the peasants live in Park Slope."

I liked that Horizon was not an Open Road music purist. So many of the people on Tour, like the people from my high school that I started out with, would only listen to the Road, or one of the jam bands closely associated with them. Truth be told, as much as I loved the Road, as much as their music could feel like it penetrated my very soul, I didn't subscribe to some unwritten rule that fandom was a competition won by the number of live shows in your CD collection or by how obscure of a musical reference you could conjure about the band. In fact, I always thought that the people (let's be honest, mostly dudes) who only listened to the Road or bands featuring a member of the Road entourage or bands that played with the Road, were boring assholes. And they were missing out on a lot of great music. And as much as I might not always have been in the mood for the keening vocalists of one of Horizon's indie bands, I knew I would have jumped out of the camper and walked hours ago if I had had to listen to nothing but noodling eratic jam bands for the duration of the trip.

"So where was your first show? You were on the east coast, right? So, what? Rochester? Hamilton?"

We were moving steadily now, but slowly, and we anticipated it would be at least another couple of hours before we hit the entrance to the college, where every vehicle in front of us was either showing security guards their parking passes and tickets to the concert, or being turned around to come up with some alternative plan, not on college property, thank you very much.

"Buffalo," I said.

"Buffalo? There was no stop in Buffalo on this Tour, was there?" Horizon moved the old camper gingerly forward, as it was prone to stalling at slow speeds. "Nope. But that's where my first show was, two years ago."

"You'd been to shows before?"

"Just Buffalo, winter Tour. It was a bus trip that some guys we kind of knew from school put together. We paid a set amount, and they got us the bus there and back, a ticket to the show, and a hotel room for the night. Like I said, it was winter in Buffalo, so no Field action, no Main Street. But it was a good show. Me and my friend Irene went. It was fun. It's how I got to know Alex."

I didn't expand on that; didn't tell Horizon that Alex had flirted with almost all the girls on the trip all weekend, including, occasionally, me, which made me feel good but also the opposite of special. I didn't tell him that Alex had been so cute and happy, offering everybody handfuls of the weird snacks he had brought with him—things like chocolate covered potato chips and gummy candy shaped liked ears. And I didn't tell Horizon that when the bus dropped us back in town near our suburban high school, Alex ignored all the girls trying to get his number, "We *have* to party together this summer!" dripping all over him like honey, and came and asked me if he could give me a lift home. And that we were together pretty much every single day from then on. A unit. A habit. Until he felt like more work than I had the energy for. Until I called him to come get me one night anyway and he ended up dead.

"So, how come you never went to any other shows?" *With him*, Horizon was kind enough to leave out.

"I don't know. I had a part-time job I didn't want to quit. Because my mother needed me. I didn't want to leave my little sister to deal with her alone. I don't know." The sun was getting lower in the sky. I found my sunglasses in my patchwork satchel and put them on.

"I had had a lot of fun on that trip, the bus was fun, the party at the hotel afterwards was fun, the concert was amazing—did you know that was the night the Road did *St. Paul's Tomb* live for the first time in like, fifteen years? But I felt so peripheral to it all. I knew all about Yellow Birds, of course, but seeing them for real, in their natural habitat—I felt a little like I was crashing somebody else's party. I didn't feel self-conscious, really, just, like they understood something that I didn't. And I wanted to understand it, so badly."

"So you stayed away for two years? That's not really how you become an integrated part of a scene. Besides, it takes time. Everybody had a first show at some point."

"I know, but that's the thing; it didn't seem like anybody had ever experienced a first show via a bus trip full of Twinkies from the suburbs. Everybody seemed so authentic, and I felt like an imposter."

"Wow," said Horizon drawing the word out. "Those were some kind of rose-coloured glasses you were looking through." I squinted at him, questioningly.

"What makes you think the people on the bus with you weren't having an authentic experience," he asked? "And what makes you think the Birds walking around with co-opted Native symbols tattooed on their backs, stoned out of their tree, were? And besides, it's not just about travelling in a pack and letting your hair dread." He was staring straight ahead, concentrating his gaze at the road, even though we were barely moving. Was he mad? The heat in the van as we inched along was becoming more stifling and I was feeling irritated—by it, by the close quarters and by this conversation. I tried to tell him that he wasn't getting my meaning, but he interrupted me.

"How do I look to you, Kait? Do I seem authentic enough for you, or are you going to try to find somebody in Olympia who hasn't grown up and lives in la la land full time? Maybe someone with less baggage but more band t-shirts? Maybe Skate will be there. You can go have some authentic fun with him."

Whoa. Horizon's tone was measured, even though the words stung.

"I don't even know what your baggage is!" I said to him. "Unless you mean your goddess junkie ex-girlfriend? She sounds like a great time. Are you going to go have some authentic fun with her, or did you not bring your needles?" Horizon shifted the camper into park and we jerked to a halt. We had barely been crawling along the highway, but the car behind us honked at our sudden stop anyway. He turned to me and his expression was intense but it wasn't anger I saw in his eyes; it was surprise and pain, like I was a hunter whose sloppy shot had just grazed its prey. It disarmed me.

"That was low," he said. I swallowed hard, not quite ready to abandon my sense of righteous anger.

"So was what you said." We were silent for a few minutes, staring out our own windows. I wanted to get out of the van, out of the heat, out of this situation. I felt a lightheaded again, from the confrontation and the waning adrenaline that still crackled through my nervous system like electricity after a storm. I heard Horizon turn in his seat.

"I'm sorry," he said, his voice back to its normal timbre. But when I glanced towards him, I saw the fire had not quite gone from his eyes. I swallowed hard. *Already?*

"I'm sorry, too," I added, not really feeling compelled to say it with meaning yet. "But you have to tell me what happened with you. She'll be in Olympia, and I know you have a messy history. But I'm pretty sure whatever I'm imagining is way worse than what really happened, and I don't feel like going into this unprepared."

The car behind us beeped again. Traffic was moving. Horizon sighed, turned back to the dashboard and put the camper in gear. We went about twenty feet before we stopped. Horizon shook his head a little and exhaled audibly. He was trying to shake off his irritation, or maybe just stalling.

"There's no tragic tale to tell, Kait. I don't know what you heard from other people, but I promise you, their version is more exciting than what really happened." He turned his head only slightly, but his words came right to me.

"And I'm not a fucking junkie."

My heart dropped in my chest and I wondered if I was asking too much, demanding a confession he was not ready to give. It was confusing. How much was an exchange of our bodies worth? Were we bartering for intimacy? Was I asking this of him because I had just shared something so personal? Horizon refused to turn his eyes from the road and I pushed down a fear that despite the easy closeness we had developed in the time we had been together, this was a boundary he wasn't ready for me to step past; that I was trespassing in a part of his life that was too private to give me access too. But in that moment, I decided that it was necessary. For this to feel real and for me to be able to feel safe, feel trusted—and to trust him.

"Tell me what happened then," I prompted. When I thought the silence was going to last forever, Horizon spoke.

"I met Larissa through some friends at a Christmas party."

"What," I said, before I could stop myself, "I thought you guys were high school sweethearts or something."

He turned to me. "Seriously, Kait, right now I don't care to know what version of my life story someone else told you."

"Ok, I'm sorry. I won't—go on."

"We hit it off. We were together for the rest of the year, we both graduated from our *different* schools, and then we went on Tour. But Larissa was supposed to go to Europe with her parents that summer as a kind of grad present-slash-they wanted to keep an eye on her kind of thing, and she blew it off." She was eighteen, he said, it was her call, but her parents were both doctors and very rich, and they were mad. To them, Larissa was a perfect little thing, who made them look good, but they put a lot of pressure on her. Too much pressure." I nodded despite wanting to see Larissa as a villain, knowing all too well how difficult it could be to live in the shadow of your parents—whether you were saddled with their overachievements or their struggles.

"She was already a serious pothead and doing a lot of other things that they just didn't see, or didn't want to see, before we got together. But they figured I was the problem because I was their daughter's boyfriend and I was not rich.

"Anyway, we went on Tour and she decided she wasn't going to go to university in the fall. I knew I wasn't going. I got in to engineering at UBC but I deferred, because I had to work for a year. My parents don't have a lot of money, they work hard, but there was nothing there for me, and I didn't want fifty-thousand dollars in student loans by time I graduated, so that was always my plan." Horizon glimpsed at me when he said that, and I could see the pride and the hurt in his eyes. Before I could stop it, tears sprung to mine. He turned away again quickly, and I think I blinked them back before he saw. On the side of the highways, someone was doing tricks on a BMX bike. Others were stopping to watch. They applauded the tricks the biker landed, but applauded the tricks he didn't land even more enthusiastically.

"Larissa was supposed to go to school in Toronto—OCA. Art school. I didn't know that she hadn't told her parents she wasn't going to go."

"You were in Toronto! I heard it was Boston. I can't believe you were in Toronto!" I interrupted before I could stop myself.

"Kait." Horizon said.

"I'm sorry, it's—you were in Toronto!"

"That's not the—" Horizon shook his head. "Listen, that's not the point. The point is, yes we were in Toronto, because I figured I could work there as well as I could work in Vancouver, and also, being away from Vancouver made it easier to forget that I was supposed to be a student, not a bloody waiter."

"You were a waiter?" I was incredulous now. I couldn't picture Horizon as a waiter. But I couldn't really picture him doing anything in real life, away from Tour. Tour was where we came to forget about real life.

"Kait, yes. Shut up and let me tell you the story. We both worked at the same restaurant. And you know what there is at restaurants?"

I shook my head no.

"Drugs. Lots of them. Lots of late nights and lots of partying and lots of going to crazy clubs afterwards for more partying, and Larissa loved it. She was having a fucking ball. Anyway, we took some time off and went on fall Tour and the partying continued. We came back for the winter and I went back to work, but she didn't. She just partied more. And her parents were bankrolling her, because they had no clue that she never actually attended school. And I had no idea that they still thought she was going. I thought they were just sending her money because that's what rich parents do." Horizon shook his head and put his arm out the window to adjust the mirror before he continued. "They finance their child's fucked up life because they think she's just trying to figure things out. What did I know? Anyway, that winter was crazy, and I was so unhappy. Larissa just did lots of drugs and stayed in the house, and I worked my ass off. But the money from her parents was paying all of our rent, and I brought home food from the restaurant and got good tips, so I knew that as fucked up as things were getting with Larissa, I was at least saving money and doing what I said I was there to do."

"Are you telling me you never did drugs?" I asked. There's no way the truth could be so far off from the story I had heard. Horizon shook his head.

"No, I did, I did. It was part of the culture. I mean, I always smoked pot, that's not it, but yeah, I did some coke at the restaurant, and drinking. Like everybody there. But Larissa had gone way past that. She was doing speedballs. It wasn't enough. She was taking pills. It wasn't enough. So then it was heroin." He stopped here, knew that was what I was waiting for.

"And you?" I asked gently now. Horizon nodded slightly, quickly.

"Yeah, I did some of that, too. You have to understand, Kait, it was there, all the time, and she wanted me to do it, too. To be close to her again, she said. And I wanted that too. It's complicated." I waited for him to go on, tried to block out the ambient noise of the cars and the music and the people going by.

"Anyway, at first I didn't do much partying, just a night here or a night there. The plan was to go on spring Tour, then I would work through the summer, then that was it, I was going back to Vancouver in August, to start school. But it kind of overwhelmed us. All of it. I got sucked in, too. We didn't go on spring Tour. We didn't go anywhere. We stayed in our apartment, getting high."

The heat in the van was excruciating. I willed the traffic ahead of us to move, even a little, to provide any breeze. Any movement.

"I hated it," Horizon continued. "I did. I knew it wasn't what I wanted, it wasn't who I was, and I hated myself and I hated Larissa. So one night, in May, I did the only thing I could think to do. I called her parents. Told them what was going on. She hadn't been back home in months, since a really quick trip at Christmas, but things had gotten a lot worse since then, and how they didn't know that she had never gone to school—well, people see what they want to see, you know?" I nodded here, feeling a little sick.

"Larissa's parents were at our door the very next night. Less than twenty-four hours after I called them. And it was horrible. I hadn't told Larissa that they were coming, and I hadn't told her parents how bad things really were. That night was so awful, Kait. Her parents flipped, of course. Her mother cried, her father was raging at me. How the fuck did this happen to her, he kept yelling. *To* her! She did this to herself, I yelled back. I told him, I called you, remember? It was just such a mess. They totally blamed me, threatened to call the cops. And Larissa was screaming at all of us that she hated us all, that we had no right, that we should all get the fuck out or she would kill us—it was insane, it really was.

"I don't even know how it all ended, just that this went on pretty much all night. Her mother packed up her stuff, her father was on the phone with people, Larissa was going between puking, passing out, and raging at us, and I was sitting on the floor, in my room, crying, shaking like a baby, trying to figure out how I had let this get so out of control. How my life was so fucked up."

I swiped at my own tears that were falling now, sad and ashamed that I had demanded this from him, and that I had believed a different version of this story so easily. Horizon looked over at me, gave me a little smile and squeezed my leg reassuringly. I stayed silent, determined to allow him to finish the story at his own, uninterrupted pace.

"They were going to call the police, have me take the fall for having the drugs there, all of it, but Larissa's mother convinced her husband to call my parents first. They were so fucking disappointed. I still feel so guilty about how much I disappointed them. But whatever they said to Larissa's dad persuaded him to not have me arrested, at least. In the morning they left, the three of them, Larissa too tired and fucked up to really fight, her dad had given her a sedative, I think, and I found out later that they went straight to some fancy rehab in Minnesota. I guess Larissa's dad wasn't as huge of a dick as I thought, because he handed me a cheque for five-hundred bucks, and told me to get my ass home, my parents were waiting for me. He added that he never wanted to see me around his daughter again or he would call the police then murder me before they got there." Horizon huffed out a laugh, and I did too.

"So I did. I went home. And my parents were mad, but mostly they were scared, and glad I was back. So I began seeing a shrink, and did this, like, outpatient rehab because we couldn't afford rich-kid Minnesota rehab. I don't think I needed to go away. I just needed to be away from Larissa. She needed to be away from me. We triggered something destructive in each other. Getting clean physically sucked, I was so sick, but I knew that was coming, so I could deal with it. Mentally though, it was tough for me. I got depressed. I had to deal with the guilt and shit with my parents, but I did it. And then, that fall, I went to school, just like planned. Sure, I was on Zoloft and felt old and tired, but otherwise, just like planned."

"Wait," I said, not worried as much about the interrupting anymore, "You did go to school? Are you going back in the fall again?" Horizon shook his head. "I'm done for now. I finished the year, but I deferred again. I just—I needed a break. I felt like an imposter at school; I had an ok time, but I never really made any friends. I didn't want to party, go to the bar like everybody else was doing. I needed . . . this. For a while, anyway. I can always go back, or really, I think I can already go get a decent job whenever it is I feel like reentering the real world. But you know—*a map won't tell you where you really need to be.*" He was quoting another Road song, a pretty popular one called Rest Stop, and we both knew what the next line was: *And baby, right now, I just need you here with me.*

Horizon put his hand to my cheek. I put my own hand on top of his, smiled, then took it to my lips and kissed it.

"So," he said, "how's that for authentic?"

My heart flipped and I kissed his hand again.

This could happen, I thought. *I would love you.*

After the intensity of the morning, we had sat in near silence for a long while, letting the sounds of the people and the music coming from the vehicles surrounding us be our soundtrack. We needed to rid the atmosphere of our ghosts, and reset things in the front seat. I was ready to change the vibe, make it lighter.

"What foods do you think of when you think of your childhood?" I asked. "What foods did, like, your mum make that you miss?"

"Hmm," said Horizon, "my favourite childhood food, huh? Is it a cop-out to say Froot Loops?"

"Yes!" I said, pleased that he was playing along.

"Okay, okay, let's see . . ."

His elbow rested on the window ledge next to him, with his arm extended up, touching the top of the open frame. As he was thinking about his answer, he drummed his fingers. "Ok, then I think it's Mac n' Cheese Hamburger Helper."

"I'm sorry you had such a devastatingly boring childhood."

Horizon laughed. "Honestly, it wasn't good to begin with, but then my mother cooked the meat until it was grey. To top it off, she would add garlic powder and paprika, as if either of those could improve the taste. It was as terrible as it sounds, really. To this day, I can't stand ground beef. But that's what I think of."

"Yeah, that's awful. I hope you were able to salvage your meals with as many Froot Loops as you wanted for dessert."

"Nope; dessert was a version of Jello salad much of the time. You know, like a neon lime green wreath with canned tangerine sections trapped inside of it."

"No! Those are truly disgusting meals. Jews do not eat that kind of food."

"No? What kind of food do Jews eat?"

"We eat disgusting food too," I said. "But you know, not out of a box. My grandparents were all peasants, Polish and Russian immigrants, and they cooked like peasants. They wasted nothing, and refrigerated everything. Even cereal and tea bags, right into the fridge. My mother cooked like a peasant with a firm 1970's housewife sensibility. Her favourite thing to eat is pickled cow's tongue."

Horizon wrinkled his nose a bit. "Yeah, that's kind of gross. So is that your childhood food memory?"

"God no, I wouldn't eat that. But I still like my Jewish peasant food: chicken soup with matzo balls, knishes, brisket. And ketchup stew."

"Ketchup stew?" Horizon sounded skeptical. I appreciated that, of all the foods I had listed, this was the one he had questioned the validity of.

"That's where the peasant really meets the seventies housewife. My mother thought ketchup should be used to enhance almost every dish, so she made a perfectly nice beef stew, then stirred in a ton of ketchup. It's actually better than it sounds."

"It can't be. It sounds terrible."

I gasped, exaggeratedly. "Don't yuck my yum!"

"What? You *yucked my yum* repeatedly."

"No I didn't. I commiserated with you and yucked your yuck. I actually liked my childhood meals. Yours were a culinary nightmare."

Horizon shook his head at me, suppressing a smile. I sighed audibly and sat back in my seat. "Seriously, I would kill for a bowl of matzo ball soup."

"You would kill for one?"

"Well, just a chicken. It's been years since I've had some. My mother doesn't really cook any more, and certainly nothing with as many moving parts as that. She seems to live on toast and tea and paranoia and rage now."

"Yikes, good times." Horizon grimaced.

"Right? What do you think a therapist would say about ketchup stew?"

"Probably not as much as she would say about the paranoia and rage."

I was happy that our reset had worked, and reached forward for the magazine I had stashed under my seat. "Yeah, you're probably right." I flipped through the pages and let my thoughts drift, from home, to the camper, to the show we would see that night.

Bob Marley said that when the music hits, you feel no pain. That's what it's like to be at an Open Road concert. You don't watch an Open Road show—at least, there's not much to see. Five fat middle-aged men on a stage, looking down at their instruments, maybe a collage of psychedelic fractals projected onto the giant screens behind them. It's all about the magnificent collateral damage after the music hits you. And the music does hit you: it ambushes you, envelops you, takes you hostage, quite literally moves you, first with a wall of sound, then with the undeniable compulsion to communicate the band's words and notes back to them with your body. Maybe you just sway or bob or nod, but most don't. Most are taken to communicate through big, full-body gestures. There is an entire group that follows the Road called the Spinners, who whirl like Dervishes, arms above their heads, heads tilted up, eyes shut in beatific reverie. And they spin. And they spin and it is beautiful and dizzying to watch the kaleidoscope because they wear long, full, colourful skirts, even the men, all the better to dazzle you with, and they seem to never stop.

There are less organized groups of people spinning, and skipping, and staggering and even though most people engage in their dancing in a purely individual, almost isolated way, it is a collective. Hit by the same music. Pummeled by the same words, thrown by the same crashing, building, climaxing jams.

And you feel no pain.

Horizon shifted into second gear and up ahead, the entrance gate to the university's adjacent parking lot finally came into view.

10

I HAD BEEN worried about being in actual show with Horizon. I liked to dance, no matter how far my quest for space to do so took me from the action of the stage. What if Horizon was an audiophile, more intent on being front and centre, right by the band or, like some nerds, right next to the mixing and taping boards, as if he had some hand in the sound engineering of the show? What if this was where we finally discovered we were incompatible? But once again, my fears surrounding our connection was unfounded, and Horizon was happy to let me lead us where I wanted to be, which that night, was on the low grassy hill, beyond the seating of the concert bowl, where we could eke out a spot and dance with a little bit of room to ourselves.

Even after we were sitting down and settled into our spot, I was distracted, hyper-aware of everybody walking by, everybody who moved in our direction. Was Eartha here? Was Larissa? The vigilance was becoming tiring and making me anxious, and Horizon was quick to notice.

"What's wrong, Kait?" He asked as he stretched out a bit, claiming some extra space for us or maybe just relaxing. I hugged my knees, scanning the crowds.

"Nothing. I was looking for Eartha. She knows I'd be on the lawn."

"Do you think she got in?" I nodded quickly, still not turning away from the horde. "Maybe."

"Okay. Are you comfortable? We should have brought a blanket, this grass is itchy. We'll bring one tomorrow." He had picked at a blade of grass, tickled my arm with it.

"I'm good. Just people watching."

"Me too."

But when I had turned to him, he was looking just at me, and his eyes were a little darker than usual as he squinted a bit in the drooping sun. He had seemed serene, unworried, so I had relaxed a little. I didn't even know what Larissa looked like, and I wasn't sure whether I had been trying to find her, or trying not to. Concentrate on the person who is here, I told myself. And loosening my body up a little bit, I realized that watching the crowd wouldn't get me any answers anyway; if I wanted to know if Larissa was in the vicinity, I only had to watch Horizon. I'd know, I was sure of it. And with that decision made, I stopped watching for her completely, and allowed myself to just enjoy it all. Being at the show. With Horizon. As the sun set. In Washington. Having any one of those things makes you lucky, I told myself. Having all of them makes you the luckiest goddam person in the world.

Right at that moment, the amphitheater had lit up, and the band ambled on stage as we all jumped to our feet. Horizon grabbed my hand and his topaz eyes shone.

"Here we go," he said.

At an Open Road show, your ticket in was your ticket in, and every concert was treated as though the entire stadium was general seating, no matter what your pass stated, or how much you paid for it. If you wanted to sit, you found an empty seat. If you wanted to be in the open area, you moved. Every once in a while, a rookie would come up to somebody and try to turf them based on what was printed on their ticket, but there was truly no point. You figured out pretty fast that that was not how things worked out here.

And that was fine with me, because I never wanted to sit anyway, and if I did, the grass—or a hallway, or an aisle—was suitable. Like so many other aspects of the shows, it probably looked chaotic. But the inside of a grandfather clock looks chaotic too. As long as all the various pieces move the way they're supposed to, it keeps perfect time. At a Road show, the pieces move in sync. Horizon and I seemed to as well. He wasn't a flagrant dancer—I didn't expect him to be—but he did his own thing, moving mainly his upper body, head, and shoulders grooving together in time, with an occasional sway of his hips that was pretty damn sexy. And I did my thing, kind of skipping in place to the more upbeat songs, hands in the air as though we were at church, praise dancing to the sermon on stage. To some, I think we were. Every now and then, Horizon and I would pull together and I would stand in front of him with his arms around me, my head resting on his chest, or I would stand beside him and his hand would sit on that spot on my back, that just-so spot above the tailbone that symbolizes intimacy. The perfect spot. Any lower and you know it's just lust; any higher and it looks like politeness. But that spot, in the small of your back—when a hand is there, it means there is affection, familiarity. You can judge a relationship by noticing the very simple act of where one person's hand rests on another person's back.

That hand on my back was so reassuring. It asked nothing of me, but connected me to him, us to the music, the music to the whole universe, it felt.

The Olympia shows were some of the best I had ever seen. Ernest must have done precisely the right amount of drugs to keep him spontaneous but not sloppy, and though they didn't pull out any particularly rare songs, they performed the pieces that typically did the best live, but in a surprising order. Be on Tour long enough (or listen to enough recorded shows), and you knew that, even though the set list changed daily and was unpredictable, there were conventions the band always stuck with. You got to know that *Pretty Polly* always followed *Deal on Fifth*, and that *Indigo Mornings* always followed *Pretty Polly*. But on the first night of Olympia, they decided to forgo the *Deal/Polly/Indigo* standard and opened second set with *Pretty Polly* straight into a pretty funky cover of Dawn Penn's *You Don't Love Me (No, No, No)*, which excited the crowd to no end and kept the energy up through what is typically a mellow second half.

By the end of it, Horizon and I were both a sweaty, happy mess, holding hands again as we made our way back to the Field discussing how soon it would be until recordings of the night's show would star circulating.

"That's going to be trading fast," Horizon said, swiping the hair away from his eyes, the exuberance of the crowd still buzzing through us as we made our way out of the stadium.

He meant the live tape of the show. Chances were that even most people in the Field would have heard at least a muffled version of that night's concert, but everybody—inside and outside of the show—would feel that it had been special. Already we were hearing declarations like, *So-and-so's going to be bummed she missed that one*, or, later, in the Field, *Shit, if I had known it was going to be that good, I would have hustled harder to get in.*

Some people like to go straight to the party after the show, singing, smoking, shouting on Main Street or at a bon fire or a drum circle in front of someone's car somewhere on the Field, pushing the euphoria to it's outer limits, these pockets of energy pulsing deep into the night. And I knew that after a show like the one we had just seen, the party would spill into all corners of the Field, a miasma of drug- and music-fuelled afterglow.

But that wasn't what I wanted, not that night, or almost any night after a show. As much as I inhaled some sort of primal life force from the music and energy while I was right in it, I also needed desperately to exhale, to process it all after it was over. Eartha had recognized that in me right away, seemed to need it as well, and she and I would sneak away from the crowds for a while, find a grassy patch or an uninhabited picnic table to sit at, or fence post to lean against, and welcome the comedown slowly, gently, without being amped up again like an electric current coming from the jagged, messy elation in the Field.

Horizon, I felt certain, would be okay with a retreat from the crowds, and he was.

"Do you mind if we just go back to the van for a bit?" I spoke directly into his ear, loud as I could above the din of the exuberant crowd around us. My voice was hoarse and my throat was sore, though I didn't even really remember yelling at all during the show. My jaw also hurt from clenching it, though I don't remember really doing that, either. But I remembered smoking a joint during intermission, and though it hadn't tasted like anything besides shwaggy home-grown, there may have been something else in it. That would account for the sore throat and clenched jaw. And maybe a little bit of the *show's over* melancholy that was setting in.

"Are you alright?" Horizon asked, matching my volume.

"I just like a bit of a break right after a show."

Horizon turned away from the direction of Main Street, towards his camper. The rows behind each side of Main Street were narrower, somewhat quieter, though many people still set up a shop or stove to sell stuff, like me and Eartha had with our quilt and stools and hair-wrap shop. When you were vending, being closer to Main Street was a boon, but when you had no interest in the hustle, it was better to be a few rows back, where there was a bit more privacy, and a lot less partying. So our spot, secured in what we were told was "long-term" camping, was about five rows back from Main Street, and closer to the edge of the entire Field. It was a prime spot, shady thanks to a large maple tree in full, leafy bloom. One more advantage to being somebody who thought ahead and was prepared and somewhat strategic in his travel plans. We never got a nice spot like this with Easy. More likely, he would have had to park much closer to the entrance gates, with people and cars constantly going by, or in the mud or near the port-o-Johns; wherever they pushed the straggler's vehicles, which Big Blue Bertha always was.

"You don't have to come if you don't want; I'm okay on my own," I shouted through the people moving in front of us, causing us to extend our arms and occasionally break apart from each other. Fast enough though, Horizon would find my hand again and fasten it in his. He turned back again to face me and closed the space between so people couldn't walk through us.

"I want to come with you, Kait. Are you sure you're okay?" His expression of concern surprised me and I smiled reassuringly, not wanting him to think I truly wasn't okay. I was fine. I was.

"No, no, I'm good; I need a little decompression time after a show."

We kept walking, the crowds around us thinning as we made our way further beyond the mouth of the amphitheater entrance and Main Street, but Horizon soon stopped in front of a group of guys heading our way. He dropped my hand and embraced one of them.

"Albie," Horizon and his friend clapped each other on the back.

"Zion. Man, how are you?" Albie was tall with shoulder-length dark hair and a wide smile. I didn't recognize him, or his name. Horizon also greeted the three guys with Albie, and they chatted for a minute about how amazing the show had been and how good it was to see each other again. I stepped up beside Horizon.

"Hi, I'm Kait." I waved and Horizon put his hand on my back in a small gesture of apology and presentation.

"Ah, sorry! Kait, this is Albie, he's an old friend. Albie, Kait. And this is Matt, Fong, and Nathan." He gestured to the group.

"Hey," I said. Albie had a drum hanging from a strap around his chest, and a six-pack in one hand.

"Listen," he said, "Why don't you come hang out and we can catch up and you can tell me where you've been, dude." He slapped Horizon on the arm good-naturedly.

"Yeah, yeah, totally," said Horizon, "We're just going to go back to the van for a sec-"

"No," I interrupted. "Go, be with your friends, and I'll come find you in a bit. Seriously, it's all good."

Horizon waited a few seconds, perhaps wondering if I meant what I was saying. He must have decided I did.

He handed me the keys to the camper. "Follow the sound of the drum when you feel like company."

He had that sparkle in his eye again. Albie banged on the little talking drum at his side for emphasis. A third of the jokers out here were banging drums, so I knew I would just be walking the rows until I found them. Horizon leaned in and kissed me quickly.

"See you soon," then he walked off with Albie's group. I heard them laughing almost immediately, and I was happy to see Horizon so animated and relaxed with other people. I made it back to the camper in a few minutes, glad that he was off with some friends, glad that I could have a bit of time to myself.

After changing and drinking about a gallon of water, I lay on the bed and stared out the skylight of the pop-up top. The camper was stuffy, so I left all the doors and windows open for a bit, but once the cooler night air displaced the staid remains of the daytime, I closed everything but the glass sliders behind the bed and the pop-up. It felt like being in a cool, dark cocoon, the sounds of the party distant enough to act as familiar white noise, barring the occasional punctuation of an enthusiastic whoop filtering in. I was soon so comfortable that I contemplated staying in the loft, letting the party go on around me, letting Horizon have his night without me, and me having mine without him. It would have been fine to do so, but I worried that eventually Horizon would be concerned that I hadn't come back. And I worried that he wouldn't be. So I lay on the bed, delaying action and fighting the urge to doze off. A knock on the side of the camper brought me back from the edge of sleep, and I sat up quickly.

"I'm here, Horizon," I said, shuffling off the bed to unlock the door. But it wasn't Horizon standing outside the door.

"Hey baby," Earth said in a husky voice. I vaulted myself out of the camper and right into her, nearly knocking her down. I hugged her tight, tiptoes nearly dangling as I hung from her arms and it felt like it had been much longer than the week or so since I had last seen her.

Soon we were sitting comfortably in the camping chairs Horizon had unfolded earlier in front of our space, and all thoughts of wandering the rows of partiers to find him were gone from my mind.

"I have something for you," said Eartha, reaching into the bag at her feet. She rummaged for a minute, then brought out two large lumps, each wrapped in a napkin. I immediately knew what she was holding, and if the shape of the items hadn't given it away, the aroma certainly did. "Eggrolls," I practically drooled, reaching out for the gift. It was only then that I realized how hungry I was.

Getting food after a show is a must, but meeting up with Albie had distracted me from that part of the plan earlier. I had figured we would grab a grilled cheese on the way back through the Field, or maybe a veggie dog, or if food had been elusive or a hassle, there was always a bag of apples and some potato chips in the van. But the eggrolls on the Field were a rare treat, and they were my absolute favourite; fat and greasy and filled to bursting with bean sprouts, cabbage, carrots and an elusive, but absolutely tantalizing blend of spices mixed through. Wan and Pixie, the husband-wife team that made the eggrolls, weren't at every show, but I was always on the lookout for them. They dressed like ragtag fairy tale characters and if they had told me they had been on Tour since the first time the Open Road ever played, I would have believed them. And they made the most delicious giant eggrolls.

"So, how's the honeymoon," Earth asked, pushing the stringy end of a bean sprout back into her mouth.

"Good," I said, mouth full.

We talked easily as I tried not to rush the inevitable disappearance of my eggroll. Eartha told me the news from Big Blue Bertha; how they had spent the hiatus between shows at a KOA near Eugene overrun with Birds; how the communal showers at the campground had become the scene of a Turkish bath/low-level orgy ("I don't know," said Eartha, "ask Skate about that one."), how Easy had freaked out when they heard they were turning people away at the gates in Olympia—unsurprisingly, nobody in the van had tickets or camping passes, and how, at the last minute, somebody had come riding up the highway on a bike looking to sell a three-day pass that for some reason they could no longer use, and pooling their money, Bertha's crew had made it happen.

The only thing that surprised me about any of Eartha's story was that the rider was not on a unicycle with a chimp on his shoulders. That's the kind of circus it was on Tour.

"But seriously, how's it going with you? Is it working with Horizon?"

"It is; it's good." I licked the last of the flavourful oil from the eggroll's crispy skin off my fingers. Eartha waited for me to go on. "He's not—he's not what I thought," I said, meaning, he's not what *you* thought.

"The stories about him were blown up; exaggerated. He told me everything." Eartha raised her eyebrows. I tried to sound casual, like I wasn't trying to convince her of anything.

"But it's been really good. We click."

"And have you seen Larissa?"

"No, I don't even know if she's here. And we haven't exactly been trying to find her." Which was not exactly true. Eartha might have guessed as much.

"Ok; well you seem good," she said.

"I am good," I answered. We chatted for a little while longer, sometimes stopping to watch the people trickle by. Two shirtless men with long, scraggly hair and beards stopped in front of us.

"Sisters," one of them said, bowing, hands together.

"Hey," said Eartha, clearly not wanting to engage.

"May we invite you to join us for midnight prayer," he asked.

"No thanks."

He bowed again. "Blessings." The other one reached into a satchel that was slung over his bony shoulders, and held out two water bottles. We each took one.

"Thank you," I said. The Pilgrims moved on. Eartha shook her head. "Wingnuts."

"What's it say?" I gestured at her water bottle.

"Okay, quiz time: bible verse, or Open Road lyric?"

I put down the water bottle I was holding and wiggled my fingers, weaving them together into an accordion and stretching my interlaced hands out before me as if I were prepping for a fight. "I'm ready."

"*I'll consume you with my soul; I'll roll you up, I'll smoke you whole.*"

"No! They put that on a water bottle? Nobody likes that song! Gross!" We both laughed, knowing the line came from a late-70's-era Open Road song called *Jelly Roll,* a kind of psychedelic-disco number from an album entitled, *Standing Room,* widely regarded as one of the few—but colossal—misses in the vast Open Road repertoire.

"What the hell is the bible verse?" I asked Eartha. She turned the bottle.

"*The acts of the flesh are obvious. Galatians, 5:19*"

"Also gross. And I've never heard of Galatians before."

"Me neither, but they sound like pervs."

We were still laughing when Horizon came back. "Hey, Eartha, how are you?" He said, walking up to me and putting his hand on my shoulders. It felt nice, but also proprietary. *She's mine*, the hand seemed to say. He kissed the top of my head. "I figured you had found a friend. Or fell asleep."

"Hey," I said, reaching up to touch one of the hands on my shoulders.

"How's it going, Horizon," Eartha greeted him.

"Good, good. Did you see the show?"

"Of course not," Eartha said, getting up.

"Where are you going," I asked her.

"Figured this was my cue to leave."

"No—"

"You don't—" Horizon and I talked at the same time, and I was glad the message from both of us seemed to be the same.

"Don't go," I told her, "Stay and hang out. I miss you."

Eartha looked from me to Horizon, then sat back down. "Phew, good. Because I miss you like crazy, too Kaity-cat. I honestly don't know how we managed to get along without you. You are like a balancing force for good in the van."

"I was?"

"Yes. You *are*."

I appreciated Eartha letting me know my place in Easy's van was still there should I need it, and I was certain she was also letting Horizon know it too.

I was with my two favourite people in the world at the moment, and I was afraid our gathering would fizzle with tension all night, but Horizon wouldn't take the bait, and soon enough we were enjoying a natural, comfortable conversation. Eartha stayed for a long time, all of us laughing and talking, as if this was the hundredth night the three of us had spent together, not the first. We talked until night's cool darkness pulled a blanket over the Field, and the pockets of music and drumming dropped away like pebbles down a hillside.

We slipped into an easy rhythm for the next few weeks, as we travelled up and down the northwest states, with trips to shows as far east as Montana and Wyoming. Our days were spent on the road or in the Field, and nights were almost always spent at the shows, or when we were between Tour dates, hanging out with the Birds that were travelling the same path. It was a happy coincidence that we seemed to meet up with the same people over and over, and happier still that we actually enjoyed the company of the people that we kept seeing at the rest stops, the campgrounds, the Benny's.

We hung out with another couple from Lafayette, Arkansas, who we both really liked. Esme and Darcy were both jewellery designers, Esme crafting necklaces and bracelets out of found metal objects, managing to make discarded washers and wire look dainty and elegant, while Darcy honed ear spikes and rings out of foraged bone and wood. They were both funny, sarcastic, and down-to-earth, and I loved watching the easy way they had with each other; loved listening to them tell stories in their lilting rural accents.

"We're the only gay people in Lafayette County," Esme told us one night.

"Except on Friday nights when all the other gays tell their wives they're going to play poker and then go to the bar in Lewistown." Darcy's laugh was robust and kind, and we couldn't help but laugh with her. It was good to meet different people; new people who got to know us just as Kait and Horizon, without history or context.

Many Birds didn't stray from the coast during the Tour because it wasn't worth such a long drive for only a handful of shows, and sometimes because the vehicles they travelled in couldn't take the wear and tear. Big Blue Bertha certainly couldn't anymore, and it had already been established when I joined Easy's group that there would be no jaunts further east than Idaho or Nevada.

Easy had told me that Road tour zig-zagged like this to get some of the Birds off their tail, give the circus a rest. And that it was up to us to be good fans; to give them what they wanted. I wasn't at all sure that such a plan had been so deliberate, and when I mentioned Easy's theory to Horizon, he smirked.

"Or maybe the Open Road is not the only band touring right now, and sometimes venues can't always be booked in a neat little geographical line." I said.

We were travelling from Laramie, Wyoming to Denver, where the Road was going to play two shows in the legendary Red Rocks Amphitheater. It would be my first time in that venue, and thinking about Easy made me miss that crew and especially Eartha again. I was bummed that I wouldn't be there with her. Shows in Red Rocks were always said to be some of the best, and also the place where the Road historically played *Sand Creek*, one of their few overtly political songs about the 1864 massacre of two hundred Cheyenne and Arapaho people. It's more aggressive than most of their other songs, drums like the hoof beats of a hundred charging horses, lyrics scathing and snarling, culminating in a growling crescendo of guitars that crackles along with Ernest's most angry, anguished roar. The song sent shivers down my spine, and I really hoped I would get to see it live.

Eartha and I had once eaten mushrooms and lay on top of a picnic table, listening to a recording of a live version of the song on repeat, over and over again for hours, until the batteries in the boom box died and some unseen person in a tent nearby had yelled, "Thank god!"

We had laughed so hard we almost fell off our perch.

But there would be no Eartha at Red Rocks, and though I was sad about that, I was excited to see it with Horizon.

We pulled off the highway into a service station, already littered with other Birds streaming out of their vehicles for gas and toilets and snacks. We saw Esme and Darcy there as well, and promised to meet up at a rest-stop just over the state line in a few hours, where we would figure out which campground to go to for the night. I went to use the bathroom while Horizon filled the tank.

On my way back, I replayed the short chat I had just had with another Bird at the bathroom sink, who had told me that the best place to camp would be the KOA off exit 38, as it was just a tad further from the highway than some of the other campgrounds, and less likely to have booked up by the time we'd get there. I was eager to tell Horizon, and pleased we could get on the road with a loose plan in the works, but as I turned the corner around the grungy building to walk back to the camper, I saw him standing still and erect, arms folded tightly across his chest. He was talking to someone, though from the angle of my approach, the pumps obstructed my view and I couldn't tell who was on the other side of the conversation. I had never seen him looking so serious, and I swallowed hard, surprised and alarmed.

It's the Shaker, I thought, and without me there, the interaction had obviously become even more intense than it had been on the beach. I steeled myself for the confrontation, and strode in quickly, hoping to seem confident and not scared. But as I moved past the blind spot of the gas pump, I stopped short, jarred. It wasn't the Shaker Horizon was standing with, but a woman, slim and tall, in a long flower-print sundress, with silver bangles on her wrist, and dark square sunglasses pushed up on her head to keep waves of mahogany hair off her face. She was naturally tan and beautiful and self-assured, and her body language was infinitely more relaxed than Horizon's. I knew her at once.

Larissa.

I couldn't move for a moment, so I stood watching this tableau wishing I had stayed in the bathroom long enough for her to leave. *Would he have told me about seeing her?* The acute stress response is always said to be fight or flight, but there is a third response that most of us fall prey to. We freeze. As our brain, our heart, work to fire synapses, to beat, to catch up with our eyes, we shelter in place. Do nothing. It seemed Horizon had frozen as well, because, although I was sure he could see me in his peripheral vision by then, he didn't make a move towards acknowledging me. But Larissa did, turning directly towards me, catching me, it felt, as if I were an intruder.

"Hi," she said, in the most matter-of-fact way I had ever been greeted. I tried to match her steeliness.

"Hi." I faltered. But at the sound of my voice, Horizon seemed to reanimate, dropping his arms and finally turning in my direction. "Kait . . ."

"You must be Larissa." I walked up to them and held out my hand, a blatantly formal greeting for a group that thought nothing of hugging—or fucking—strangers. Larissa hesitated for a second then shook my hand, and I realized that I was gripping much harder than she was, as if I had something to prove, and she shouldn't bother wasting her strength on trying to be alpha here. Which meant that she automatically was. I dropped my hand.

"Well," she said, much more breezily, "I gotta go. You guys have a good show. Nice to see you again, Zi." *Zi*, short for Zion, a nickname for the nickname. I had never used it. She did. Of course. *Zi* didn't say anything back, just watched her walk in to the gas station's store. I watched him watching her, and despite the dryness that had crept into my mouth and the heaviness that had overtaken my limbs, I walked up to the camper.

"You okay?" I asked.

He paused for a beat, then turned to me and smiled his normal, charismatic smile. "Yeah." He rubbed my back reassuringly and opened the camper door for me. I climbed up and he pushed the heavy door shut. But I saw that before he walked to the driver's side, he hesitated. He had turned and was staring at the store.

My head began to swim and I suddenly felt unmoored from my bearings in Horizon's world. *It's just the perception*, I told myself, *nothing has changed.*

But everything had.

11

WALKING INTO RED Rocks for the first time was as magical as everybody had assured me it was. Built into natural sandstone outcroppings, being in the open-air theatre felt like being in a great urn; a cave that sloped up to the sky, a sky that felt higher here against the stone walls; brighter blue against the red. The amphitheater felt ancient; colossal, and I understood why it had been given its nickname, The Garden of Titans.

But the show that night was disappointing. Everything felt a little off. The band, whose sets were never planned in advance, were out of sync with each other, and it sounded like they were jockeying for leadership on stage. Ernest would start plucking a tune on his guitar; Jeff, the rhythm guitarist would tentatively join in, and the audience would cheer in recognition. But then Joey, the bassist, would launch into a completely different song. The keyboardist, Barbara, who was a fairly new addition—and Joey's current girlfriend—would side with Joey and back up his riff with the keys, and poor Greg, the drummer, would half-assedly hit the snare for a minute or two until the tug-of-war declared a winner and the band started to play an actual song. But even then, Ernest's voice was unsteady and without enthusiasm.

And in this most miraculous of venues, each and every flat note carried straight up the bowl, bouncing off the rocks and hillside accusingly. Horizon and I seemed to absorb, or perhaps mirror, the frustration happening on stage and had barely talked during the first set. There was none of our usual affection; no grabbing his hand when the noodling onstage turned into a song I loved; no swaying shoulder to shoulder; no passing bottles of Holy Water back and forth. None of the little things we had been doing these past weeks—things that had become our shorthand, our way of checking in on each other during the shows. I tried to convince myself that there was no malice indicated in our silence; that we just needed some space for our private thoughts right now. That a third person had not taken up that space. The weather was also cooling, casting an unseasonably damp chill to the air.

By beginning of the intermission, clouds, thick and heavy, moved into the sky above us, creating a ceiling over the recessed amphitheatre. The feeling I had when I first entered Red Rocks, of being in a glorious fortress, protected, began to morph into the feeling that I was trapped.

"Can we try to find a different place to sit," I said to Horizon, gathering up the little pile of my things—patchwork satchel, Holy Water, sweater—at my feet.

"Why, what's wrong with where we are?" Horizon gestured at our section, perhaps trying to gauge the need or even possibility of an upgrade from the spot we had claimed. We were in the middle of a row on the side of the stage we preferred—Ernest's side—about two-thirds of the way up the bowl.

"Nothing," I answered, "I'm not feeling the vibe here." I made my way towards the aisle, Horizon waiting a beat and then following as we snaked a path down the terraced walkways to a less congested space in the middle of a row. These seats were a little closer to the small area that served as the venue floor, a flat shelf cleaved from deep within the rock. Horizon voiced no opposition to our relocation, and for a few minutes the amphitheatre felt magical again. I took a deep, cleansing breath, hoping the change of scenery could calm my restlessness and reset the evening.

Intermission ended shortly after we moved but the band hadn't improved with the break, and my mood soon darkened again as well. Being in the theatre with its bleacher-like shallow benches and steep stadium seating meant there was very little room to move or dance without falling off your perch onto the person below you. I didn't feel like dancing, but the Bird that had moved into the space directly behind us did, and after the fourth or fifth time he lost his footing and ended up nearly on top of me, I whipped around.

"Can you please fuck off!" I hissed at my assaulter. He stared at me in stunned silence for a minute, then closed his eyes and continued swinging his body around, albeit with a little less of the fancy footwork.

"That was nice," Horizon said, and I couldn't tell if he meant the dancer falling on me or my reaction to him.

"I have a headache," I said, caring little that it was neither an apology nor an explanation.

"It's just the altitude," Horizon offered.

"I don't think that's it."

"Then I can't help you."

I glared at him. "I never asked you to."

"Sure you didn't," he said, and bent down out of the wind to light a joint. After a minute, he offered it to me.

"No thank you," I said coldly. He shrugged and took another pull.

"Hey," the guy behind me leaned down between us, and I glared at him too. "Can I have a hit of that?"

Horizon looked at him for a minute, then sighed and shook his head with an air of defeat.

"Just take it," he said, holding the joint out.

"Hey, yeah, thanks man," the dancing freak said, clapping Horizon on the shoulder and accepting the gift.

"It's fine," Horizon said, "just stop knocking into my girlfriend already."

Then he turned straight ahead, but took my hand in his.

A truce.

The show ended with the clouds turning stormy grey, making the night seem even darker and bigger than it already felt in the giant rock bowl of the amphitheater, and the rain hit us just as we were walking into the Field. The drops were cool and fat, and though some people were trying to keep the party going in the mud, I didn't think either of us was into a rain dance that night.

"Can we just go back to the campground?" I said, as we hopped around puddles, trying to keep our feet dry, and failing.

"Yeah, I think that's a good idea." We were holding hands again, our truce intact, but this was the most we had said to each other since we filed out of Red Rocks. As we got into the Field, a river of slow-moving vehicles was already forming, trying to make their way out of the day-use parking spots.

"We're not getting out of here for a while," he said, gesturing to the departing cars. "Might as well go dry off and get comfortable."

"Sounds good." As we walked, I tried to gauge how big of a set-back this day had been for our relationship. We passed car after car, each full of Yellow Birds, many idling, stuck in line as they waited for their chance to leave through the one exit point, and for a brief moment, panic enveloped me. I became accutely aware of the relatively short amount of time Horizon and I had been together, compared to the great distance there was right now, here in Colorado, between us and anyone else I knew.

I wished that Eartha had made it to this show. She was my friend and advisor. And insurance policy if I needed to find another way to the next show. Or somewhere else. But almost as quickly as the panic had risen, I tamped it back down, reminding myself that I was in charge of my journey, and if it felt like too much or too little or unsafe or like I was standing in the shadow of something I would never understand, I could go. I could leave. A shiver rippled through me as though my body was absorbing this new perspective. I wasn't stuck and there was always another direction I could go. Horizon, perhaps thinking I was trembling from the cold, moved his body closer to mine as we picked our way through the Field.

Soon we were in the camper, the door shut against the damp and dark. As Horizon turned on lights and heat, I took towels and blankets from the storage under the bed. We moved around each other deftly, easily, and I realized how very much this space felt like home.

No, I thought, as I stood in the dim light of the camper, soggy and cold. I didn't want to go anywhere else; didn't need an alternate exit. Not now.

By time we made it out of the Field and took the short drive to the campground, the rain had stopped. We hadn't talked much since we left the show, but the ice between us seemed to have thawed. We were tired; exhausted, I reasoned. Tour was like that: transient living was fun and liberating, but eventually it jangled nerves, at least temporarily. You have to wait it out, like the rain. Tonight was our night to reach that limit. It was just from Tour fatigue, not each other, I told myself. And it definitely wasn't from running into Larissa.

Once we were settled back into our site at the campground, Horizon opened the side door of the camper and sat on the ledge. I walked by behind him, took my favourite afghan off the bench, wrapped it around my shoulders and sat down next to him. He lit a cigarette and took a drag, the cherry casting a dim light in the grey outside. I reached out my hand and he passed me the smoke.

"What if I loved you?" he said.

It was so unexpected that for a second I wondered who he was talking to. I held the cigarette between my fingers and laid my head on his shoulder.

"What if you did," I whispered, and we stayed there, not moving as curls of tobacco smoke rose like an offering and dissipated into the night.

Later, when we reached for one another, it felt urgent, necessary. He kissed both of my cheeks, both of my temples, my stomach, my breasts, moving up and down my body like it was a ladder, and when his kiss landed between my legs I wrapped them around his chest, locking him on that wrung and allowing him to show me what his love was.

I didn't want to go to the show the next day, go back to Red Rocks, but we had a camping pass to stay in the Field that night and the next, so we would have to vacate our campground off the highway no matter what. The sun shone high and bright in the sky when we emerged from the camper, rosy-cheeked and satiated from forgiveness and lovemaking, and it tricked me into thinking that the residue of the previous day had been burned off like the morning dew.

Parked and settled in the Field, we walked Main Street holding hands, sharing an organic soda we bought from a vendor, checking out the merchandise, admiring crocheted shawls, silk-screened t-shirts and beautifully woven baskets. I lingered over an elephant-grass basket, red stripe running its circumference, bright and crisp, with a light green linen lining and smooth brown leather handles. The basket was soft and sturdy and earthy and confident.

"I'm going to get that for you," Horizon said.

"You are?"

"Yes. I want to."

"You do?"

"I do."

"You are very sweet," I said, and leaned over to give him a kiss.

"I just want you to hold our stuff," he said, playfully indicating the sweaters he had slung over his arm.

The day progressed in a light, comfortable way. The tension between us was a thin footnote, no longer a bold headline and I was sure it would dissolve completely with a few more hours of peace. Holding Horizon's hand, swinging it lightly, I felt secure and happy. I took his question from the night before as an answer, and though I had not yet echoed any of his words—the important ones, the three that could compel people to make the best or worst decisions of their life—I thought I would before the day was over. I wasn't trying to be theatrical, planning a big moment, manipulating the circumstances of the day so that when I said it back, the setting was as significant as the words, but I was thinking a little bit about timing. I hadn't said it when he did and I was proud of myself for that; even though I knew I was already in love with Horizon, had felt like I had already given him so much of my heart and my mind and my body, I couldn't quite give him the words. It wasn't just about waiting for him to say it first; it was about getting through that discomfort together, that first test. Today, I assured myself, as we moved gingerly together through the makeshift bazaar of the Field, today, if he says it, I'll say it back.

We found my favourite food vendors, Wan and Pixie, and gave them each a hug before Horizon and I happily tucked into an eggroll each. Was the secret ingredient nutmeg, mingling with the mushrooms and bean sprouts inside the giant, crispy golden skin? Wan and Pixie would never tell.

"This is the finest five bucks one can ever spend," I said, mouth full, wiping a bit of oil and eggroll juice from the corner of my lip.

"Well," Horizon said, pausing to take a bite, "I once ended up at a crazy strip bar in Vancouver with some assholes I knew from school, and one of the women on the stage danced to Cherry Pie while wearing gold sparkly deer antlers on her head, and the warm beer I was drinking cost me five bucks, so that was up there, but this—this eggroll is a close, close second."

"Nothing can compete with Cherry Pie and a naked woman wearing sparkly deer antlers."

"And warm beer."

"And warm beer. You gonna finish that?" I pointed at the nub of his eggroll, golden and glistening in the napkin he held.

"Yep," he said, popping the crust into his mouth.

When I woke up very briefly in the ambulance after the car accident, I had approximately three seconds of confused, ignorant bliss while my senses worked to acknowledge and process my surroundings, careening me into the present, the here, the now, and informing me with exact and lightening-sharp clarity, where I was and what had just happened. That the fog never lasts is the cruelest of mother nature's survival tactics. Yes, people must assess their environments quickly in order to make the decisions that ensure our existence persists, but that reptilian instinct also does us a grand disservice in times of trauma, when a haze, an inability, at least temporarily, to understand what the fuck is happening here, would be merciful. I recognized the procedure my brain was going through in the ambulance: I had undergone the process before. When my father finally left for good, told me on the phone, calmly, in measured tone, that he wasn't coming back, I had felt it. The three seconds of catch-up, of bliss, before the haze departs and reality assaults you.

When we turned the corner after finishing our lunch, Horizon stopped abruptly, dropped my hand from his and I was thrust into those hazy three seconds. Then the cruel acrobatics of my senses playing catch-up ended, and I knew I would mourn those three seconds, like I did after the accident; like I did after my father left, forever.

Larissa, standing in front of a van underneath a white canopy, a makeshift store-front peddling imported goods: bags and wallets from Guatemala, their telltale bright colours and patchwork patterns a ubiquitous aesthetic among Birds; tams crocheted in the swirling colours of the Jamaican flag, worn most often to lift a white boy's white-boy dreads from off his sweaty white neck; Tibetan prayer flags tied to poles of the tent, bisecting the billowing canopy. I could smell the heady scents of nag-champa incense and patchouli oil permeating the space and they, along perhaps with the recently guzzled giant eggroll, and the sight of the only woman in the world I did not want to run into that day, encouraged a swell of nausea to roll over me like a wave I did not see coming. I had turned my back to the ocean.

Because it was not just Larissa standing there, not just the sight of her alone that induced the temporary impotence of my senses and the roiling unease in my guts that followed. I saw what Horizon had seen. A baby boy stood next to Larissa, holding a tiny, pudgy fistful of her batik-patterned skirt. He seemed like he was about two years old, and he was gorgeous. Kewpie doll lips, and a mess of downy-soft sandy brown curls flopping over his eyes; eyes that were bright and searching and unmistakably the color of topaz gemstones. I knew those eyes.

Larissa saw us one beat later, and reached immediately for the child. She swung him onto her hip in a natural, practiced move and wrapped both arms protectively around him. The little boy did not protest, perched safely against his mother's warm body. I turned to Horizon who seemed frozen in place, staring at Larissa and her baby.

"Hi," she said plainly and directly to Horizon. Horizon said nothing for a minute, then seemed to regain animation, like the tin man, finally oiled.

"Who's this?" he asked.

"Donovan," she answered, and in a world of names given, taken, made up and borrowed, his was perfect.

"And where did Donovan come from," Horizon asked quietly, and my heart lurched. It was a strange question to ask about a baby, about another human as if humans just materialize from some vast inventory, like imported prayer flags.

"We have to go," Larissa said, and quickly moved out from under the canopy, still clutching the baby to her. She turned into the aisle and walked away and though she did not seem to quicken her pace, she moved purposefully away from where we stood. Horizon walked after her and I, forgotten by him for the time being, followed behind. Larissa turned between two parked cars into what formed an alley bisecting rows of Main Street.

"Larissa! Larissa, stop!" Horizon called and thankfully, she did. The futility and silliness of a chase at this point was clear and I allowed myself a second to admire her for not being a total drama queen though the opportunity presented itself. She turned around and looked at Horizon, then me. I tried to will myself to feel relevant in the moment, while also wondering what the hell I was possibly doing here, besides watching how this all played out. There were a few people cooking food on a Coleman camping stove behind a car about ten yards down from where we faced off, but otherwise, it was mercifully just us in the little row for the time being.

"Larissa . . . what the fuck, Larissa? You told me it never happened. You told me you got rid of it. Larissa," Horizon had his hands on his head, raking his fingers through his hair. There was something in his voice I hadn't heard before. There was anger yes, and panic, but that wasn't it. He was pleading with her.

"Oh my god, Larissa please. Please just tell me the fucking truth. Is he mine? Just tell me, please . . ."

And her clear, calm reply: "He'll never be yours."

12

WHEN MY MOTHER began collecting ceramic bells, and then broken picture frames, and then mismatched teacups, and then empty coffee canisters, we knew it was because she needed to have control over her things. She needed to have stuff that she loved and that she decided could love her back; stuff that could never be unpredictable or leave her like my dad had. We knew where the compulsion came from, but knowing did not make it any easier to live with. Not with the stuff, and not with my mother, who eventually transferred any affection she once had for people, to her things. And though her affection for my sister and me always seemed forced at best, we felt it being taken from us in tiny slices with each passing day; with each old radio added to the heap.

First she stopped asking to see any forms we brought home from school. Then she stopped asking who we were talking to on the phone. Then she stopped asking us what time we were coming home, or even where we were going. At first these things felt like freedoms, but really, they were cuts. Small cuts; paper cuts. But get enough paper cuts and you can still bleed to death.

So when I overheard a few of my classmates talking about seeing some Open Road shows after graduation the next week, I interrupted and asked if there was room for one more. That night, I told Janine that I was going on Tour for a few weeks, but then I'd back. *Besides, you'll be babysitting almost every day this summer,* I said to her, *You won't even miss me.*

What about Mom, she asked and I paused in front of my closet where I had been pulling sweatshirts and dresses off of hangers to stuff into my backpack. *She'll be okay. She might not even notice I'm gone.* I said it as a joke, but I wasn't even sure our mother realized we were home at that moment.

She made it to graduation, fussing constantly over her dress, my sister, the contents of her purse, and I was equal parts annoyed and sad that she couldn't just enjoy herself, be happy for both of us. My father was the unexpected hero of the day. I was surprised and pleased when he had told me he would be there, but downright shocked when he quietly but resolutely helped manage the day—manage my mother, ensuring we all got where we needed to be, picking us up on time and politely shaking hands with the teachers and parents that came up to chat with us at the reception after the ceremony.

When he dropped us back at the house later, he asked me to stay in the car for a moment. *How's your arm,* he asked, bending his own and pivoting it up and down like a wing, mimicking the movement he must have assumed still gave me trouble. *Dad, it's fine,* I answered. He hadn't really been there after the accident; he had called often but had only come down to see me once, right after the first surgery. I found his concern embarrassing. *You did good today.* I peeked out the car window at our front door. *Thanks, Dad.* We didn't say anything for a moment and I shifted in my seat. *I should go,* I said to him. *Your mother's not doing so good.* Ah, we had gotten to the point. *Nope,* I said but a protective flush rose through me. I didn't want to talk about my mother with him. He was one of the reasons she wasn't "doing so good." *Why don't you girls come up north this summer?* He had asked us this before. We had said no before. *Janine's working,* I said. *I'm going to see some Open Road shows. Travel around a bit.* He nodded slowly, didn't push for a different answer. Then he reached into the breast pocket of the sportcoat he was wearing and handed me a folded piece of paper. A cheque. *I'm proud of you, kiddo.* I noted the amount. It was't enough to pay for university tuition if I decided to go, but it was enough to get by for a while. *Thanks, Dad.* He asked me to check in with him while I was away; I promised I would. *This isn't a healthy place for you girls to be,* he said, glancing at the house. *I agree,* I said.

There were no feelings of animosity as I watched him drive away from us once more. After all, it was exactly what I would be doing in a few days. He didn't seem to turn and look back. I was sure I wouldn't either.

My story was not unique. You didn't have to be on Tour long to find out that many had a similar tale to tell. The hometowns were different; the families were different, the details were different, but the need to leave something that was hurting us was familar. And if anybody bothered to consider it, we knew what people thought of Tour. It was Babylon, it was hedonism. It was a waste of time and youth. But we weren't walking away from reality. This was real. And we were where we needed to be, away from the things making us unhealthy or unhappy. My mother needed to be in the basement with her collections. My father needed his own sheltered existence in a lab hundreds of miles from his family. Me and Eartha and Easy and Horizon—this was right where we needed to be.

And then one day your ex-girlfriend shows up on Tour with your baby.

"I'm not going to go in without you," I said, and handed Horizon the water bottle I was holding, a Pilgrims bottle. We sat in front of the camper, the mountain air cooling in the late afternoon breeze.

This ship's a-sinkin'; I hope you can swim – Glory, The Open Road,

Perfect. I didn't even want to know what the bible verse was. Horizon took the bottle but didn't drink. He held a cigarette in his other hand, unlit, and his eyes were red-rimmed, though I hadn't seen him shed any tears. But he was shaken to the core; that I could see.

"You should go. I'll be all right; I just need a little time to myself." That stung a bit, though I understood.

"What should I do with the extra ticket? Should I wish-list somebody?"

"Sure," he said, "that sounds great."

Wish-listing meant giving away a ticket for free, another Open Road construct that capitalist normal people couldn't really understand. The term, of course, came from a song in which Ernest sings to a lost love that her return is at the top of his wish list. At shows, you would see dozens and dozens of people walking around with signs declaring their desire to receive a wish-list ticket, which I always found desperate and kind of cheesy, no matter how clever the sign. I preferred the method of silently holding up three fingers, a W, signaling the need for a ticket. It seemed much more dignified and breezy to me.

At that point, I had never been the recipient or the gifter of a wish-list ticket, and even though what I really wanted was to see the show with Horizon, I wrung a tiny bit of happiness out of our messed-up situation from the thought of bestowing a show on somebody.

I left Horizon at dusk and he assured me that he would be alright; that he was mentally exhausted and was just going to stay in the camper and try to figure out what was going on and what he needed to do. Larissa's news had been a storm coming through, and without any preparation, we were simply left to assess the damage, get ready for the clean up. What I didn't know when I left him, seemingly in quiet, if decidedly complicated, thought, was that we were really in the eye of the tempest, and the destruction was nowhere near complete.

It was like there was a neon sign over my head projecting the words, I HAVE A FREE TICKET, because the wish-listers were all over me as I walked the rows of the Field. *I wish I may/I wish I might/see the show/with you tonight*, read the sign being held up by a kind of handsome guy with no shirt and pukka shells around his neck. Ugh, so . . . obvious. No wish for you, I thought. The signs meant that these people never came to the shows with any tickets; never planned or hustled or made an effort to get in, just thought they could show up and party as much as they wanted, and then, if they felt like it, get in through the generosity of whatever sucker found them charming or cute. No. Holding up three fingers might actually have signified even less of a plan; even less care put into trying to get a ticket, but it still seemed cooler to me; a secret handshake that only we knew and only we could return.

How I wanted Eartha to be here, wanted the whole crew to be here. I wanted to see her so badly; tell her what was going on with Horizon and Larissa and that whole fucked up story. The enormity of the situation, of the addition of a child into the whole complicated mess, was something I needed to digest and understand. And Horizon wasn't talking to me about it, so I needed Eartha. But I would have been happy with any familiar face at that point; Skate's protective friendship or Easy and Vivi's bossy but loving familiarity. I would even have been happy to see JuJube; would, I felt with a sudden knot of affection rising in my throat, actually love to sit with her and shoot the shit in the weird wonderful way only JuJube possessed. I would have been happy to see anybody I knew at that moment. Well, anybody but Larissa, and the fear that she would be around the next corner crackled through me, interrupting my thoughts.

"Shit! Sorry!" I rubbed my forehead where it had just collided with—a shoulder?

"No, I'm sorry, girl." I recognized the voice, and still rubbing the sore spot, looked up. It was one of the water guys that had come by in Olympia when I was sitting outside the camper with Eartha. A lifetime ago. It was the taller Pilgrim, the one with the dark curls. He put a hand on my shoulder, steadying me.

"No, it's ok. I'm sorry."

"Nah, I plowed into you; I'm sorry."

I gave my forehead one more rub for good measure and stepped away. He dropped his hand. "Anyway," he said, "you'll recover." I nodded and we both stood there for a second. "Where's your friend?"

"Eartha?" I asked, as if he knew her.

"Is that his name?"

Ah. "Horizon. He's . . ." I turned away, towards the row I had just walked, as if there was someone waiting there, and I felt my eyes get hot with the sudden sting of tears. I blinked them back and turned towards the pylon I had just run into.

"He's not feeling well. I'm trying to give away his ticket." He nodded, and I knew why I had told him that. "Do you want it?"

"It's not my night to be in the show," he said. I was confused for a second or two and then understood.

"I'm not suggesting you work or something. I'm saying you can have the ticket just to enjoy the show. You can go in with me. Or," I added quickly, a momentary panic flushing my blood stream, "I mean, go in with whoever you want. Doesn't have to be me. I don't care." I was babbling. He laughed.

"I just banged you on the noggin and you want to reward me with a wish?"

"Yep, pretty much. You don't have to take it." I turned to walk away. He put his hand on my shoulder again.

"Nah, nah, nah, girl, I'll take it. Thank you."

"My name's not girl," I said.

"Sorry—I'm sorry. What's your name?"

I hesitated for a second. It may as well be *Girl*. "It's Kait."

"Well, It's Kait, I'm Dov."

"Like the bird?"

"No, no 'e'. It's Hebrew. It means bear."

"Are you a bear?"

"If I have to be. But actually, I think I'm usually more like the bird."

"You're flighty?"

He snorted. "I'm fast and I have good vision. And I like to get high."

This time, I snorted. "Well, Bear, here's your ticket."

I took the envelope out of the bag that was slung over my shoulder and held out the slip of paper. It was a beautiful light blue woven card stock with embossed fireworks exploding behind the printed words. Special edition, like most mail order tickets. Special edition. Like my trip with Horizon until . . . I shook the thought away. It felt like I was giving away a tiny piece of him. Dov held out his hand in acceptance, and with a deep breath I hoped he hadn't heard over the din of the Field, I released the ticket.

"When are we going in?"

"Excuse me?" I said to Dov, who was all smiles.

"Didn't you say I should go in with you?" His head was cocked a little to the side. Did I actually want company? Did I actually want him as company? I scanned the people walking by. A woman was heading towards me with the strap of her tank top pulled down, holding an infant like a football as he latched onto her breast. My heart sank.

"Yes. Yes, I did say you should come in with me. But you can't fucking preach at me or anything." I gestured to the Holy Water poking out of the pocket of his hoodie. He raised his eyebrows and his hands in a gesture of surrender. I adjusted the bag on my hip, letting my shoulders, which I had been tensing—clenching, almost—drop. "Let's go, Bear," I said.

"Lead the way, It's Kait," he said.

Horizon was exactly where I had hoped but did not actually expect him to be after the show—sitting in one of our folding chairs outside of the camper, smoking a cigarette. He got up when he saw me approaching. There was another chair next to him. Waiting for me, or vacated by someone else? Probably both, I thought, and admonished myself for caring. He dropped his cigarette and ground it out under his shoe.

"Did you have fun?" he asked and wrapped his arms around me. I was a little buzzed still from a joint I had smoked with Dov during the first set; the high usually didn't stick around for so long, but it had been strong, and I hadn't sweated it out dancing like I normally would during a show. I hadn't danced much at all, though on paper it had been a good show. But I felt displaced there without Horizon. We had a routine, a shorthand at the shows that I had gotten used to and which made attending a show both more bearable and altogether elevated from any other experience. And I felt a little of the same with him here now. Where was our shorthand, our routine? Attending, or not attending the actual concerts together was the germinating kernel of our unconventional relationship from which the more mundane and also more extraordinary aspects of our partnership radiated. We had never tried to have one without the other.

I tried to push the haze away, and we embraced for what felt like a long time. We were reassuring each other; finding footing together before separating, acknowledging the evening we had spent without the other.

We rocked a little together, like dancing, and I never wanted to lift my head from where it lay against his chest. He rested his cheek on the top of my head, then lifted it, kissed my forehead.

"It was good," I said, trying to sound happy, neutral, reassuring. I sat in the chair next to him. "They played *Don't Get Around Much Anymore.*" A crowd favourite, energetic (for the Open Road, that was, whose energy levels were best not compared to other bands).

"Nice."

"And *Sparrow* into *Flower Child*, just like in Olympia. And the first set was so long, I think people were wondering if they were ever going to stop. It was almost too long, but then, intermission was really long too, and everybody was talking about whether this would end up being the longest show they had ever played. And I saw your friend Albie. He said he might stop by." I was babbling.

"Cool."

"And anyway. I missed you." I took a drink from the bottle I was holding.

"Holy Water?"

I held the bottle like I was just noticing it for the first time. "Yeah."

"So," Horizon took another cigarette out of the pack and lit it. "Who did you give the ticket to?"

I swallowed, blaming the sudden uptick in my heartbeat, the momentary unease, on the buzz I still had. Fuck this, why should I feel weird about who I gave the ticket to? I held out the bottle of Holy Water and shook it in Horizon's direction. He made a face. "A Pilgrim?"

I opened the bottle and took another sip. "Yep. A guy named Dov." I replaced the cap and rummaged in my bag for nothing. "Me and Eartha kind of know him, and I ran into him walking around. We were chatting and I gave him the ticket." I shrugged. No big deal.

"That's fine, Kait; you don't have to be weird about it."

"I'm not."

"It's fine."

"You already said that. And I know it is. You're the one that didn't want to see the show with me. Dov did. He got the ticket. It was great. How was your night?"

"He went in with you and everything?"

"Yep."

"That's nice."

"It is nice, Horizon." And fuck you, too, I wanted to add.

"Kait," he said, "You know I don't care if you see the show with another guy; I just don't trust *these* guys. All their religious bullshit. Did he try to convert you?" I sighed. Would I have been happier if Horizon had actually been jealous; had worried that a guy would try to hook up with me and not just convert me?

"It was fine. He wasn't like that. It was just two people seeing a show, not a church service."

"So no Spinners there today?" This was Horizon's way of changing the tone of our conversation, his way of getting us to move on. The Spinners, we knew, did in fact treat an Open Road show like a church service; treated Ernest like a god to be worshipped. It was weird.

"They were there of course."

"Good; the world is not ending tonight. But hey—" he stared at me intently and I tensed again. "Which group has a better chance of surviving the apocalypse—the Spinners or the Pilgrims?"

I relaxed and rolled my eyes at him, appreciating the levity.

"Well, the Spinners have the direct connection to their god and never seem to get dizzy, which is quite the superpower, but," I picked the bottle up from where I had set it down beside me. "The Pilgrims have the water." I opened it up, held it towards Horizons in a "cheers" gesture, and drank what was left of it.

"Now," I said, capping the bottle, "I gotta go lay down." I walked the step to Horizon's chair, leaned down and kissed him on the cheek. He put his hand on my arm and pulled me closer, and I kissed him on the lips. It was such a nice kiss, his lips were always so soft. I could taste cigarettes and beer and it didn't bother me at all in the moment. "I'll be in soon," he said. I nodded and went into the camper. In the dim light and close space, I felt dizzy, so I kicked off my sandals and climbed into the bed, not even bothering to change out of my clothes. I hadn't really asked about his night in our brief conversation, and he hadn't really told me. I turned onto my side, away from my thoughts, and fell immediately to sleep.

The sound of voices outside of the window woke me up, but I couldn't tell if it was ten minutes or two hours later. The general din of the Field seemed to have quieted down for the night, and I could see the moon, cleaved in half by an ancient process, high in the sky from the open hatch above me. So many stars out here, but my eyes couldn't focus enough beyond seeing them as pinholes of glinting light. Horizon's voice and one, perhaps two other people with him. Male, both; Albie probably, and someone else I didn't recognize. The tones were soothing. Shooting the shit, the occasional laugh. Nothing serious. Nothing dangerous. My head was still spinning a bit. I fell back asleep.

The opening of the camper door was the next thing to awaken me. Again, I had no idea how much time had actually passed, though it felt like I had just opened my eyes a moment before. "Hey . . ." I said, shielding my eyes from the beam of the night's dim but distinct light penetrating the dark of the van. Horizon closed the door as gently as he could, but I was pulled further from my slumber.

"Sorry, Kait," Horizon whispered.

Sleep still only a moment behind me made my words sound thick. "Come to bed."

"I am." He sounded calm as he slid onto the bunk, his breathing so regular and recognizable, so soothing to me.

"Who were you with?" I asked.

"Albie. A friend of his."

"Good. Did you have a nice chat?" Horizon gave a little chuckle. "We did." He kissed me on the forehead, then turned onto his back. "Bright night," he said. I murmured my agreement and turned onto my back as well. I nudged my shoulder under his and he reached across to me, tapping his fingers up and down my arm as if counting the stars.

"Do you know what a group of stars is called?" I asked. He didn't answer me, just turned towards me.

"A galaxy," I said, and giggled. He gave a little shake of his head at my lame joke, but kept smiling.

"I think that constellation is Orion's belt. It's supposed to be quite visible from here." He pointed up, towards the open hatch. We both watched the patch of darkness above us for a while, quiet.

"What else do you know about the stars in the sky?" I asked him after a few minutes.

"Nothing, really," he said, "Only that every time I look for them, there they are. And I have never, ever been able to say that about a single other thing in my life, ever."

We were quiet again for a little while, unmoving, until finally I turned to him. He was still looking up, out at the stars.

"What if I loved you?" I whispered.

"What if you did?" he whispered.

I rolled on top of him and he put his hands on either side of my hips, pulling me further in to his universe.

13

THE NEXT MORNING we knew we had to talk, but it felt like neither one of us particularly wanted to interrupt our peace, our post-coital intimacy, for such a practical discussion topic as what we should do about Horizon's newly uncovered paternal role. Or rather, what Horizon should do about it, and whether I would land anywhere within the sphere of navigating his strange, new reality.

So we ate a breakfast of pancakes that I cooked and coffee that Horizon brewed and we sat in our camping chairs and watched the Field wake up, stretch towards the brightening sky and shake off the previous night. People were moving leisurely as this was not a travel day; one more night, one more show, and then the frantic load-up, the searching for lost shoes and lost travelling companions and lost money and lost hope that we could just stay here, like this, in the imperfect, perfectly acceptable camp we made with the other hopefuls. But we would feel the same way about the next place as well. When you lived this life, even temporarily, you had to think of the transitions not as a break in the life, but just as a shift in the mechanism that kept you going; a quarter turn of the landscape and you realign the compass, point it home again.

Early on, in the first weeks I was on Tour before joining Big Blue Bertha, I used to have a moment upon arrival at any campground or Field or motel, anywhere new, when I wished it was already over. That the mechanism was ready to shift again and shows had already ended and we were heading out. To be anywhere else but where we were. To be home. But then we would set up camp or pitch a tent or check in, and then we would go to the Field and see the show and party afterward and fall into my cozy sleeping bag or luxurious $39 a night motel room bed, maybe alone, maybe not, and then I would wake up and have a different moment. When I would wish that it would never end. A small perfection, indifferent to whatever challenges lay in the day or the road or the decision ahead.

A moment like this, eating pancakes and drinking coffee in a camping chair, with a boy I had admitted to loving, avoiding the thing that was already consuming our moment of perfection even as it occurred.

We spent the day at the camper, didn't walk around the Field, didn't try to find people we might know or a party we might want to join. Horizon worked on a coolant leak he thought might have sprung somewhere deep in the bowels of the old vehicle, his body half hidden under the front of the camper, legs sticking out, one bent at the knee, a number four. I straightened up inside a little, having mainly been the one to render it untidy. I folded and packed the clothes that I had flung over the back of the passenger seat, or on the corner of the bench; I collected the various hair elastics and pens I shed on almost every surface, and I made the bed, all the pretty blankets and quilts smoothed and flattened and folded. We were the picture of domesticity, checking in with each other when one needed a wrench or the other shook the dirt off the rag rug. We would talk, I knew we would, but I had to give Horizon time, had to respect that it was his decision when. For now, we could pretend that life was the same as it had been before we knew. It was calm. It was careful. It couldn't last.

Larissa appeared at around two. Me and Horizon were both sitting in the camping chairs by now, reading. He was in the middle of a sci-fi book by a writer I didn't recognize, and I was reading Alias Grace, the new Margaret Atwood. I saw her first, a figure in my peripheral vision heading towards us in a way that seemed like it could only be on a deliberate path. She was alone. Ah, two o'clock. Maybe Donovan was napping. With whom? I shook my head once, I didn't care. It was this sudden flick of my head that aroused Horizon's attention, and he raised his head up as well, saw what I had seen. Who I had seen. And then he didn't move and Larissa was in front of us.

"Hi," she said, looking from me to Horizon.

"Hi," I said, and Horizon glanced at me. Was I supposed to be meek? Mad? Start a fight? Pretend I wasn't there? He said nothing.

"So," Larissa said, "I think we need to talk if that's ok." Her tone was much less combative than it had been yesterday, but Horizon's face was like stone. I wished that he seemed angry, or even like he was in despair, because the mask he was wearing was unreadable and impenetrable. I wondered, involuntarily, if Larissa knew what his expression meant. And with a flush of resolve of my own, I stood.

"I'm going to go," I announced. Horizon reached out and grabbed my wrist, and I was surprised by the show of vulnerability, demonstrated in front of Larissa. I felt a rush of affection for him and a desire to stay, but I knew I could not be a shield, or even a filter between them. They had to deal with this, now, and I didn't want to hamper the discussion. Or even witness it. I resisted the urge to touch him back, to make either of us seem more vulnerable than we already were.

"I'm ready to stretch my legs for a bit," I said.

I reached into the camper, put down my book and grabbed my bag and the bottle of Holy Water, refilled from the night before. "I'll be back soon."

I put on my sunglasses so that my expression was now also hopefully unreadable and I turned and walked down the row. I was careful not to rush, not to stagger at all or seem unsure of where I was headed. I had known this moment was going to come, and I wanted Larissa to know I knew, to see me as cool and composed and as prepared as I could be. But my heart was racing and my mouth was dry, and I didn't dampen it with a sip of water because I was sure I would drop the cap from my shaking hands. I turned out of our row and leaned against the trunk of a parked car.

When I had taken a drink and my legs had stopped vibrating, I considered where I should go. The last thing I wanted to do was be around people who would distract me from thinking about Horizon and Larissa, stop me from conceiving, over and over in imagined iterations, how the conversation they were having was playing out. The impression it may have given Larissa when Horizon grabbed my wrist. He needed *me*. I hoped that in leaving, I sent a message to them both that my allegiance was to Horizon, that I was being mature and accommodating and practical because no conversation they could ever have would shatter my sense of security that me and Horizon were solid. I hoped.

But I also couldn't help but worry that Horizon might feel abandoned by me, because in all honesty, it felt to me, a tiny bit, like that was what I was doing to him. Abandoning him with a very new, traumatic situation and forcing him to confront it after twenty-four hours with somebody who had had more than two years to think about exactly how this might play out. My stomach lurched at the thought, and I resisted the urge to run back to the van.

I made my way through the rows of the Field, forcing myself to walk slowly, as I had nowhere to go, and looking up at no one, as I had no one to look for. My mind flashed from thought to thought, marching through the scene that could be happening at our camper, and back to more selfish thoughts of where I would land when the chips had fallen. Would he get back together with her? Would he be a father? Would she let him? Was I going to have to fucking go to the show with a stranger again tonight? I barked a laugh at my ability to be so selfish.

"Better to laugh, right?" The guy that had obviously heard me was the usual kind of Bird, shirt off, sitting cross-legged on a ratty blanket in front of a ratty car, surrounded by other ratty Birds.

"Always, man, always." I said. I walked away, and then turned back. "Hey, do you have the time?" I asked ratty Bird.

"It's time to get ill," said one of the rat Bird's friends. I rolled my eyes. "Quarter past four," rat Bird said. Holy shit, I must have been walking in a trance for it to be that late already, I thought.

"Thanks," I said, and headed back up the row in the direction of our camp.

There was nobody sitting in front of the van. He went with her, I thought, to properly meet his son. My throat hitched at the word, and I wondered if I should just start packing my stuff. In the two hours I had been walking and obsessively turning the scenarios over in my mind, I had not considered that he would leave here with her, that they would do anything *but* talk. I felt as dizzy as I had after the show the night before, and I wondered if I should sit down on the chair outside or go straight inside to lay down. Inside! Of course that's where Horizon was. So stupid not to even check. I pulled open the side door and stuck my head in, convinced that I would see Horizon laying on the bench, or the bed, exhausted by what he had just been through and understandably, needing a rest. But the camper was empty. I swallowed hard and backed out again. He did go with her. Well, I wasn't going anywhere else. Like a parent sitting at the table waiting for a child who had broken curfew to get home, I would sit with a firm, impassable expression on my face and wait for him to come back and tell me where he had been. Even, like that parent, if it took all night.

Naturally, my resolve to remain stern dissolved within minutes. I was so not ready to be some kind of weird stepparent, and my mind went back to narrating imaginary conversations that hadn't happened and never would happen. Conversations with Horizon, with Larissa, with Eartha—well those conversations would probably happen, and I ached to have my friend with me, even if the only thing she was going to tell me (as I imagined possible in one such narrative) was to get back into Easy's van and get the fuck away from this messed up nonsense.

They would be in Phoenix in four days, the next stop on Tour; I thought that maybe I should spend my time not sitting around here waiting for the fallout of a bomb to decimate the lovely little world we had created, but to go back into the Field and find myself another ride to Arizona.

I had almost made up my mind to do just that when Horizon turned into view. He was alone, but he was holding something.

"I brought us something to eat," he said, depositing two eggrolls and two cans of Mountain Dew on the little plastic table next to my chair.

"Where were you?" I asked, a little too much of that stern parent coming through.

"I went to get us food." He pulled the tab on the can of pop.

"But where are you coming from?" I demanded.

"What? Nowhere. From here. Larissa left a little while ago and you weren't back yet, so I got us a snack. I thought you might be hungry. I'm hungry."

Hungry? I had been on the verge of stress barfing for the past two hours, but leave it to a boy to prioritize snacks. Nevertheless, smelling my favourite Field eggrolls did make my stomach growl despite the stress, and I tried to calm down enough to acknowledge the thoughtful gesture.

"Thank you." I opened my own can, and took a big sip of the sweet, cold, pop. But I wasn't going to let the silence or the denial creep back in.

"Horizon," I ventured, "what happened?"

Horizon unwrapped his eggroll and took a bite. Chewed, swallowed, buying the last few seconds of life between us as it had been.

"We talked. I think we came to an agreement."

"So . . . so, he's yours?" I swallowed hard, felt nauseous again. Horizon nodded, couldn't say any affirmative words, but had the decency to at least look at me.

"What's the agreement?"

Horizon held on to the eggroll.

"She doesn't need any money from me, doesn't want any, but she'll put my name on the birth certificate and it will be known that I'm the father. We're going to get a custody agreement in writing, but for now, I'll go to Vancouver for a few weeks. Get to know him a bit. Figure out what the fuck I'm going to tell my parents. But Kait . . ."

I swallowed, heart beating hard again.

"Yes."

"I think I have to move back to Vancouver. I can't live in Toronto if he's there."

"I understand." I said, much more quietly than I had intended.

"I'm sorry. I know that we never talked about that."

"Horizon, we never talked about any of this. Anything at all."

"I know," he said.

"Where did you expect to live anyway, when this . . . when this was over?" When Tour ended and life with me ended. When this game of make-believe we were playing, ended. Horizon peered at me, like he wondered why I was asking the question.

"Where did I expect to go? Wherever you were."

I swallowed hard. Would I ever believe in this?

"Then I can go wherever you are."

"Vancouver?"

"Even Vancouver. It's a little damp for my taste, but the coffee's good." He smiled a wan smile.

"I can't make you do that."

"Nope. You definitely can't. But if I want to move to Vancouver to support you and your love child, I guess that's my decision." But my joke went over flat, and Horizon just held his eggroll.

"What about school?"

"I'll see if I can transfer my acceptance or I'll just apply again in Vancouver. What about you?"

"I don't know if I'll be able to go back to school."

I jerked my head back a little. "Why? Why wouldn't you be able to go back to school, Horizon? You don't have to give up everything you've worked for. You don't even know if she's going to actually let you have access to this kid. You don't know if she's going to actually put you on this kid's birth certificate."

I could handle a change to a plan I never knew Horizon and I had, but the thought of Horizon changing the plans that he had, to stay in school, to achieve something, made me angry. He said something quietly in answer to my outrage, but I didn't register his words.

"What?"

"I said, he's not *this* kid. He's *my* kid. My ***kid***. Do you even get that? How huge that is?"

"Do you?"

Horizon's face was a mask of defeat. Of pain.

"I don't, Kait. I don't get this at all. I can't even fucking believe any of it." He dropped his head and I went to him, put my arms around him. He was silent, still.

"I'm sorry. Horizon, I am so sorry that you have to deal with this, but you do have to deal with this. And I'll help you. It is what it is and we can deal with it. Together."

I hoped my words were reassuring, helpful, or at the very least, soothing at that moment, but Horizon was so tense under my touch. Finally, he relaxed. He lifted his head, put his arms around me, and pulled me into his lap. He buried his head in my neck, my hair. I felt silly in his lap, this position was too casual, too lighthearted for the conversation we were having, but I tried not to think about the incongruity. If Horizon needed to bury his head in my neck while I sat in his lap like we were at a bonfire, so be it. After all, we're in the Field, on Open Road Tour. And Horizon had just given insanely big, life-changing news. The whole thing was incongruous and ridiculous.

"I love you, Kait," Horizon said to my neck. I believed him.

"I love you too," I said. I believed me.

We sat still for a long time, barely disturbing our ridiculous tableau.

I had already decided that I wouldn't go into the show without Horizon that night. If he didn't want to go in, we could give away both tickets and stay at the camper. In my contingency planning, I momentarily thought about just keeping the tickets, not giving them away; tucking them back into the little box the tickets were kept in, but almost immediately I realized that the unused tickets would become souvenirs of this shitty, shitty day, and that was definitely not what I wanted. I would just give them to the first people I saw who needed wishes. But the whole contingency plan was unnecessary, because Horizon began to put our stuff away and get the camper in order at around five o'clock.

"What are you doing?" I asked.

"Well," he said, "I thought we should probably pack up before we go to the show, so we don't have to do it in the dark. Tomorrow's a travelling day."

"You're going to come to the show tonight," I asked.

"I am. I want to. Is that okay with you? I need a change of scenery."

"Then we should leave now and go to Mexico," I said.

"How about the show tonight, and then we finish Tour, and then we see about Mexico in the fall?"

"You want to finish Tour?"

He did. Larissa was going back to Olympia the next day, then she'd head to Vancouver a few weeks later. With Donovan, of course.

"Which is what she says she always had planned," he added, seeing the look of skepticism on my face. "I told her I'd be there by the end of September."

My heart bounced in my chest, his words charting a course I could choose to follow or abandon, but it was the course he would traverse.

"Ok," I said. I would not clarify as to whether that meant I was agreeing with the plan, or just acknowledging his words. We were both quiet for a minute, but as Horizon turned back towards his task of packing up our gear, I broke the silence.

"So you're going to be a dad."

"I guess I already am."

"Mazel tov," I said, and folded away the chair I had been sitting on a moment earlier.

We tried. We tried to have fun, to melt back into our show routine, to rely on the well-choreographed steps and fluent shorthand we had established to ensure each other's separate comfort as well as our shared enjoyment of the night. But he was distracted throughout the entire first set. The band played *Shooting Star,* a sweet slow melody and I clapped enthusiastically.

"I love this song," I said leaned into Horizon, but he was fishing for something in his pocket and inadvertently elbowed me in the ribs.

"Sorry." He pulled a few bills and a lighter out of his pocket, counted the money and stuffed it all back in. I figured he was planning to go buy a beer from the concession stand, but he remained where he was. I took a long swig from the Holy Water bottle I was holding, then pointed to its label.

Today, tomorrow, forever, right now
Write me our story; play me our vow. – Shooting Star, The Open Road

"Horizon look, it's good luck," I said. There was common Yellow Bird lore that when a song the band was playing matched the lyrics printed on your bottle, it was an auspicious sign.

Horizon took the Holy Water from my hand, quickly read the words on the label and shook his head. "I don't know about that, Kait," he said and handed it back to me.

"Don't tempt the gods of the Holy Water like that." I was doing my best to keep things light.

"You mean The Pilgrims? Sure." Horizon's tone was flat.

"Maybe we'll have better luck with the actual bible verse then; hang on—"

"Kait," Horizon interrupted, "I don't really care what it says. Besides, this song isn't great."

I gave him space. It seemed like we both needed it. Everything we we were doing was like a dance whose steps we couldn't keep straight. Everything we were saying sounded like an unfinished sentence.

During intermission, I went to use the washroom, splash water on my face. When I went back to the area Horizon and I had been in, he was gone. Assuming he had also gone to the washroom, or to get that beer, I waited for him. After fifteen minutes or so, I walked around the section, through the bleachers, wondering if this hadn't been where I had left him after all. Everything that had seemed familiar suddenly seemed different. I silently cursed the mayhem that dominated Open Road shows and wished, for once, people had to stay in their ticketed seats. Had we been six rows up, or twelve rows up? Were we on the south side of entrance number four, or the north side? And if I was having trouble fixing our location on this writhing jellyfish of a human map, it seemed likely that Horizon was as well. Hadn't we both been distracted, preoccupied? *Stay in one place*, I counseled myself, like I was five again, and I didn't know which way to cross the road. *He'll find you.* Unless of course he had given himself the same advice while standing on the opposite side of the concert bowl. I kept weaving my way through the crowd, sure I would spot him in the next momentary clearing.

The collective noun for jellyfish is a smack, a smack of jellyfish, moving like one in the ocean, in this arena. So it didn't feel strange when I smacked right into someone, body to body, face to chest.

"Sorry," I said as I tried to veer out of the collision course.

"I'm not," came the reply. I looked up. Dov stood in front of me, smiling.

"Dov. Hi. I ran right into you. Again."

Dov's expression morphed into an appearance of mild concern. "You okay?" he asked. "Alone again?" My stomach dropped a bit at what felt like an accusation.

"Nope. Peddling your salvation bullshit in a water bottle again?"

Meting out small cruelties feels like putting your hands under the tap before you realize the water is too hot. So by time what I said registered, my face mirrored Dov's, and I felt bad until he surprised me by coughing out a laugh.

"What's going on?" he asked, and rubbed my arm in a congenial way.

"I don't know. I've lost Horizon somewhere. I don't think I care. What are you doing?" I raised my eyebrows questioningly. "Peddling your salvation bullshit in a water bottle again?" He laughed as I had hoped he would, and shook his head.

"Just enjoying the show, It's Kait."

All around us, the crowd suddenly erupted, the sign that the lights around the stage had gone dark again and the second set of the show was about to start.

"Well, I may as well try to do that too," I said, turning. "Come on."

If Horizon was still here among the jellyfish, I was sure we'd eventually smack into each other too. For now, I was fine to make my way back to the sea.

The second set was an hour-long exercise in breaking my heart. The Road played their saddest songs, at least the ones I considered sad, about lost love and untenable love and dreams that would never be realized and losing it all at the bottom of a bottle. It was delicious sadness, and when Dov saw the tears slipping down my cheek, he rubbed my back and didn't tell me the song sucked. It felt normal, and I didn't think about it not being Horizon's hand on my back too much, and I kept crying, and Ernest kept singing about poor Dinah who dies penniless and heartbroken in a fire that all my tears could have extinguished.

No sign of Horizon. I shuffled out of the stadium with Dov, accepting the joint he lit along the way even though I remembered how awful and disoriented his weed had made me feel the night before. Lightning in the distance portended another coming shower as we made our way slowly back to the Field, speaking little, except for the occasional, *sorry*, when one or the other of us was jostled, or *thanks*, when the joint was passed back. I felt drained: from the music, from the joint, from the millions of times I squinted at the crowd around me to try to spot Horizon throughout the second half of the show. From trying simultaneously to accept and stave off the reality of the past few days. My head swam as we were swept into the tide of people, and I just stayed close to Dov, allowing him to break the waves just ahead of me. Commotion was all around us, the naked abandon that followed the close of every show; the happy noise that usually felt so comforting. But as we turned towards the outskirts of the Field, where Horizon's camper was, the rain began to fall and the energy of the crowd changed perceptibly, though it was not due to the weather.

Punctuating the dark was a different sort of light than the usual illumination from battery powered camping lanterns or cook stoves. This light was blue, then red, and seemed to come from far above our heads, like a lighthouse's signal. And like the notice to a passing ship of inclement weather or treacherous tides, I knew the light was for me—was beckoning me but was also a warning that I was about to be slammed against a rocky shore. I lurched forward but Dov put out an arm and caught me. "Kait, wait."

But Horizon is there, I wanted to scream. Dov turned and bent down a little so we were eye to eye.

"I'll find out what's going on, but you shouldn't go down there. Do you know where our bus is?" I nodded, unable to make any words come out as the crowd in front of us parted briefly and I saw a venue security car and an ambulance parked in front of the camper; an impossible tableau.

My mind flashed to the story I had heard about the Yellow Birds in Philadelphia. We would all get caught up in this, they would grab us all. My head swam with the chaos of processing what I was seeing just as the full force of the high from the weed we had smoked was taking hold. My heart raced and my thoughts crashed into each other, shattered before any could take hold. Birds—kids, we were just kids—were running everywhere, but I couldn't make sense of which direction they were trying to go. *Where was Horizon, where was Horizon.* Philadelphia. The bust, the round-up, the imprisonment in the van, the OD. The kid that died. The kid that died.

"Kait, go!"

My feet slipped on the rain-slicked grass as I ran.

PART III

THE PILGRIMS

14

"HOW DO YOU know it was Horizon?"

I asked Dov to go over the events of that night again and again as we made the long trip from Red Rocks to Tamsen, Washington aboard the Pilgrams' converted school bus. The details changed little with each telling: Rain, lightning, a crowd, a commotion. Police, ambulance. Horizon—yes, he was sure it was Horizon—in the ambulance, a few other guys he didn't know in the police car. People scattering, people yelling, people staring. The emergency vehicles eventually driving off, and then a strange quiet that blanketed the Field, followed Dov back to the bus where I was waiting. And then our leaving. Our leaving.

"We had to go, Kait. It wasn't safe. There was nothing you could do."

How many times could he tell me before I believed him, forgave him for taking me from Horizon? Forgave myself.

The trip out of Colorado would take three days, and I was determined to spend as much of it as possible in a haze, trying to overwhelm the lucid moments that were spent vacillating between bouts of pure exhaustion and pure panic. I ingested every pill offered from an outstretched hand, every flask proffered from beneath a seat, and every hit of a joint passed my way. At one point I was about to accept a spliff making its way towards me, but Dov intercepted it as he walked down the centre aisle of the bus.

"Wait, don't," he said.

"Why not?" I asked, frustrated that he was interrupting my opportunity to blur the edges of my reality with some of the Pilgrims' strong weed.

"Where are your people, Kait?" Dov asked.

"My people?" Did he mean Eartha?

"Where are your parents? Do you still talk to them?"

His questions were so strange and surprising that for a moment, I didn't think I heard correctly. We didn't ask people questions like that on Tour. *Where are you from*, sure. *What's your family like*, maybe, when the conversation moved in that direction. But never *Where are your parents*, because the most obvious answer, and maybe the most complicated for so many of the younger Birds you found at Open Road shows was, *Not here.*

"Yeah," I said, not willing or sure I should go into any details. "I still talk to them. Why?"

"I think you should call them the next time we stop. You should let them know where you'll be."

"No thank you," I said, and looked over the back of the bench seat I was perched on to see how far the joint had travelled past me. Dov put his hand on my arm and I jerked it away.

"Please fuck off," I said sharply, annoyed by Dov's paternalistic concern and the abject reality his suggestion would force me to confront. My parents? They had nothing to do with this. *I* wanted nothing to do with this right now.

"Kait," said Dov, "You're going to call home when we stop. You've got to let them know you're alright before we get to the farm. There's no house phone there." His tone was gentle but resolute, and it occurred to me that I was existing in a liminal space, a gap between places. And I had no real idea of what the place on the other side was going to be like—or if I was even going to be allowed in. Dov's request was one of the entry requirements. I could call my dad—he never answered anyway, was never available—leave him a message with the barest of details. Doing this should meet Dov's condition while also keeping the promise to my father that I would check in once in a while. It had definitely been a while.

"Fine," I said. And hoped we'd stop soon so I could make the call, get back on the bus and say yes to whatever substance, with its promised oblivion, was passed down the aisle to me next.

In my first week on the farm, Dov and whatever other Pilgrims bothered to take an interest in me told me that they'd reached out to the community, put out a message and assured me we'd get a message back soon. The communication system on the farm seemed to be headquartered in a little outbuilding on the property that was probably once a shed but was now used as an office. As Dov had warned, there was no phone inside the house, but people came and went from the office regularly, and it seemed a few Pilgrims were delegated to administration duty, though I didn't yet understand the nature of the work assignments here.

The important thing was that Horizon would know where to find me if he wanted to find me, they said, but he needed time. He had to heal his body, his heart. And me? I was being protected, wasn't I? Being given shelter and the opportunity to be part of the community, being given the opportunity to heal my own body, my own heart. Among friends.

"Friends," I said to Dov. "Does Tzvi fuck all his friends?" I had been taken to meet the Pilgrims' enigmatic leader the night before. A girl named Naomi, with mousy, bedraggled hair, bedraggled dress, bedraggled mind, had come to the room I was staying in without knocking, sat down on the mattress I was laying on and rubbed my back. "Come little bunny rabbit, come, come, come."

It was like she was reciting a children's poem to me. And what was I at that moment, after all, besides a broken, crying child lying on an old mattress facing a wall, because it was easier than having to face whatever it was that had led me there? Naomi had been assigned to me, it seemed. My ambassador as I "settled in." I was staying in a room with another girl named Brady. "You're in Shoshana's bed," Brady told me.

"Where's Shoshana staying" I asked.

"Somewhere else," said Brady.

Dov checked on me often but there was a weird separation between men and women in the house. I was the women's problem. Dov would see me in common areas but he didn't come up to the floor of the room I was sharing. The girls' wing; Shangri-la, they called it. The boys' wing was called Babylon. It seemed strange that the boys' idea of a paradise didn't include girls. The rest of the house was rambling and ramshackle. White clapboard on the outside, the farmhouse was three stories of wide-planked hallways and chilly rooms, a maze of cubbys all separated from each other that led to a feeling of being both cramped and vast. I didn't ask Naomi where she wanted me to go, but since I had not been summoned anywhere else since I had arrived, it wasn't hard for me to guess. We walked down the dim hallway of the old, creaky farmhouse out of the Shangri-la area and down a narrow staircase to a landing with two doors that met in the corner, both closed.

Naomi pushed the one on the left open. *Nobody knocks*, I thought. Tzvi was sitting in an armchair with a notebook in his lap and a pen in his hand. There was a desk in the room with an old wooden stool in front of it, two shelves stacked with books above it, and a double bed that ran along the length of the wall under a window that was open partway. It was the neatest room I had seen in the house so far.

Tzvi was Steve, the leader of the Pilgrims. The people in the house called him Tzvi; outside, to everybody else, he was Steve. *Only those who are true shall know him truly*, Naomi had told me. She did not proceed to tell me what it meant to be true, but judging by what I had seen, it had something to do with singing some sort of hymn together before meals, gardening, taking care of the chickens, repairing a barn to prepare it for livestock, and putting together the supplies that the Pilgrims took on the road with them—Holy Water and first aid kits.

Like the room itself, Tzvi seemed incongruous with my idea of who and what the Pilgrims were. I don't know what I was expecting in a cult leader—David Koresh with his huge glasses and Texas lilt? Charles Manson with his swastika and burning insanity? Ernest with his grandfather's beard and potbelly? Tzvi was not any of those things. He was young. Maybe five years older than Dov or Easy, but he seemed pretty normal. He was handsome, with dark eyes and his dark hair pulled back into a loose ponytail.

"Kait," he said, putting his notebook and pen down on a small wooden table next to the chair. I noticed that there was also a glass chillum in an ashtray and a lighter on the table. Tzvi motioned to the stool by the desk. "Sit down. Please."

"Sure," I said, glad the stool was on the other side of the modest room. We still felt too close together. I resisted the desire to turn behind me and scan the books on the shelves above the desk, believing they would give me clues I wanted to figure out what this guy was all about. Would they be religious scripts? Spiritual, at least? Or would they be something surprising, like business philosophies or movie star biographies? You can learn all you need to learn about a person by seeing the books on their shelf. And if they don't have a bookshelf, well, that's all you need to know as well.

"Why are you here, Kait?" Tzvi was looking at me intently, but there was no predatory edge to his manner.

"Dov brought me."

"We're glad you're here; we want you to be here, but if you're going to be here, we want it to be for a reason. Everybody is here for a reason. Maybe that reason is a safe place to grow; maybe that reason is to learn how to help others grow here or when we travel. Maybe it's just that some shit has gone down and you can't face going home."

"That's not why I'm here," I snapped. Tzvi's expression didn't change. Probing but benevolent.

"We know you've just been through some trauma, Kait, and we want to help you heal, want you to have a safe place to be while your friend heals—but if you're going to be here—if you're going to partake freely in our life and hospitality, you're going to need to know the real reason why. And you're going to have to get out of bed and participate. Can you do that?"

Tears sprang to my eyes at the mention of Horizon and my abandonment of him, so all I could do was nod. I'd figure the rest out later.

"Great." Tzvi reached for his notebook and pen. "Go rest. Tomorrow, you start work in the chicken coop with Brady and then you'll take part in the Kula ceremony with the rest of us." I was dismissed.

I had a better look at the bookshelf on my way out of the room. Steinbeck. Kesey. Kerouac.

He was making this up as he went along, just like every other asshole out there.

15

"WOULD YOU LIKE some coffee? You have time."

I took stock of the kitchen. Plates had been scraped but were piled in the sink. Soiled dishrags sat in a heap on the counter, as though the person that had soiled them believed that their half of the job was done and that surely someone else would come and dispense with the rags. Nobody would, so there the rags sat, moldering on the counter. One mess cleaned, another made. I understood the compulsion to finally ignore this never-ending cycle; let the rags pile up. I had lived in a home where that compulsion had taken over many spaces. Anywhere else, it might seem like laziness, like unfinished business or a mind unable to cope. But here I imagined somebody had convinced himself it was deliberate: a protest, a philosophy to halt the toil, to accept the mess, to not think of it as a mess. Once I might have considered this myself; taken a moment to drift into a state of circumspection and applaud my ability to not let such earthly, insignificant distractions as filth get in the way of a good philosophy. Now, I was simply exhausted by it. Exhausted by it all; by the mission statements, by the philosophies, by the addictions and the excuses and the lifestyles we constructed just to hide our pain and our vulnerability. I was tired. I had been tired since I got here. Maybe it was the weight of my treachery. Maybe it was all the weed I had been smoking and the pills I was taking, the stuff I accepted to try to lift that weight. Banish it. It didn't work. I was still tired. My treachery, still crushing.

"Thanks Bear," I said, "I'd love a coffee."

When the coffee pot was emptied into our mugs, it left behind a coppered patina of old, burnt grounds banding it, and it was this small neglect, this sepia-hued residue of utter disregard for cleanliness, which strangely, considering the scale of disregard for order and cleanliness blanketing the entire house, repulsed me more than anything else. Repulsed me and also ignited a twang of homesickness. Because if I was going to be in a place where people were blind to their own chaos and neglect, I might as well be in my mother's home.

Dov and I took our coffee cups and walked through the canteen which opened into the de facto living room ("The crash pad," Dov said). These rooms took up almost the entire back half of the big house, the only spaces that weren't closed in, closed off like the rest of the rooms. We walked out the double doors to the rear porch, which sloped towards the earth on one side, giving it the impression of being more like a haphazard ramp than a terrace. It looked over the pasture, the half-finished barn and beyond that, the gorgeous Cascade mountain range, draped in hemlock and pine so thick its face appeared black from where we sat on the soft wooden stairs leading from the deck.

"Kait, you know that's not what Tzvi is about; that's not what this is about," said Dov, referring to my comments about Tzvi and the loose boundaries between friends here.

"Watch the ceremony tonight; really watch it and try to understand why it's so important to us." He took a sip of his coffee and looked to me. "It's about connection. It's about connecting us to the past and to the present and to each other. And it's about trust. You could use more of that, you know." His tone was gentle and lacked accusation but I wasn't feeling receptive.

"So this is a sex ceremony?"

Dov froze mid-sip over his coffee mug.

"No, Kait. It's nothing like that. It's a bonding ceremony that allows two people to get to know each other on a deep level. It's not about sex. That can be included, if they want it, just like any two people could choose to have sex. But they could also choose not to include it."

"Except, they don't choose; Tzvi does."

From what I understood, the Kula Ceremony was an exchange of a ring from one person to another and signified the coupling-up of two Pilgrims. They could stay in a room together, the only sanctioned room for a couple to be in (besides Tzvi's), ate together, studied together, slept together. One bed. But they only had sex if they wanted to. Tzvi had to okay the exchange before the ceremony took place, and he was the only one who could call a ceremony, deciding how long that couple had to be together. It was usually once a month, Dov had told me.

Later, as we worked together in the chicken coop, Brady quietly told me that sometimes Tzvi called a ceremony after a week. Sometimes it would be months, and once in a while, he would gather everybody for a ceremony a few days after the last. But mostly it corresponded with a new moon or an eclipse or something. I didn't know if tonight held special meteorological symbolism and decided not to ask Brady. We gently wiped the dirt from the eggs we had collected with a scrap of cloth. Later, we would be building boxes for a dozen additional chickens that would be added to the coop the next week. It wasn't crowded in the coop, but Yonatan, who was in charge of the chickens, believed that if there were not enough boxes for each hen to claim as her own, the flock would be unhappy and become violent with each other. He was in a battle over this point with a woman named Melodie, who also worked in the coop and grew up on a farm.

"One box for five hens," she said, "one for three at the very least." Yonatan wouldn't concede. *Brood*, I wanted to tell them. *It's a brood of hens.*

I knew nothing about the ratio of non-violent hen to nesting quarter, so I just did what I was told and prepared to build the boxes, wondering why the Pilgrims didn't care to apply this lodging math to the people that lived, overcrowded, in the house.

"Why would he call a ceremony more than once a month," I asked Brady.

"Well," she hesitated. "Sometimes maybe he can tell that the couple isn't working together in the best interests of the group, or maybe they're even getting too close, and that's not what this place is about."

"Is he afraid people are going to fall in love?" I asked.

"No . . . it's more like, we want to be sure that we are all equally in love and learning from each other, I guess. No favourites."

"That's kind of fucked up," I said.

"It's not," she said, "it's really nice. And when we exchange the Kula ring, Tzvi also gives a woman his Kula necklace, signifying their partnership until the next ceremony."

Now I understood. It wasn't just about monitoring the chemistry between the Pilgrims exchanging the Kula ring; the arbitrary timelines had to do with Tzvi wanting a new concubine. Sometimes a new ceremony was called within days. I had been here two weeks, and this was the first ceremony that had been called since I got here.

"Who has the Kula necklace now?" I asked.

"Shoshana," said Brady. The girl whose bed I was sleeping in. Brady turned back to the nesting box and reached for another egg.

The ceremony was held outside, in a clearing with a giant fire pit near the sheds on the east side of the property. We were all sitting on blankets spread out on the ground circling the fire. Dov was on one side of me and Brady was on the other. Cross-legged, sprawling, leaning back, leaning on each other, it appeared to be like any other gathering around any other campfire. It was a damp, chilly night so some people had additional blankets draped over their shoulders or wrapped around outstretched legs. Everybody participated in the ceremony, Naomi had told me. She meant everybody that was at the house at the time and not working on Road Tour, in the city on a provision run, or, I suspected, out meeting with the growers who supplied the vast quantity of weed the Pilgrims smoked and sold. No growing on the premises—selling was business but cultivating was too great of a risk. These things seemed to happen in shifts, work details with up to ten or twelve people away at a time, depending on what they were out doing. Tonight there were about twenty people at the house, so not everybody but most, I thought. I still couldn't get a handle on how many Pilgrims there were—everybody was coy about providing an actual number. I had missed the last shows. Summer Tour was almost over.

My heart sank. If this part of Tour was over, Horizon was supposed to be back in Vancouver, dealing with everything. And I was supposed to be with him. But Horizon had dealt with everything that had happened by fucking himself up on god knows what and I—well I was here.

Brady passed me a joint that had come around. I inhaled deeply and thought about Horizon; what he had done to me, what I had done to him. *Same/same*, I thought, and took another hit.

A guy named Beckett had a guitar, and he strummed something I didn't recognize, but the Pilgrims did, because soon they were all singing. It was soulful, like an old folk song or something, and I had to admit, the group sounded pretty good; passionate. A passion of Pilgrims. After that song ended, another. It was one I recognized immediately, an Open Road song called *Trust* that you had to go pretty deep into the playbook to know—definitely not what you'd consider a greatest hit. And like the previous tune, the Pilgrims sounded so good singing it. The lyrics in *Trust*, which I had always considered nice but a little cheesy, sounded sweet and sincere that night, and I didn't even realize I was softly singing along until Dov reached for my hand and squeezed it. I squeezed it back and kept singing though I wouldn't raise my voice at all, and realized I felt—not good, exactly, but the best I had since I arrived. Calmer. I gazed up at the sky, starless under the cover of low clouds and framed by the silhouettes of so many tall trees. Maybe there was something to this place. Or maybe it was the fire cutting through the damp night, or the crickets chirping or the strumming of the guitar.

"Or maybe it's all just a line, connected," Dov said to me, and I smiled at him for real, for being able to understand what I was thinking and for convincing me that whatever happened that night, I would embrace it; allow it, believe it.

It wasn't until much, much later that I realized Dov wasn't reading my mind; he had just been singing the last line of the song.

"This ring I give is imbibed with the gifts of sacred love, wisdom, pain, and pleasure of those that have worn it previously. In this exchange, I ask that the person who accepts the Kula ring accepts the gifts it represents, and fills it with their own love, wisdom, pain and, pleasure, sharing our purpose and intentions. Thank you, Grey, for sharing this gift with me and for allowing me to pass it on." Grey gave Lindy a look of angelic sincerity and nodded. Grey was cute, a tiny bit pudgy with a beard so blonde it was almost white. I liked his style, wearing overalls like a friendly goat farmer. Or maybe a friendly goat. He was sitting five or six people away from me and the fire threw a golden haze over the exchange. I wondered if Lindy had truly been happy to have Grey pick her, or if she had just grinned and beared their partnership all month. But no, I reminded myself, the Pilgrims are here because they believe in this—they *like* this. They like being part of a group. They like Tzvi calling the shots. Lindy turned ninety degrees away from Grey until she was facing someone else. I didn't really know the guy, though I recognized him as one of the Pilgrims that was always at the Open Road shows, giving out Holy Water. Were these always hetero couplings? What if Lindy wanted to hook up with a girl?

I turned to ask Dov about it, but when I saw his face, I stopped myself. He was staring at Lindy's back, crestfallen. I almost gasped. Dov loved Lindy! I snapped my lips shut and turned abruptly from Dov, not wanting him to notice me watching him; not wanting him to feel embarrassed that I guessed his secret. Was it a secret? Or did all the Pilgrims already know how everybody actually felt about everybody else. Maybe this was all just a perverse game, but I was intrigued. Always eager to talk, I knew Brady or Naomi would satiate my curiosity about these love connections later if I asked. Lindy was addressing the guy in front of her.

"Cedar, will you accept the Kula ring?" Ah, right, Cedar; that was his name. Dov must be pretty tight with him since they were always at the shows together. Did Cedar know how Dov felt about Lindy?

Did Lindy know how Dov felt about her? Did every couple have sex or did some just stay platonic? No, I was sure Tzvi arranged these matches for maximum intimacy, maximum complication, maybe. To tie everybody to each other and to this place, become a many-armed creature with Tzvi and this farm, the body. Entangled. I tried to repress my interest the sociological machinations of the ceremony and see it for what I assumed its intended purpose was as a community equalizer of sorts, but I just couldn't. I was almost giddy with the sophomoric urge to talk to Eartha about it all. *Eartha.* My heart sank as it had so often recently. I missed my friend so much. Why wasn't I with her, gossiping about this crazy place? Why wasn't I with her, period? Surely she would have heard what happened at Red Rocks by now; what happened to Horizon. News like that travels through Yellow Bird circles quickly, and we were supposed to see each other again at the Nevada shows. Would she be looking for me, or would she assume I was with Horizon? And what would she think if she found out I wasn't?

I stared at the bonfire and in the flames conjured the scene so clearly. I could hear the conversation happening outside of Big Blue Bertha the first night of the Vegas shows, picture it perfectly: Everybody sitting around a fire in the cookstove, Vivi leaning into Easy's lap; Jujube weaving colourful threads into a bracelet by the firelight. Skate would be mad at me as usual. Mad that I went with Horizon in the first place, mad that I left him. *She always leaves. She always takes the easy way out.* Eartha looking straight at the fire while she defended me. *Remember Philly? Remember that girl? You don't stick around when there's trouble like that. Even if . . .*

Even if the person you say you love is the one in trouble.

Dov had assured me so many times that they would understand, would not have wanted me to get into any trouble that night. Understand that I needed to be safe. To get whole again. This was the place I needed to be. But the things I imagined Skate saying were true. The things I imagined were true. I left everything behind. And so far, I had not returned to anything. Anyone. How long could I wait before there was nothing to go back to.

My head was swimming from the weed, from the ceremony, from the loneliness and shame that clouded the visions of my friends until the flames incinerated them completely.

I didn't hear Tzvi saying my name.

Dov nudged me and I looked at him. He was nodding towards the fire. No, not towards the fire; towards Tzvi and Shoshana, standing in front of the fire. In front of me. Tzvi had his hand outstretched, beckoning me. I stood up unsteadily, looked around at everybody staring at us, at me.

"Kait." Tzvi still had his hand out. Unsure of what else to do, I took it. "Shoshana would like to pass the Kula necklace to you. Will you accept it?"

I recieved the necklace with a stammer that simulated confirmation. And with my head still swimming and everybody watching us, expectant, the feeling was almost . . . reverent. I accepted. And then I was sitting back in my spot again, and Dov seemed surprised again but squeezed my leg in a reassuring way and Brady was picking at something on her foot and the ceremony continued. That was it. What was I supposed to do? I was living here, eating their food, reading their books, working in their chicken coops, taking advantage of their strange but undemanding hospitality. Undemanding until that point anyway.

A number of people stood up to declare "Gratitude and Intentions," which gave the impression of being confessional: Lior was grateful that the remaining lumber for the barn had been delivered and unpacked despite his forgetting to organize a crew to be home when it arrived; since it looked like the rain would hold off, Naomi intended to finally cut the lavender and sage to dry for medicines and smudging the new barn, and John wanted to announce his intention to take a name this week and to offer his gratitude to all those who had supported him on his journey. A whoop went up around the circle, and Tzvi stood again, clapping.

"John, we're honoured to accept your intention. We'll set the Sabbath table this Friday so you can take your name in the eyes of our creators and everyone present. Nice work, man." Tzvi clapped John on the shoulder.

"Let's close our Kula ceremony with the *One Way*. Beckett?" Tzvi nodded at the guitarist and he began strumming the opening chords of a protest song by a Hasidic reggae singer that was popular with Yellow Birds and, I was not surprised to find out, Pilgrims. In the days I had been with the Pilgrims, I couldn't really glean their true connection to Judaism, beyond some of the Pilgrims using Hebrew names and the printing of Old Testament passages on the holy water. And since my own connection to Judaism, besides it being the religion I was born into, was tenuous, I didn't worry too much about it. Every Jew, Christian, Yellow Bird, and Pilgrim was a disciple. We just didn't always know which god to follow home.

16

TZVI'S ROOM AGAIN. Cast in purple shadows from the bulb of a small lamp on the table, it seemed just as tidy as the only other time I had been in there, but even smaller now. Closer. I sat on the bed after Tzvi patted the spot beside him. My heart was racing now that we were alone; my mouth was dry.

"Drink more," Tzvi said, motioning to the mug of tea I was holding. "It will help."

Help with what, I said and giggled.

"What's so funny?" asked Tzvi, smiling himself. I realized I hadn't said that out loud.

What kind of tea is this, I asked, but maybe I didn't. My limbs felt loose. I sipped. He took the mug from my hand and placed it on the table.

"I'm glad you accepted the Kula necklace, Kait. It's very special to us." I nodded. The light was playing tricks on me. I tried to focus on Tzvi, the things he was saying, and not on the shadows moving around the room. *Can I lay down now?* He kept talking, slowly. Or maybe it was my hearing that had slowed.

"Think of it as a bonding agent, not just meant for me to get to know you, but for you to get to know me. We function better when we're all connected, when we feel as close to all as we do to one. Do you understand?" I nodded, the easiest thing for my body to do at the moment. Tzvi moved closer to me, stroked my arm. It felt good. I closed my eyes and made the shadows go away.

"We're glad you're here, Kait. We hope you get what you need. But if you're going to be here, you have to give as well."

"I'm working in the chickens," I said thickly. I put my hands over my eyes to make it even darker.

"That's good. That helps everybody. But you need to open yourself up to your pain and acknowledge it. You need to connect to your pain and connect to the people here if you want it to get any better." Gentle pressure on my arms and I was lying on the bed. He stroked my hair, ran his hand to my shoulder, did it again, ran his hand to my elbow, did it again, to my wrist.

"You know what we teach here, Kait: love the stranger because we were once the stranger. There's no room for judgment, for boundaries. Isn't that why you're here? Isn't that why you go to the shows? So you can be where you're not judged; where you're understood. Where you're not a stranger." His hand, my hip. His hand, my leg. I ached for something that felt different, for one exquisite spark that could extinguish the panic and guilt I had been feeling, and maybe, maybe relight the embers of calm I had felt earlier, at the ceremony.

"I always feel like a stranger," I whispered.

"I can change that tonight if you'll let me." His lips my neck. His hand, my shirt. My hand, his back.

I let him.

When I woke up, I was alone. After a disoriented moment, my physical and mental faculties merged and I remembered where I was. Tzvi was gone and so was the haziness that had been with me the previous night. The mug of tea had been replaced by a glass of water. I was naked and felt warm and comfortable. The sex had been slow and quiet. It had been good. Tzvi was a surprisingly decent lover who had treated me with just the right amounts of attentiveness and intensity. A momentary heat rose in me once again as my mind flashed to the fire and the ceremony the previous night. It had been good to feel something other than unmoored, disconnected from my surroundings.

And then a surge of anxiety wound through me, taut as a snake coiled round its prey. Horizon. Had I just betrayed him? I could believe that being away from him right now was for my safety, my survival—but being with another man . . . No. That was survival as well. Being here meant being a part of the Pilgrims world and last night was the invitation to truly step inside that world. If I had turned it down, where else would I go? And I hadn't wanted to turn it down. I wasn't going to stay here forever but maybe, like Dov said, this really was where I needed to be right now. Once we figured everything out and Horizon and I could be together again, we would each have to accept the things that happened after he decided to leave me at the show that night.

If we were going to be together again.

But as soon as I got up and got dressed, that tenuous feeling of belonging was replaced with a sense of insecurity. What would my reception be like downstairs? How would the rest of the house view me? While I had the Kula necklace, I was invited to stay in Tzvi's room when I wanted, provided he wasn't working, and to spend the nights with him when I wanted.

"This is your choice, Kait. It's all your choice." He had swept his hand in front of him, a gesture of infinity, but I didn't even know what having the Kula necklace really meant yet.

I hadn't even realized that Shoshana and Tzvi had something going on previously, which must mean that having the necklace was a subtle, normal thing not to be flaunted or treated as an advantage. The Kula ceremonies were meant to be a bridge to greater equality and connection, so I reasoned, acting as though Tzvi anointed me with exceptionality would be the antithesis of the ceremony's purpose. Business as usual. I decided I would be on the lookout for signals from other people that might help me set or adjust expectations.

Trying to figure out the social order of the Pilgrims was baffling so far. In new situations I usually tried to watch for a little while, see who emerged as the alphas in the pack and who naturally deferred to the alphas. I was content to let others work out the power struggles and be a happy member of the herd for the most part, as I had in Big Blue Bertha, as I had at school, as I had at home, but the farm seemed to operate differently. Besides Tzvi, I couldn't figure out who the alphas here were. He seemed to have closer confidantes—Dov, Shoshana, a few others, but besides those few who worked quite closely to Tzvi, there seemed to be no hierarchy. Everybody was an active participant in life on the farm or at the shows, and in the ceremonies. I worried that Shoshana might resent me, but she had simply resettled in a different room and, while not exactly friendly to me, certainly wasn't unfriendly. She had seen this before, I imagined; they all had. But I hadn't. Tzvi's and the Pilgrims' quest for equality, for an egalitarian society (more or less), seemed to be working. If everybody was part of the herd, there was no herd.

Still, I hoped that I could wring an advantage out of my access to Tzvi. So when the evening meal that night had finished and everybody was sitting around the crash pad, smoking joints, and listening to music and shooting the shit, I sought out Tzvi. I found him on the back deck with Dov. A misty Pacific Northwest rain was falling softly, accounting for the crowd inside. They were talking about a plan for the next day; a trip to a nearby farm to check on a crop it was growing for the Pilgrims. Not wanting to interrupt, I went back inside.

Lindy and Cedar got up from where they were sitting on the floor and, holding hands, headed to the stairs.

"Ooooh," came a singsong from one of the other boys.

"First comes love," someone sang,

"Then comes marriage," more chimed in, and a dude named Leary interrupted—

"Then comes Cedar working his ass off on a construction site because the mortgage is due and Lindy is pregnant again and wants a bigger house and a better car and her mother's coming to live with you."

Laughter from the crowd as Lindy turned and smirked, giving the room the finger as Cedar rolled his eyes, leading Lindy upstairs. With their departure, more people turned in for the night. I glimpsed out the door from the canteen to the back porch, but it was empty now. No sign of Tzvi or Dov.

I hung around the crash pad for a few more minutes, accepted a pass of a joint from Leary, then got a glass of water to help banish the pasty feeling the weed left in my mouth, and went upstairs. But instead of heading to my room in Shangri-la, I stopped on the landing outside of Tzvi's room. Light filtered out from under the door. After a moment's hesitation, I knocked quietly.

"It's Kait."

There was no immediate reply and I was about to open the door, when Tzvi spoke from the other side.

"I'm working right now, Kait. Good night."

I felt immediately stung but hoped he wouldn't hear it in my voice.

"Good night, then."

I waited for any other response, but none came so I tiptoed away from his room and proceeded up to the girls' floor. I was grateful that I had gone upstairs a little early, so I could feign sleep when Brady came in.

I felt sheepish the next day, trying hard not to think of Tzvi's dismissal as disinterest in spending time with me. He was busy; he was working. If *all this* was my choice, then it was his, too. He couldn't force me to be with him and I couldn't force him to be with me. But something that would have left me feeling relieved only a short time before now felt like rejection.

The next day, Tzvi didn't talk to me or even acknowledge me at all around the house, but that didn't seem unusual; I had rarely seen him mingling with the others during work hours. As for the rest of the Pilgrims, they were in a flurry of activity by noon and it bolstered my mood to see everybody so happy and busy.

"What's so exciting?" I asked a girl whose name was Lior or Liora or something like that as I poured a coffee during my lunch break. But when she told me what was going on, any exuberance that I had felt a moment before quickly retreated and my spirit fell like an arrow, sharp and piercing. Open Road Tour was ending that night, and all of the Pilgrims still out at the shows would be heading back here over the weekend.

Heading home. Where I should be going with Horizon, because Tour is over, because even though things got complicated, we were going to figure it out; go home and deal with it all, together. Because we had a plan. We had a plan.

I didn't realize I had let go of the coffee cup until I heard the shatter of the ceramic on the floor. It took a second longer to register the heat of the liquid burning my foot.

After I washed up from work in the coop, I dressed for dinner, putting on the nicest thing I had at the moment, which was a white linen shift with delicate embroidery around the neck and around the hem. It had been on a hook in the communal women's clothing closet that any of us could pick from, and was designed more like an old-fashioned nightgown than a dress, which may have been why it had not been taken by anyone else by time I found it. But still, I had been surprised that it was unclaimed, left hanging there like a seasonal decoration at the wrong time of year. It was so pretty and impractical. On the back of the door in my room at my mother's house, an intricately patterned caftan hung from a hanger. Deep azure blue, persimmon, and gold, with flecks of green and yellow, I had found it a thrift store where you pay for your clothes by the pound. The rectangular length of fabric had a deep v at the neck and wide unsewn openings for the arms, but hung perfectly flat against my door like a flag. I loved it the second I saw it and, like the white dress, couldn't imagine how somebody else hadn't already grabbed it. Even after many months of looking at it from my usual perch cross-legged on my bed, it made me happy. I must, I decided, have a very different idea of what's beautiful compared to other people.

There was a very small yellow stain near the bottom of the white dress, but it still felt clean and pretty when so little else in the house did. JuJube would never have stolen a dress like this from me. I raked my fingers through my hair, trying to tame the waves a bit, then pinned it up in a loose twist. The slight but constant dampness in the air here was good for my skin and hair, kept my cheeks a healthy pink over the olive tones, kept the curls springing from where I tucked them behind my ears. There was a little compact mirror on the dresser and I moved it through the air so I could see my reflection in small round glimpses. Lip and chin. Eye and temple. Collarbone. Good effort.

My intention in dressing up—as much as one could call a stained dress and unbrushed hair, dressing up—was to appear as presentable as possible and go talk to Tzvi. If there was any favour to curry in wearing the Kula necklace, I was ready to exploit it that afternoon.

I wanted to talk to him about what happened at Red Rocks; what happened to Horizon. Try to find out what he knew, and then help me devise a plan. *So I can focus my time here in a meaningful and productive way,* I would say to him; assure him that I could be a better citizen of the farm if I knew when I should leave it. People here were big on intention and choice so that's how I wanted to steer the conversation. My heart was beating fast, but my confidence level in navigating the forthcoming meeting was high. I would tell Tzvi what I wanted, in clear terms. And in clear terms, I expected, he would tell me what he wanted from me in exchange for his knowledge and help.

Right before I left my room, I hastily remembered to put on the Kula necklace, a symbol of my allegiance to him—and hopefully visa-versa—even though I hadn't touched it since the night it was given to me, assuming the significance lay in the taking and not necessarily the displaying of the thing.

I didn't hear the voices in Tzvi's room until I was standing on the landing in front of his half-opened door. Not wanting to intrude, I panicked a bit and turned to go, moving clumsily and causing the old floorboards outside of the door to groan. From inside, Tzvi called to come in.

"Kait. What is it?" Shoshana was in Tzvi's room. They were both standing by the desk and turned towards me when I entered. He did not sound pleased to see me and Shoshana did not look pleased to see me, though whether her dour expression was directed at me or Tzvi, I couldn't really tell.

"I'm sorry. I didn't mean to interrupt. I'll go," I said, fully expecting Tzvi to tell me to stay, since I was already here, in his room in the late afternoon, wearing his Kula necklace and the pretty white dress.

"Yes, thank you," he said, and nodded at the door.

My neck reddened with humiliation and I retreated back to Shangri-la, all of my previous bravado extinguished like a candle's flame in the path of a whisper. In my room, I removed the Kula necklace and dropped in my drawer of the bureau. Then I changed out of the white dress and put it back on the hook in the communal closet.

17

"HEY, KAIT."

I looked up, shielding my eyes. The flat clouds in the late-day sky reflected a dark blue-grey light. It had made me notice the wild lupines growing in tall blue spikes around the outbuildings. How coordinated. Mother nature was a decent decorator.

"Hey, Bear."

"How are you?"

"Did you know there were robins here?"

"Robins?"

"The birds. I didn't know there were robins this far west. They seem so out of place and exotic here. At home they seem so ordinary."

"So doesn't seeing them here make you feel more at home?"

"Right now they make me feel more out of place."

Dov sighed and turned to me.

"Kait, why are you here?"

"Why the fuck are you here?" I snapped at him. He didn't flinch.

"Because I believe in this community, and I believe in God and what we're doing, and it's my home right now. And maybe I'm looking for something and hoping to find it here. And maybe you are too."

"I need to find Horizon," I said. My shoulders dropped and I couldn't stop the tears.

At dinner, I didn't really talk to anyone unless a moment of the conversation was directed right at me. After my quiet, unenthusiastic replies, it didn't take long for people to stop including me in the conversation altogether, which was all about the returning Pilgrims and the upcoming naming ceremony for John. Tzvi, at the head of the table as usual, had not insisted that I sit to his right, like Adam's rib, where the woman with the Kula necklace usually sat at meals. It was not my hand he took during the prayer before the meal, nor my direction he turned even once during the lively talk of preparations.

The work teams would have to be rejigged with the house full of returned Pilgrims, so almost everybody should expect a change in detail, Dov told us. Naomi would sort out sleeping arrangements, and Liora (Ah, not Lior. I made a mental note) and Leary would be coordinating harvest.

"Priority," Leary said with authority, and the Pilgrims at the table nodded in assent. I had no idea what they were talking about—we had a vegetable garden that could sustain the house, but it certainly didn't seem like something that two people needed to handle or gather serious support for, but I didn't want to let my confusion show or ask anybody what Leary meant. It was beginning to seem clear to me that I wasn't truly a member of this household anyway, not equal in status—and certainly not elevated at all. I poked at the vegetarian curry on my plate, but there was no room in my body for food when doubt and loneliness were already taking up so much space.

I was not on canteen duty that night, so when plates were being cleared, I pushed back my chair, intending to go outside in the fading light with a group of women to help braid the garlic that had been pulled out of the garden earlier that day. But as we were all leaving the dining room, Tzvi called my name, startling me.

"Come with me."

I swallowed, unable to discern whether the sudden dip in my stomach was fear or pleasure.

"Shut the door." The light on the desk was already on in Tzvi's room, cutting the dim light; anticipating his return. He sat in the chair. I stood in front of him, not speaking.

"Where's your necklace? You had it on earlier." So he had noticed.

"It's in my room," I said.

"Go get it."

I considered what he was actually commanding, then opened the door I had just shut. When I returned with the necklace in my hand, I closed the door behind me.

"Put it on," said Tzvi. I did. He walked over to me, put his hands on my head and ran them down through my hair, combing it with his fingers. His gaze was not unkind, but it was intense, as always. He sat on the edge of his bed.

"Now take everything else off."

I did, slowly.

"Get over here."

I did.

With Alex, sex had been sweet but clumsy; young people hampered by horniness and inexperience and embarrassment, but also a tremendous sense of not wanting to make the other feel uncomfortable, trying to reconcile our clothed easiness with the awkwardness that being naked together brought. I was better at it than he was. My body seemed to know what to do and temporarily gave my brain permission to slow down, relieve myself of my thoughts a little while and enjoy it.

That same permission, that freedom, that ability to get my brain to just shut the fuck up for a while, no guilt, no regrets, no wondering what my next move should be, allowed me to unquestioningly explore my sexuality after Alex; on Road Tour. It allowed me to hook up with guys when I wanted to. To say yes when I wanted to and allow myself the enjoyment of being desired, that power and pleasure, and then be fine when I left, or when whoever I was with left me.

And then Horizon, and it was something else altogether. Something new. It was good, it was so good, and my body wanted that pleasure from him and to give him that pleasure, but it was something else as well. We fit together. There was an equality in it. The sex was as good as the conversation; was as good as setting up the camper in the rain; was as good as just holding hands and walking through the Field together. I didn't want him to leave. I didn't want to leave. But I had. I had left him.

I wanted help from Tzvi, I needed it. But as he pushed me forward on his bed, held my shoulder, and thrust into me, I needed something else that I thought he could give me as well. I was desperate for that shut off in my brain, to be relieved of my thoughts for a few moments. I needed distraction. I needed absolution.

"Can I ask you a question?" I was lying on my side in his bed; he was sitting up drinking a glass of water. Outside, the night had descended but I didn't know what time it was. We had smoked a joint some time ago; had sex again, slower, but we hadn't fallen asleep. I could hear some people talking outside; wondered if they had heard me.

"What's your question, Kait?" he passed me the water glass; I drank.

"Are you actually Jewish?"

"In the simplest terms, yes. But what we believe here, what we practice here is not traditional. You can see that." I regarded his back. His body was slim and muscular, with broad shoulders, the body of someone that does physical work, though I hadn't really seen it yet. He had several birthmarks and a fan of freckles near his neck, probably from the sun. His weight was substantial on top of me; not unpleasant.

"What do you believe?"

"I'm not proselytizing at you, right now, Kait. If you want to know what we believe, come to Sabbath dinner on Friday and support John as he takes his name and commits to our life here. Then see how he is embraced, how that connection strengthens, and you'll see why we do this."

"John's definitely not Jewish. So like, does he get circumcised when he takes his name? Is it going to be a bris as well?"

"Is that your idea of a joke?"

"Are you still with Shoshana?" Now he turned to me, didn't say anything for a moment.

"You don't get to question me like that."

"What do I get to do?"

He showed me.

Later, still dark but we had fallen asleep. I got up, pulled on my t-shirt, grabbed the empty glass and went to the bathroom. When I came back, Tzvi was laying on his back, still. I sat on the edge of the bed this time, drank some of the water. Tzvi turned on his side and stroked the back of my arm, kissed me just above the elbow, then reached out his hand and I gave him the glass.

"I need to know where Horizon is. I need to know he's safe."

He reached across me and put the glass on the bedside table.

"He's safe."

In the dark, I doubted Tzvi could see the stunned look on my face, but he must have known that the information shocked me.

"I have a number for where he should be now. Dov will take you into town tomorrow and you can try to get in touch with him." He lay down on his back again. There was still space beside him. I lay down as well.

"How did you do that?" I asked.

"It wasn't hard, Kait. We know a lot of people. And I told Dov that if you were going to be here, we needed to know the cops weren't going to come looking for you, so we needed to know what happened to that kid."

That kid. My heart sank a bit, but then I thought about what Tzvi had just said. Horizon was okay. I was going to speak to him again.

"Thank you," I whispered.

We slept.

Dov was waiting for me in the morning, sitting in the canteen with his coffee, leaving me to wonder when Tzvi had put this plan in to place, and when he had intended to tell me if I had not asked about Horizon in the middle of the night. But thinking better of using this time to question either of them, I poured a coffee and tried to calm my nerves. We hadn't talked since I snapped at him on the back porch the day before, but Dov seemed his usual serene self.

"You good?" He asked. I nodded, sipped my coffee. It was tasty, I liked it when Dov made the coffee. He seemed to be the only person who cared to measure the grounds into the filter using the scoop, and not just filling it by look or feel as most of the other Pilgrims did. And Dov always cleaned the pot first, preferring not to have yesterday's scummy leftovers become a bed for today's brew.

"You know, Kait," said Dov as he turned to rinse his mug under the tap, "that first time I spoke to you, in Olympia—do you remember that?" I nodded again, blew on my mug to part the steam.

"You gave me and Eartha Holy Water."

"Yeah, but that wasn't the first time I saw you. I had noticed you for weeks, saw you doing hair wraps. Saw you hanging out. Before Horizon."

"That makes sense. We see so many of the same people at the shows."

"Yeah, but I had been noticing you. It just took me a long time to talk to you, to try to be your friend. But then we saw those two shows together—"

"We saw one show together."

"Well, we went in to one show together. And I had a great time with you. At both shows."

"I had a good time with you, too Bear. I'm glad you were there. Especially . . ."

"I'm glad I was there too, Kait. So glad. And I'm glad we're both here now."

"Dov . . ."

"Listen. All I'm saying is that you're safe here. You're safe with me. And if things don't go the way you want them to; if the news isn't good, well, you will always be safe here, and I will always be here for you. With you." I was taken aback and a little confused.

"What about Lindy?" I asked. Had I imagined everything at the Kula ceremony when she gave the ring to Cedar?

"Lindy?" said Dov, "Lindy's my sister. Did you think—no, never mind; I don't want to know."

"Oh my god," I said, "No, you don't want to know!"

He looked up, a bit shyly. "Does that change anything for you?"

"Bear," I said gently. "You have been such a good friend to me, and I appreciate that so much." I shook my head, felt a hitch in my throat. "But I still love Horizon, even if this doesn't go well."

Dov hesitated. "I know, I know. But Kait, love is only one part of it." He wiped his hands on his jeans, then clapped them together.

"Ok; you ready? Let's get this show on the road." He held out his hand to me, squeezed mine when I took it.

I removed the piece of paper from my pocket and unfolded it. The phone number belonged to Horizon's parents in Vancouver, which I had guessed as soon as I saw the area code that Tzvi had written down. Punching in the numbers, first the ones on the phone card Dov had given me, then the 11 on the slip of paper, my nerves ramped up. My heart started beating in my ears and quick waves of nausea washed over me. I had no idea who was going to be on the other end of the line, and I was afraid I would faint before I could find out. Finally, all the numbers dialed, I heard a ringtone.

"Hello?" It was a woman's voice. Horizon' mother, I assumed.

"Hi—hi," I stammered, "Um, I'm looking for Horizon Evans. This is Kait."

"Kait," Mrs. Evans said, as if she already knew me. Flashes of the small, capable woman Horizon had told me about came to mind, and my idea of her was both supported and weakened by the voice on the other end of the line. I took a deep breath and started talking.

Horizon's mother was firm but compassionate. She sounded composed; I was a mess. But Horizon would be fine, and that was what mattered. She told me the story in a calm, matter-of-fact tone. I said nothing as she spoke.

Horizon had taken ecstasy at the beginning of the show that night, which I hadn't known. It was already hitting him when he went to the bathroom during the set break (when I had lost him), but he wasn't feeling good from it, he was probably getting dehydrated, and while he was in there, he saw someone he knew who offered him cocaine. He took it, hoping to help keep his trip positive.

They were in the bathroom for a while and when they came out and couldn't find me, he and the guy with the coke went back to the camper. They continued to do lines. When Horizon began to slur his words, the guy got worried. When Horizon slumped over and wouldn't wake up, the guy panicked, gathered up as much of his gear as he could find, and left.

After the show, but before I got there, Albie and Fong had gone straight to the camper to hang out with us. They were the ones that found him; they were the ones that called the ambulance. The police, who were already at the show, got there first. Horizon had had a small stroke, the effects of the cocaine and whatever it had been cut with, compounded by the MDMA raising his blood pressure. He was taken to the hospital and stabilized, and after spending the night in intensive care, was moved to a regular room. His parents were called that day and arrived in Colorado the next, so they were spared seeing the worst of it, as if your child pale, weak, and in a hospital bed was not bad enough. The police did not press charges, but took Albie and Fong into custody that first night, until they were convinced that someone else had provided the drugs.

Horizon wouldn't, or couldn't, tell them who it was. He was in the hospital for two more days, but as soon as possible, his parents brought Horizon back to Vancouver. His mother flew with him; his father drove the camper. They knew everything. About me, about Larissa. About Donovan.

"Can I talk to him?" I finally squeaked out. But he wasn't home; He was at the clinic with his father, for physiotherapy and then counseling. Did I understand that Horizon had a long road ahead of him? Not only his recovery from the stroke, which had weakened the left side of his body, but from the drug use; and from the trauma of discovering that he had a son.

"So that we can all hopefully have a good relationship with my grandson," she said.

"Do you think he wants to see me?" I didn't know if I should ask, but I also didn't know if I would ever get another chance. A pause.

"Where are you, Kait?" His mother asked.

"Tamsen, Washington," I answered.

"Is that where you live?"

"No, I'm just staying here." Another pause.

"I don't know if seeing you would be good for Horizon yet. I don't know if he's ready to face you. He needs to get stronger."

"I don't—I don't want him to be worried about me," I finally said. "I'm so sorry about everything." I was sobbing, like a child.

"Kait," Mrs. Evans said, "I'm not sure you have anything to be sorry about. This is just going to take some time. We need him to get better." I wondered if I was part of the *we* she was talking about. I nodded into the phone, still crying.

"Is there a number we can reach you at?" She asked. I shook my head though she wouldn't see it.

"No, no I don't even have a phone right now. I don't have anything. It was all in the camper."

"Ok. Ok, Kait, how about if you give it a couple of weeks. Can you call back in a couple of weeks and we'll see where we're at?"

"Will you tell him I called?"

She softened. "I will. Soon, sweetie, I promise."

"And Mrs. Evans?"

"Yes, Kait."

I sniffed and felt my throat hitching.

"Tell him I'm sorry."

"Oh, honey," she sighed, "Why don't you go home too?"

"How did it go," asked Dov, handing me a cone piled high with a twist of vanilla soft-serve. After he dropped me at the post office, Dov had gone to run some errands. "Meet me at the ice cream shop," he said, nodding to a storefront across the street that advertised thirty-one flavours. "We could probably handle a treat."

We hadn't talked much on the forty-five-minute drive into town. Waiting for Dov, I had watched the people walk by and the cars stop for gas at the pumps next door. And I replayed the phone call over and over in my head.

"Thank you," I said, and tasted the ice cream. It was cold and smooth and soothed my throat, which was sore from the little talking and lots of crying I had just done. "It was all right."

"Are you all right?" Surely he could see I wasn't. I nodded quickly, afraid to talk and summon more tears. Dov didn't ask me any more questions, so we sat together in a companionable silence until our cones were done.

"You were right to help me get out of there," I said to Dov on the way home. He reached over and squeezed my leg gently, but didn't say anything.

My head was spinning. I wasn't sure what to do now. My instinct was to run away; to get to the highway and hitchhike to Vancouver; it wasn't that far. But then what? Although I had Horizon's parent's address, his mother had made it clear that it was too soon to see him. So I was going back to the Pilgrims, because I didn't have anywhere else to go, but what was I going back to? It felt like everything had changed. Being with Tzvi had felt necessary for my—what? Survival? Maybe. But now it just felt like another betrayal—of Horizon's loyalty, of my own capabilities. No, no, I will not condemn myself for this, I thought, and I shook my head, banishing the guilt from my mind at that moment. Dov, my steadfast new friend, was ready to be my knight in shining armour, but the thing I really needed was, for once, to fucking save myself.

Pulling into the farm, I could immediately sense tension, as more people than usual were standing around together talking during what was supposed to be a productive time of day, and those that were actually working were doing so with more purpose than I had ever seen, head down, movements stiff.

"What happened?" Dov asked Lindy as she approached the car. I saw between them a resemblance I hadn't noticed before. It was obvious now that they were siblings. They even glided in the same graceful way that some tall people moved through the world.

"Cops," said Lindy. "They just left a little while ago."

"What did they want?" asked Dov. "Where's Tzvi?"

"He's in the office." Lindy nodded her head towards the outbuilding situated between the house and the barn that housed the business supplies the Pilgrims needed; a computer, printer, fax machine, files—and a phone whose use was not generally offered to the other Pilgrims, necessitating our trip into town that morning.

Dov shut the car door and headed towards the small building, leaving me with Lindy.

"What did they want?" I asked.

"They were trying to find someone. A runaway or something. It happens every now and then, some kid goes on Tour, doesn't come home, so their parents start searching for them, and the cops love to come here, like we're body snatchers or something. The problem is, once they're here, they like to nose around as much as they possibly can without a warrant, trying to get people scared, to say something incriminating. You know how cops are. It just puts everybody on edge."

"The person they were looking for wasn't here?"

"No, no, we had no idea who the kid was. Somebody named Ari."

I nodded at Lindy, and walked inside. Everything that had already happened that morning came rushing over me; the phone call, the fear and relief, the blasts of adrenaline, the ice cream. It all churned like a sea inside of me. I barely made it to the bathroom before I vomited until I was as empty as the promises I made.

18

"TZVI WANTS TO see you, little bunny rabbit." Naomi stood in the doorway. I don't know how long I had been sleeping, but the light filtering into the room was the orange of early sunset. It hit the dust flying in the air and cast a terracotta reflection, like tiny sequins were falling to the floor. I sat up slowly, feeling hollow both emotionally and physically. My hair was damp with sweat, from the effort of vomiting and then from the crying that had finally exhausted me to sleep. I tried to clear my head as I followed Naomi down the hall like the small, helpless animal she thought I was.

"Did you get the answers you were looking for?" Tzvi was at the desk, writing in something like a ledger; scrutinizing pages as he flipped through them. He didn't look up when he spoke. I had not been invited to sit down.

"How did you get that phone number?" The words felt like sandpaper against my raw, battered throat.

"Why don't you answer my question?"

"Why don't you answer mine?"

He turned in his chair.

"This house is a sanctuary and all are welcome, but we're not here to clean up anyone's mess. When Dov brought you here, we needed to know that your problems wouldn't become our problems. So we had our brothers and sisters still on the road check into things. We've been doing this a long time, Kait. We know a lot of people. It wasn't difficult to find out what we needed to know in order for you to safely be here." His glasses magnified the intensity in his eyes.

"You're a smart girl, Kait. You can see that we want to operate here without outsider interference. We certainly don't want the police dropping by, looking for someone that we've welcomed into our home, do we?"

I was thankful there was nothing left inside of me, or I might have been sick again. I swallowed, trying to move saliva down my dry throat.

"No, of course not." I hoped I sounded confident; normal. I moved towards him and put my hand on his arm.

"Thank you for what you did for me today. For what you've done for me since I got here. I'm grateful."

Tzvi stood up and walked slowly towards me, so that I was forced backwards until the back of my legs hit the side of the bed. I struggled to remain upright. He reached out, ran his fingers up and down my arms like a bow gliding across violin strings.

"Why don't you stay here for a bit; show me how grateful you are?" Involuntary feelings of arousal betrayed me but I stepped around him.

"I have shit to do," I said, as I walked out of his room.

He found me again a short time later, washing chipped dishes in the big sink. "Wear your necklace tonight. And a skirt. Be modest." I cocked my head towards him at the incongruity of the words he spoke. "Tonight?" I asked.

"It's the Sabbath and John is taking his name tonight. You will be part of the ceremony."

"I will?"

"You will. We'll begin just after sunset."

"What do I have to do?" I tried to seem compliant after our last exchange, weighing my need to have a place to live while I worked out my next steps against Tzvi's unequivocal power to toss me out the door.

"You'll sit to the right of me and you'll be a part of this community you're so grateful for. You'll drink from the cup I give you and smoke from the pipe I give you and you'll do whatever it looks like you're supposed to do as we support John through his journey. Do you understand?" He left before I could answer. I turned back to the sink and unplugged the stopper, watching the filmy water slowly drain out.

The people that had still been on Road Tour had arrived home that afternoon, emptying out of the second, smaller school bus the Pilgrims used, so the table was the most crowded I had seen it since my arrival. The seven returning Pilgrims were greeted warmly, but not with much fanfare. They seemed to integrate back into the fold easily enough, this was their home after all, but it threw me off balance a little bit to see faces I didn't recognize, or only recognized peripherally. Nobody was especially friendly to me, though there was no rudeness, either. When people came and went from their lives so frequently, it made sense that the rotating cast would not make much of an impression. I did, however, wonder if this was why Tzvi had told me to wear the Kula necklace. Perhaps it sent a message to those who had been away that I was not just the typical temporary squatter.

One of the Pilgrims that had just come back, sat to my right. "Giacomo," he said, leaning into me. I recognized him as the Pilgrim that had been with Dov in Olympia. "Kait," I said. I was about to attempt some small talk, ask him how the end of tour was, but just then, Naomi and a few of the other women stood and began to sing.

I recognized the song immediately; a prayer in Hebrew, and it stimulated a group of memories I had long relegated to the dust pile of my mind. I knew this prayer, had heard it often, but not for many years. The rest of the group followed with the prayer in English, reading from little spiral bound books that had been scattered down the length of the table, while Tzvi lit the two candles on the table in front of him.

Blessed are you, creator of the universe, who sanctified us with the Commandment of lighting these Shabbat candles.

Next, Tzvi poured wine into a heavy cut glass chalice and passed it around. It was much bigger than the Kiddush cup that I remembered from Friday nights at my grandfather's house when I was very little, but then, so was this gathering. As we each sipped the overly sweet wine, Naomi led once more in Hebrew, then we followed, reciting once more in English.

Blessed are you, creator of the universe,
who gives us the fruit of the vine.

Although my family was never overly religious, and became more and more secular as the years demanded a deeper commitment either towards or away from Judaism, the familiarity of the occasion was comforting and I felt a fondness for the group once again. All the women were dressed in relative modesty, as Tzvi had instructed me to do, wearing skirts that covered calves and shirts that covered midriffs. The guys all wore shirts, which was their threshold for occasion-worthy propriety. I drank deeply from the glass of wine that had been placed at my, and every, table setting (not as sweet, I gratefully noted) and smiled warmly at Naomi, who had sung the liturgy quite nicely. I was actually happy to be sitting by Tzvi;

to be given a place of importance at the table, and tried not to think of the fact that I had been commanded to do so. Nobody else knew about our earlier exchange anyway. As I was one of the few actual Jews at the table, I could claim my right to be here just as much, if not more than the others—this was *my* ritual.

But my feeling of familiarity and belonging was disconnected almost immediately, as Tzvi opened a box that was on the table and took out a pipe. He packed it tightly with weed and lit it, taking the first haul. The group chanted.

Blessed are you, gardener of this sacred plant,
may it be your will that it lead to my healing.

Ok, I thought, maybe not quite so much like it was when I was little.

After the pipe was passed around the table, with a pause to be repacked as necessary, the crew that was on canteen duty for the week began to bring in the food. It was a feast like I hadn't seen before at the house. Our meals were usually simple affairs—a spicy curry or chickpea burgers, always vegetarian, sometimes as humble as our own eggs topped with a pesto made from purslane foraged on the property. Tonight, the abundance of food was almost startling: there were steaming tureens of white bean and kale soup, platters of lentil loaf with miso gravy, a beet and carrot salad with a tangy, citrusy dressing, bowls of steamed vegetables dotted with herbed butter and plates heaped with the pickles that had been put up over the last week or so. Many of the ingredients came straight from the gardens here, and the dishes were met with enthusiasm and impressed exclamations from the group. The three Pilgrims tasked with feeding us stood in the doorway between the dining room and the canteen, looking gratified, before wiping their hands on dishcloths and joining us at the table.

The meal was joyous and unhurried, everybody talking and laughing with each other. Conversations overlapped as jokes and anecdotes bounced up and down the rows of Pilgrims sitting on both sides of the table. The newly-returned Pilgrims shared endless comic tales of triumph and toil on the road that had the group roaring in laughter, myself included, even if I didn't quite understand the genesis of some of the gentle razzing. The earlier stress of the visit from the cops seemed forgotten, or at least, had been washed away by camaraderie and food and a few more rounds of the pipe being passed.

As chairs were noisily being pushed back from the table to make way for full bellies, and scavenging fingers finally ignored the platters of picked-over food, Tzvi stood up. The banter around the table quieted.

"Brothers and sisters," he began, "let me start by thanking our creator and our three chefs for the delicious feast we've just enjoyed." Whoops and claps erupted around the table. "Kristin, Cedar, and Brady, you've honoured us well."

The three smiled, nodded their thanks for the acknowledgement.

"But of course, there's a reason we all gather tonight, in the midst of our friends, in the hands of our creator and in the garden of community we have planted. And that reason is that our brother, John, is ready to commit to our creator and to our friends and to this garden that nourishes and nurtures us, so that we may see clearly in times of fog, love readily in times of hate, and rely steadily on each other as we treat this life as merely one step in our journey, Pilgrims on a path to truth and light. Our brother John is here tonight to commit to walking that journey and as he does, he commits to shining that truth and light on others, whose journey is not yet clear before them."

At this, Tzvi rested his hand on my shoulder and I froze under its weight. It was the most preaching I had heard from Tzvi or anyone else in the time that I had been here, and I tried to accept his touch as a symbol of the support and acceptance he had just been talking about, and not as an accusation. He kept his hand there as he continued.

"John, tell us the name you have chosen for your true self, and for your brothers and sisters and for our creator to know you by." John stood up, pushed his hair behind his ear and looked around the table until he rested his gaze on Tzvi. He spoke clearly and calmly.

"In the midst of our friends, in the hands of our creator and, in the garden of our community, I will walk this path of truth and light and be known by the name of Ilan, the tree."

Another whoop erupted from around the group as people banged their forks on the tabletop and shouted Ilan! Welcome Ilan! Welcome our tree! Tzvi was clapping and nodding his approval, and I clapped alongside him as John, the lanky shy boy who left his small-town home in the Midwest and worked building fences and nailing down storm-battered shingles, became Ilan, a tree, whose roots were now solidly planted and who stood as though he had been granted the freedom to allow his limbs and branches to stretch all the way to the heavens.

Soon we were all outside and a bonfire was blazing in the pit. Several people had instruments: djembes and talking drums, bongos and tumbas, and still others held percussion instruments, shakers and rainsticks and even a gorgeous West African shekere, the large round head of the gourd shrouded in a web of hand-painted beads that resembled an intricately-patterned textile. The cacophony was rhythmic and joyous, and those who weren't playing were dancing around the fire, moving their bodies to whatever beat they felt in their soul. The celebration was bolstered by the returned Pilgrims, and by passing of both the pipe and a number of spliffs, but when I was about to accept one that Leary had rolled and lit, Dov put his hand on my arm to stop me. He leaned in close so I could hear him above the din.

"It has peyote in it," he said into my ear. I hesitated for a second, then accepted the joint from Leary and took a haul. I smiled at Dov, kissed him on the cheek, and joined the circle of dancers. I might not be a tree, or a bear or the light on a path, I thought, but I could be free. At least for tonight.

The party lasted well into the night, and although I only had one or two more hits of the peyote-laced joint, I was sure I felt it in the way my body was moving, first to the drumming, then to the music that blared from the sound system Giacomo, who turned out to be the resident DJ, had set up. The fire and the bass and beats and the Pilgrims all merged into what I considered to be perfection that night, the purest escape I had allowed myself there, and hours later, when Tzvi reached out his hand to me, I took it, allowed him to lead me to his room. I felt power in the pleasure we gave each other, my body continuing to dance and my mind continuing to lead me to new places until I was sure that for a moment, I felt the connection I had been told was waiting for me all that time.

Our collective hangover the next day was fierce and obvious, with almost every one sleeping half the day away before peeling themselves from bed only to find a new place to plop down and do nothing. The crash pad was full of the most brutalized of the Pilgrims, laying on the couches, leaning against each other on the thick mats, groaning any time someone dared to crack the shade to see if it was actually daylight outside.

I was on a chair on the back porch, wearing a floppy hat to keep my eyes shielded from the sun, which, even in its Pacific Northwestern anemia, still seemed too bright. I was tired and heavy, but there was a satisfaction to the fullness; a sense of happiness and peace in my low-grade suffering that I had been a part of a special night, that I had been one of the group; and was now one of the group nursing a colossal headache. Any of the others who could tolerate a little bit of daylight were also lounging on the back deck, not talking much besides the occasional snippet of conversation that would soon dissolve into the afternoon breeze. Dov, as usual, was being productive, making pitchers of iced tea and tidying the canteen. I had no idea where Tzvi was until I saw the door of the office open. I was only surprised because he hadn't, like the rest of us, given himself the day off. He usually went straight to his office in the morning, coffee in hand to check messages, go on the only computer on the premises and do whatever work he had to; I just hadn't expected him to do so that morning. I noticed that there was no coffee mug in his hand, and then he turned back—to speak to someone? As he stepped away from the door, the person he was talking to emerged into the light. Shoshana. What was she doing in there with him? There was a momentary curiosity about whatever business they had been doing in there together, but it faded quickly. It had nothing to do me, and the night I had spent with Tzvi had nothing to do with her. I closed my eyes and lifted my face up towards the sun as it peeked through the clouds, determined to enjoy its warmth for as long as it lasted. I hoped it would last a while.

I was dozing off in my chair when the growl of a motor woke me up. A Pilgrim named Thomas was barrelling onto the property atop his ancient, rusted motorbike, which he used to make quick trips to Pumps, the gas station-slash-general store about six kilometres up the highway from the property when someone was desperate enough for basic household item that they would pay the convenience rate charged at Pumps rather than travel the 45 minutes into town.

Thomas drove right up to the house, jumped off the bike, killing its engine and letting it fall in a dusty thump to the ground.

"He's dead!" Thomas shouted as he ran onto the porch. "He's dead! Ernest is dead!"

19

IT WAS A heart attack. It was a heroin overdose. It was a diabetic coma. Nobody knew for sure, the news that Thomas heard at the store conflicting with the news that Tzvi was getting via phone calls and news searches on the computer. But one thing was certain: Ernest Winter, lead singer of the Open Road for more than thirty years and the reason for this, *for all of this*, was gone, two days after the end of summer tour.

As the day went on, our reaction to the news changed. Some people were talking or murmuring *I can't believe it*, over and over; others were consoling each other while they cried and still others were almost aggressively seeking out whatever sliver of fact they could glean of the tragedy, as if knowing the circumstances would allow them to take the steps to undo it. We came together in groups then separated again, like a puddle of oil disturbed by a drop of water as we each searched for the best way to digest the information. Still others isolated themselves from the group altogether, picking up a hammer and pounding nails into the next fence post or pulling weeds in the late-summer garden; needing to keep quiet and keep busy and let the terrible, surreal news filter into their reality while engaged in an activity that felt real, solid, secure. And as tragedies often do, this one left us feeling adrift but connected, like a bouquet of helium balloons bobbing in the air, strings tethered together so none could come loose and float totally away. It felt like time was standing still, but the hours somehow passed.

As our communal shock gave way and the first tendrils of grief wrapped tightly around us, I wondered who we were now. A grope of Yellow Birds. A worship of Pilgrims. A cortege of mourners. A sadness of orphans.

Around the house, questions of *what happened* soon turned to questions of *what now?* Summer tour had ended in Tacoma where the Open Road was based, and we heard that Yellow Birds, some who were still in the state, and some who had hastily travelled back to it, were descending on the area in a growing human memorial for Ernest. We were so close that I thought the Pilgrims would be running immediately for the road to be part of the communal lamentation and celebration of Ernest's life; that they, more than most, had rights as the most primary of mourners outside his family. Weren't the Pilgrims a presence at every single show?

Weren't the Pilgrims so intertwined with the Yellow Birds that the fabric of the scene would somehow fray if they weren't there? Sitting on the cusp of the two groups, I felt an even more desperate urgency to be in Tacoma; to be with as many people as possible that understood; that *got it.* But nobody went anywhere, not that night. And Tzvi did not call for me despite my assumption that he would, so I retreated to the mattress on the floor next to Brady, acknowledging silently that I would have preferred the possibility of finding comfort and distraction in Tzvi's bed.

Sunday dawned grey and rainy, echoing the mood of the house. Nobody had prepared breakfast, so the canteen was crowded with people cooking their own eggs, making toast or rummaging through the fridge for leftovers from the naming ceremony on Friday night. The celebration felt like years ago, but barely thirty-six hours had passed. I poured myself a mug of coffee and took a banana from the basket on the counter. Just as I was sitting down at the table where Brady, Cedar, and Lindy were gathered, Tzvi came in to the room, followed by Dov, Shoshana, and Leary.

"Brothers and sisters, can we gather?" Tzvi gestured to the dining table while a few people got up to collect those who were not already at the table or flung on a couch in the crash pad. Once every seat was filled, Tzvi and the other three sitting like a council around the head of the table, he told us the plan.

"We will be going to Tacoma tomorrow." I was relieved. Nods and murmurs of approval floated around the table as Tzvi continued.

"Those who have just returned will not be expected to leave again, but Giacomo, if you could put together a work group to resupply our Holy Water stores and restock the big bus, that would be appreciated."

"Definitely," said Giacomo, who nodded to a few other people, tapping them for the task.

"So now what?" Asked Tzvi before answering the question himself.

"We have an opportunity here and it may be the last of its kind for a while. So we have just talked to our label suppliers, and they are rushing the production of a memorial t-shirt that Shoshana has designed. It's a memorial t-shirt for Ernest Winters and it is a calling card for our community. Along with giving away our Holy Water and administering first aid as needed, we are going to sell the t-shirts at the memorial and try to make enough money to keep us flush for a while. Everybody will want one because everybody will want to prove that they are a true fan and everybody will want to prove how sad they are that Ernest has died. We won't be the only people with this idea, so we have to get there first. And it looks like there will be no fall tour, probably no winter tour. We have no idea how long it will take the Open Road to regroup—if the Open Road regroups—and we don't have the luxury of waiting for them. We have operations here that rely on the donations we bring in from shows. If there are no shows, there is no money for operations. If there is no money for operations, there is no way we can sustain our community and grow it the way we want to. Does everybody understand?"

Around me, heads bobbed up and down but I just stared at Tzvi, at Dov. I understood. We were going to Tacoma but not to mourn, but to capitalize on Ernest's death and the sadness of the Yellow Birds. Nobody said anything, but I raised my hand for a second, then spoke.

"How did you put this into motion so fast?" I asked. Tzvi hesitated for a second. Dov, Leary, and Shoshana sat, stone-faced.

"I got word of Ernest's death early yesterday morning and asked Shoshana to start working right away. We were waiting for more details before telling the group when Thomas came back with his news."

Tzvi knew Ernest was dead and his first instinct had been to figure out how to make money off of it rather than even telling us that he had died. Was I the only one that felt this information like a punch in the gut? Looking around, I thought perhaps I was. I opened my mouth to say something else, but thought better of it. Tzvi was talking again anyway.

"Brothers and sisters, we mourn for our brother Ernest Winter and we offer blessings to his family and to his fans. We wish him a peaceful journey to our creator but we know that he is basking in the glory of our creator and we know—we cannot forget—that our love for our brother Ernest Winter is the love we feel for any living being, and to treat his death as the death of any part of who we are is to honour a false prophet. I urge every one of us to look to our creator and to each other for strength and solace and to remember that our community cannot be torn down so easily. We must do what we have to, to thrive and to fulfill the promises we have made to each other and to our community and to our creator.

"We will be sending a group to Tacoma. In the next few weeks, we will also be sending out scouting groups to various tours that we may be able to secure a presence at as we have at the Open Road shows. We hope that by time Open Road fall tour would have commenced, we'll have a plan for our community's near future. This is all still in the working stages of course, but we believe a path will become clear."

Tzvi didn't ask if anybody had any questions, he just got up and left. Shoshana and Leary followed him. Dov stayed at the table. The meeting was over; the message received. People began to talk about the t-shirt, about the plan, about the future.

"Do you think we'll have to move?"

"I want a t-shirt!"

"Ugh, I hope it's not Phish tour; so many people on acid for the first time."

I got up and went outside. Dov followed me.

"Tzvi would like you to go to Tacoma. I'm going as well." I turned to Dov, about to ask why the hell I would ever be part of a plan that took advantage of one person's death and thousands of people's sadness. But something stopped me. I had a decision to make. Dov had been so good to me; had done nothing but try to help me and make me feel like this was where I was safe and where I belonged.

"Sure, Bear," I said. "No problem. I'll go."

On Tuesday morning, the t-shirts were delivered. My first look at them made me think more highly of Shoshana as the design was beautiful and thoughtful. The shirts were dark blue on the front and featured a large rectangle, like a window. The shape was bordered by towering pines and between the trees, Ernest walked into a night sky that shone bright with the northern lights swooping into one corner, and dotted by yellow pinpoint stars across the rest of the dark space. Surrounding Ernest was the silhouette of small forest animals; bear cubs and deer, raccoons and foxes. Maybe they were following him or maybe he was following them. All of the figures were outline only, filled in black but distinct in their shape. It was a reference to an Open Road song called "Aurora" whose lyrics were printed below the window in an art-deco font:

I'll look for you in the stars in the sky
In the aurora borealis,
I'll look for you in the songs they sing
And in every story they tell us.

Ernest Winter, forever in our hearts and in our songs.
© Pilgrim Press

The design of the t-shirt also answered another question I long harboured about the Pilgrims and the Holy Water when I saw the scripture printed on the back:

For you are dust, and to dust you shall return.

So not a random pairing of lyrics and verse after all. This one, I noted, was subtle as well; better to not put someone off buying it due to religious protestations. Clever. We loaded them into the big Pilgrim school bus. The same bus that had brought me here weeks earlier. Here I was, getting in it again, to go down another road unsure of what I would find at our destination. Dov drove. John, in his first outing as Ilan, sat in the passenger seat, and I was behind them, sandwiched between Shoshana and another Pilgrim on the vinyl bench seat. There were others seated in the benches in the back, where I had sat on my way to the farm. Every Pilgrim on the bus had gone through a naming ceremony; had pledged allegiance to the community. Except me. I wondered if I was supposed to feel privileged or warned in being chosen for this task.

Tzvi hadn't called for me until Monday night. I was already sleeping, knowing we'd be leaving early the next morning, but Naomi woke me up around midnight and I went, slightly nervous that Tzvi was going to tell me he had changed his mind and I would not be going to Tacoma after all. I sat on his bed while he remained at his desk, barely acknowledging me, wondering if he was coming to join me; wondering what I would say if he did. Eventually I must have fallen asleep, because when I woke up, Tzvi was beside me, snoring softly, his body not even touching mine. I manouvered my way off the bed, careful not to disturb him, and in the thin dawn light, I had gone back to my room and packed my only bag.

Tzvi hadn't asked me to wear the Kula necklace to Tacoma, but I had it on anyway, and now I pulled it from underneath my billowy top so it hung between my breasts, bouncing as the van travelled over the country roads. Shoshana turned and looked out the window and I tried not to smile as the van merged onto the highway, heading south.

By the time we got to the park just outside of Tacoma that the Yellow Birds had gathered in (or more likely, been siphoned to), the crowds were nearly as big as they were for any Open Road show. People were grouped everywhere, in cross-legged circles shielding candles from the breeze; cloistered under trees where guitarists led people in singing Open Road songs; in rows by the walking paths, canvases stretched out in front of them where messages of love and *RIP Ernest* were being painted with watercolours. And around these groups more people moved, walking through the crowds so that, if viewed from above, the impression would be of interlocking waterwheels of varying sizes being fed by a human stream. Posters, some atop sticks and some clutched in outstretched arms, dotted the headspace, paper hats proclaiming devotion and mourning, all the sad lyrics given their due. From the more artistically-minded, the placards displayed magic marker drawings of Ernest, as an old man walking through the pearly gates; as the young man photographed on their first album; as the classic silhouette, long-haired and bespectacled, guitar in hand, sketched atop tie-dyed auras cascading out to the paper's edges. Flowers, some that must have been bought from nearby florists, and some that looked like they had been picked from nearby gardens, lay at the foot of trees as if marking Ernest's final resting place, but then, the mood was of a funeral for a deity, so why shouldn't every majestic tree act as headstone?

Tzvi's plan worked exceptionally well. Moments after we entered the crowds, each of us wearing one of Shoshana's shirts with an additional pile of a dozen or so draped across our arm, plus a pack full of Holy Water strapped to our back, people approached us.

"Great t-shirt; you got more?" A middle-aged man wearing a golf shirt and jeans pointed at the bundle in my arms.

"Yes, we're selling them," I said, offering him my most charming smile. "Twenty-five dollars." Tzvi had instructed us to start at twenty-five, but to accept twenty, or fifteen, or ten, or whatever that person had; not to say no to a reasonable amount. But of my first dozen sold, I was only offered less than the asking by one person brandishing a twenty dollar bill. We were also instructed to hand a bottle of Holy Water to everyone that bought a t-shirt, and to let them know about a meeting later that day. I heard a Pilgrim nearby reciting this message, casually, confidently and knew it would never be part of my sales pitch. "Hey brother, take some water as well; and why don't you come sit with us tonight by the west gates of the park? We're doing a sunset memorial, cool? Awesome, see you tonight."

As the day went on, the crowds grew, swelling by thousands as more and more people entered the park. The cops were being cool; there was nothing going on worse than the passing of a joint anyway. They seemed busier warning members of the general public that came to the gates that they might want to find a different path to jog or walk their dog that day, but lots of people that were most definitely not Birds strolled into the memorial anyway, curious, touched, amused, or all of the above.

When we needed to, we restocked the t-shirts from where Shoshana sat with the boxes near a copse of trees by the west gate that we were directing people to visit at sunset. On my third trip back to get more product and deposit some cash, I told Shoshana her t-shirts were selling like hotcakes. She was pleased. "Well they're gorgeous," I said, "Who wouldn't want one?" Shoshana asked me if I wanted to take a turn sitting in the shade. It was the nicest she had been to me the entire time I had been with the Pilgrims.

"I'm totally fine walking around—unless you wanted to stretch your legs?" But I had a feeling she preferred to stay with the inventory and the cash, so she assured me she was also fine staying at her post.

"See you soon," I said, relieved that she had done what I expected her to do and stayed put. I needed to be out walking around. The park was huge—acres and acres that had been donated to the city by a wealthy developer a hundred years before—and the crowds were getting denser by the hour. If I stayed in one place, I might never find them, and I was sure, I was *positive* they were here.

After another hour or so, I began to doubt myself; doubt my whole plan. We were staying in Tacoma tonight and tomorrow, but expected to be packed up and on our way back to the farm with whatever money—and whatever new recruits—we could collect by tomorrow night. Tzvi's thinking was that many fine young Birds would be left feeling unmoored, sad, unsure of what their next move would be, and that we should, as always, offer sanctuary to these confused and sad souls. "Our barn could be finished by winter," he told Liora.

If something was going to happen, it would have to happen soon.

There were several times when I thought I saw them; that the girl walking away from a group of people by the fountain was Vivi; that the guy with the hair falling over his eyes sitting near a drum circle, clasping his hands around his knees was Skate. I wouldn't mistake Eartha if I saw her. When I saw her. I was sure they were here; could almost feel it.

I had sold out of my stack of t-shirts again, but I had no intention of heading right back to Shoshana. I was contemplating what direction to head in next when Dov spotted me and came over. He was eating a hotdog he must have bought from one of the dozen carts that had set up on the street along the eastern perimeter of the park. Mouth full, he rubbed my arm in greeting. "Hey, how are you? This is crazy, huh?"

A group of Birds were sitting on blankets and swaying back and forth as they sang together. I agreed and took a drink from the bottle of Holy Water I was holding.

"They love the t-shirts; I'm sold out again, too—you heading back? I'll walk with you."

"No, not yet, I'm going to find a washroom and get something to eat—that looks good." I pointed at his hot dog, hoping he would not be keen to walk back where he had just come from.

He nodded, swallowed another bite. "Do yourself a favour and head to the restroom first because you're going to be in line for a while for one of these."

"Good tip. See you later." I walked away before Dov could change his mind, moving deliberately into a large crowd of people coming towards me—and then, right into Easy.

"Kait!"

"Easy!" We threw our arms around each other and held tight while the throngs pushed past us.

"Holy shit, Kait, where have you been?" We grabbed hands and cut a path to the lawn where there was room to stop.

"Oh my god, Easy, I knew you'd be here." I hugged him again and his arm around me was like a vise.

"Well I had no clue you'd be here. We heard you were with the Pilgrims or some shit like that."

"No," I said, "Well yeah, I am, but it's just temporary and I need to leave them and I knew you guys would be here. Please, Easy, please, can I come back with you guys?" I was trying not to babble or cry, but I hadn't allowed myself to think of a backup plan if this didn't happen.

"What? Dude, you have no idea." Easy said.

A panic rose in my chest. I had misjudged this.

"Kait," said Easy holding on to my arms and shaking his head at me, "We were coming to get you."

20

EASY DIDN'T KNOW where Eartha or the others were, but we made our way towards the lot where he had parked Big Blue Bertha, Easy gripping my hand in his like a child he didn't want to lose. We walked quickly, snaking through the crowds, and I was relieved we were heading to the south end of the park, and not west where Shoshana and the other Pilgrims were more likely to be. He turned to speak to me only once, as we passed a huge cardboard cutout of a guitar that people were drawing and writing messages on.

"Can you fucking believe this," Easy said, "Can you fucking believe Ernest is dead?"

"I can't believe any of this," I answered, but Easy had already turned back to face the direction we were heading, and I was sure he hadn't heard me.

Seeing Bertha was like seeing a long-lost old friend that hadn't changed a bit during our years of separation, and for one delirious second, I imagined running to the van and throwing my arms around it. But just as I refocused my mind as much as possible to the reality that I was actually here, the side door pushed open and JuJube jumped out, so I went quickly to where she stood and threw my arms around her instead.

"What!" JuJube demanded, then shook her head and laughed her maniacal laugh and hugged me back. She pushed me out of her arms. "Nice of you to show up," she said, shaking her head again. She was wearing my patchwork dress.

"I'm going to need this back," I said, tugging on the pocket. JuJube shrugged and grabbed a can of pop from inside the van. She pulled the tab, took a long swig, then handed the can to me. She was my long-lost friend that hadn't changed a bit.

Vivi returned next, gave me a hug, whispering, "Hi, my sweet," into my ear, then, acting as if I had never left (or never returned), proceeded to talk about the candlelight vigil that would be taking place later that night, and whether or not it would be too sad to actually attend. My being back caused barely a ripple for Vivi, just as my leaving probably did the same. I knew her well enough not to think too much about it.

I didn't want to make anybody feel unappreciated, but finally I couldn't stand it any longer. I had convinced Easy, who was fairly adamant about knowing what had happened in the past few weeks, that we should all catch each other up once everybody was back here together, but I was starting to get anxious again.

"Where are Eartha and Skate?" I asked.

Facing Eartha would be the toughest part of this reunion, but also the part I was dying for. I wanted to see my friend, for us all to get the immediate catch-up over with, because I was starting to worry that the Pilgrims would come looking for me. Maybe they had anticipated my defection, but even if they had, I still had to face Dov, tell him I wasn't coming back with them. A pang of guilt stabbed at me as I thought about Dov being the one to then tell Tzvi. Tzvi wouldn't care necessarily that I was gone, just that I had left. I was absolutely sure he cared more about his ego, his image, than me. But I felt bad for making Dov deal with that. It occurred to me that I could just never go find them; just stay in the van until we could leave; it would be so much easier that way.

My mother, my schoolmates, Eartha, Horizon—I had spaced on so many people already. The default to run had been there for so long and I wasn't sure I was strong enough to stop it. But I could change it. I could change direction. I didn't have to always run *from*; I could try running *to*.

I didn't feel like I owed the Pilgrims much, but I owed Dov a goodbye. And I owed it to myself to know that I had definitively closed that door, that I hadn't just run, or the guilt and shame of it would follow me around like one more cloud in the sky. And there were so many clouds in my atmosphere already.

After chatting for a bit but trying not to talk about anything too important, I asked Easy if I could go lay down in the van. He made an arced gesture with his hand.

"Mi casa su casa."

"Thank you."

Leaving Bertha's side door open, I moved into the dim light of the van and made myself a little nest out of the sleeping bags and pillows that were strewn about. For once, the mess of the space felt comforting and not annoying, and it wasn't until I was off my feet that I realized how tired I was. The world was just becoming hazy, the din outside the van just registering as white noise, when a head full of bushy blond curls poked inside of the van, casting my nest in shadow.

"Hey, thanks for saving us a trip to Yellow Bird Jonestown," Eartha deadpanned. "Nice shirt."

I scrambled up and over to where she was, hugging her while I knelt until we both fell over into the van.

"Are you laughing or crying?" Eartha asked, wiping my face with her hand.

"Both," I said as we sat up. That's when I saw Skate standing by the circle of chairs outside the van. He was smoking a cigarette, something I had only seen him do on very rare occasions.

"Hey," I said and was about to make my way out of the van to him, but something stopped me. I would have to tread lightly with Skate; for whatever reason, he didn't seem ready to welcome me back like a prodigal daughter or escaped cult member or hobo or whatever the hell I was right now, and I would have to respect his feelings, get our friendship back on track slowly.

But first, we all sat in the chairs, and I expressed my relief at seeing them and they expressed their surprise at seeing me.

"I knew you'd still be here," I said, "Tour just ended so there was no rush to get anywhere. I figured you guys would probably take your time, hang out for a bit like always. And then when we heard that Ernest died, and it was only two days after Tour ended—well, I knew you'd just stay here. And you did."

"That's kind of the story," said Eartha. She confirmed that yeah, they had stuck around after the shows ended, but it wasn't their intention just to hang out and party. They weren't exactly sure where I would be—if I was at the shows or on my way back with the Pilgrims, and they had already decided they were coming to get me—

"We were hoping we were coming to get you and not coming to be run off the property because you had decided to become one of Steve's wives or something," said Eartha. I swallowed hard at this, wondering exactly how much about my time with the Pilgrims I would tell them. Not that much for now, I decided, my reception still being a bit of a mixed bag. I glanced at Skate. He was sitting with us, but looking out towards the park.

Eartha continued. "So we wanted to give it a few days to make sure you were back at their property. And then Ernest died." We were all quiet for a minute.

"Ugh, it's so crazy," said Vivi, shaking her head, "What do we do now?"

"I need to go to Vancouver," I said.

"Oh. Okay. You do?" asked Easy. I looked at Eartha, could tell she already knew why. I nodded.

"Horizon's there," I said. Skate snorted at this, shook his head. *Gently*, I reminded myself.

"I spoke to his mother. He's going to be all right, but I have to go see him." Now Skate got up and grabbed the knapsack at his feet. He slung it over his shoulder and finally looked at me.

"What makes you think he wants to see you?" He asked, then turned and walked towards the park. I was stung by his words, but what he said had occurred to me as well. I didn't know if he wanted to see me. I didn't know if his parents wanted him to see me. But I was done running away; done leaving the threads of my life unfinished and fraying. Even if Horizon didn't want to see me, I had to go and find out. But first, I had to make sure that one last thread wasn't left to unravel.

Eartha offered to come with me and I accepted. "I'm not exactly the most intimidating person you'll ever meet," she said, "but if this turns into a tug of war over you, I'm not letting go until your arm snaps off."

"Gee, thanks," I said.

It had gotten late and I knew that Dov and the other Pilgrims would have gone to meet up at the west gate with Shoshana for the sunset service by now. I wanted them to all be together; it would be easier to make my intentions clear to them that way.

Ilan saw me approaching first. "Hey! Where have you been?"

Shoshana was angry. "Nice of you to show up. Do you know how many shirts you could have been selling?" But it was Dov who noticed that Eartha was with me.

He stepped forward, putting himself between me and the other three. He knew.

"What's going on, Kait?"

I swallowed hard. I didn't think this part would be difficult. I had been so anxious to see if my plan would work out, to try to find Eartha and Easy, that I never pictured this part of it.

"I have to go, Dov." He didn't say anything. Behind him, Shoshana stepped forward, but Dov put his hand out, stopping her advance. He refused to look away from me, and despite everything, I felt terrible to do this to the one person that had been my true friend in the house. But I didn't feel so terrible that I would change my mind.

"You don't have to go, Kait."

"I do. I'm sorry; I don't belong with you guys. I never did."

Shoshana looked disgusted, which I suspected was the most honest she'd ever been with me. She ignored Dov's hand and stood a little in front of him. I didn't move while she spoke. "No, you didn't. You don't deserve to be there. You don't deserve anything that Tzvi gave you. You don't deserve anything he did for you."

I nearly laughed. "No, you're right; I definitely didn't deserve it." She stared at me for a beat, then spun and walked away, quickly enveloped by the crowd.

"I'm sorry, Bear," I said to Dov. I looked at Eartha and gestured that we could go.

"Kait," he said. I turned around. "It's ok. Be happy. Stay hydrated."

I smiled at my friend. Then I took Eartha's hand as we walked back towards Bertha, but after a few minutes, I put my hand in my pocket and stopped abruptly. I still had the money from the last batch of t-shirts I had sold. It was over three hundred dollars. There was no way I was going back to the Pilgrims to return it, but I still had another opportunity to rid myself of something that belonged to them. As people pushed past us, I pulled the Kula necklace out from under my shirt, took it off and threw it to the ground.

PART IV

KAIT

21

WE ALL AGREED that it would be best to leave Tacoma the next day. It seemed as though the memorial for Ernest could last a week or more. But like everything the Yellow Birds got involved in, the scene in the park was turning into a circus.

More and more people were arriving, and they weren't really typical Yellow Birds or even Twinkies. These were not just the curious onlookers or Tacoma locals who wanted to see the freak show funeral mass. This wasn't just a memorial—it was an opportunity. The vibe changed quickly. By the end of the first day in the park, the Shakers were out, understanding well that collective grief was an easy in, a gateway narcotic for their business. And the hustlers were out in full force, ready to capitalize on the unfortunate occasion. I had once heard that there were stamps the Canadian Mint used for our coins that had already been cast with Prince Charles' likeness on it on standby, so that when the Queen died, our Canadian money could still be produced with no interruption. Were there also Open Road bumper sticker makers that had future-proofed their inventory for exactly this catastrophe? The Pilgrims weren't the only ones selling memorial items—candles, hats, and many additional t-shirts, each cheesier than the last, were being peddled to the masses, and the masses were buying these items up, commodifying their sadness, proving they had been there. The machine had to keep turning, right? Everybody got something from the Open Road.

"That's what killed Ernest," said Easy that night as we eschewed all starlit memorials for a few feet of space in front of Bertha, together. Even Skate was there. "He knew the band couldn't stop even though it was killing him. Too many people depended on Road Tour—how could he let them down, even when he was tired, even when he was burnt out, even when he was a junkie and nobody wanted to admit it."

"It wasn't just his staff you know," said Vivi. "It was us, too. We made him keep doing it."

"It's true," I said. "How many nights did he get on stage and sound like shit, forget the words? But we didn't send messages that made him think he should slow down and get healthy; We cheered and screamed and ran ahead of them to the next stop on the Tour and basically said, more, more, more."

"Well, where would all these yahoos go without Road Tour?"

"Where will they go now?" asked Eartha.

When they figure it out, they should let the Pilgrims know, came the involuntary thought. "Who knows," I said instead.

"Who cares," said Skate. "I'm done with this scene anyway."

We talked for hours that night, catching up on what we had been doing then veering off onto topics both silly and serious, the way good friends can. I answered a lot of their questions about the Pilgrims but felt oddly protective of them at the same time and I refused to condemn them even when goaded by Easy or prodded by Eartha, who seemed to know that there was more to my time there than I was letting on.

"What was that girl talking about, what did—Tzvi? What did he do for you anyway, and why wouldn't you deserve it?"

"Tzvi is Steve, the cute guy with the dark hair we used to sometimes see at the shows? He's essentially the leader. In the house, we called him Tzvi. Some people have taken Hebrew names. It's a whole ceremony." I tried to remember how I thought of Tzvi when I only saw flashes of him now and then at a show or by the Pilgrims' bus in the Field. It was hard to reverse my impression of him now that I was aware of him on a more intimate level, though I didn't want to tell them how closely I had come to know parts of him.

"What did he do?" asked Eartha.

"He . . . tried to make me feel like a member of the household. I worked in the chicken coops!" I said, changing the subject. We talked a little more about how the Pilgrims made their money, which I told them was definitely from selling weed and soliciting donations at shows, but that money didn't really seem like the primary motivator for the group.

"So what is it," asked Skate.

"Building a community. Being with people that believe in the same things you do. People that can feel like family."

"Family that can just get up and leave whenever things get tough or they think something or someone better came along?"

I tried not to let Skate see that his words had stung, or that I deserved them, and instead thought of Dov and wondered if he and the others would be going back to the house with one less Pilgrim, or if they would manage to find somebody to take up the seat in the bus that I left vacant.

The crowd thinned out around eleven that night, heading to vehicles or homes or hotel rooms. Others seemed to be staying put. The cops were definitely not going to allow tents to be set up, but some Birds clearly had the intention of staying in the park for the duration, crashing on the blankets they had been sitting on all day or trying to get comfortable on a bench if they could claim one. I knew the Pilgrims had two rooms booked in a hotel off the highway, and among the things I was very grateful for that day was the reprieve from having to share a room with Shoshana. But it felt strange not to be with them anyway. The Pilgrims back at the farm would all probably be hanging out together in the crash pad right now, would be singing along as Beckett played guitar, or sitting on the drooping back porch talking quietly about everything that had happened in the past few days. I had gotten used to the Pilgrims' energy; their presence and way of moving through the world, with a clear purpose and a focus that couldn't be dislodged by what other people were doing or expected them to do. And with this dedication, this belief that the way they lived was true and important, came an insulating sense of authenticity that protected the Pilgrims from the opinions, the rules, the influences of the rest of society. I had never seen people more comfortable in their own existence. I wasn't sure if that was devotion or freedom, or both, but I was envious that they had achieved it, even if I hadn't. Even if I never could.

And as happy and relieved as I was to be with Eartha and my friends in Big Blue Bertha, I wasn't even sure I knew the rhythms my friends moved to anymore. Easy and Vivi said goodnight first, used the public restroom inside the park gates then retreated into the van. JuJube followed up with the same routine a few minutes later, leaving me, Eartha, and Skate outside. It seemed like a good sign that he stayed behind with us, but I wondered if he had gotten everything about my return off his chest. Turned out, he hadn't.

"So are you sleeping here tonight, or are you going to go look for whatever adventure is next for Kait? You've already done the van full of hippies, the tragic hero, and the cult—maybe it's time to try out being a lesbian? Is there a hot girl you can crash with tonight? Or wait—I bet you could find some crew that's on their way to Belize to build a schoolhouse in the mountains or a well for an orphanage or some shit like that. What do you say? I can help you look."

"Skate, don't," said Eartha.

"No, it's all right," I said. "Skate, I don't have to stay here if you don't want me to. I can go; I can take a bus to Vancouver. But why are you so upset when I wasn't even around that long. You guys were fine before you took me in as a stray. I don't want to upset you. I can go."

Eartha put her hand out as if to lock me in the chair. Skate shook his head.

"Here's what you don't get, Kait. You act like being a part of someone's life couldn't possibly be important to them, that as soon as you leave, they'll forget you existed. So you act like a ghost, you disappear as though the space you left will just close right up like you were never there. And you think you're doing this, why? To protect yourself because your presence in someone's life is so insignificant? To protect other people from having to deal with you? But you know what you're really doing? You know what this crazy disappearing act actually does? It makes the people you left behind feel insignificant; like *we* never mattered to *you*, not the other way around. You're telling us how little you regarded our love and energy. When you just leave, you're not saying that you know you didn't mean anything to us. You're saying that we didn't mean anything to you. Is that really what you think of our friendship? Jesus, Kait."

Skate got up and walked away from the van. I watched him go until he turned a corner and did a disappearing act of his own.

"Kait . . ."

"Eartha, stop." We didn't speak for a few minutes, just watched people filter out of the gates and down the street past where we were parked. "Is that what you think as well?"

Eartha took some time before she answered. "I think you leave first, before anybody else can leave you."

The exodus out of the park continued for some time; holding bundled blankets or slung with bags across their shoulder, people clasped hands, walked slowly, didn't talk much. I wondered where these people would go. And then it hit me that this wasn't just over for now; this was most likely over for good. We were at the very end of something, and it wasn't just going to morph into something else, like the change of the seasons. This wasn't about being sad that summer's fun was over, while looking forward to cozy sweaters and apple picking in autumn. That's not how this was going to go. Ernest was dead. This was done. Then I thought about what Skate had said, and I thought about Horizon and I even thought about the Pilgrims, and I wondered if maybe this had already ended for me. I had left first. Eartha noticed me wiping at my eyes.

"I know, buddy. It's a sad day. But I'm happy you're here."

The melancholy parade kept going, illuminated by the streetlights and the occasional flickering of a lighter's flame. So many people were already headed somewhere else.

Thanks to the traffic leaving Tacoma and a long delay at the border crossing, the three-and-a-half-hour drive to Vancouver took nearly all day. Skate wouldn't really talk to me, but he had come back to the van late the night before while we were all already asleep, and moved into the crowded space beside me. He didn't touch me deliberately, but his leg was draped over mine when we woke in the morning, and he shared an apple with me on the drive north. He, Easy, Vivi, and JuJube would head to a friend's place in Whistler with the promise of being back down in the city in a few days, and me and Eartha were dropped off at her apartment on Commercial Drive. It was a big brick Edwardian flat above a shoe store with two bow windows jutting out over the street like bulging eyes and keystones over the three smaller windows between them. We entered from a door on the ground floor next to the entrance to the shoe store, where Eartha picked up a pile of mail scattered on the floor. Then we walked up two flights of stairs. Eartha's apartment was airy and spacious, with soaring ceilings and plastered walls. The furniture was all slip covered in loose linen, probably to hide the age of the pieces underneath them, but there was a plush white shag rug in the middle of the living space, atop nicely worn hardwood floors that squeaked when we walked on them, and a large, low coffee table in the middle of the rug between the couches. Eartha showed me the small galley kitchen with a beautiful big porcelain sink that led out to a back deck on the flat roof. Outside, remnants of plants withered like dry strips of parchment sat on a low bench that ran along the back wall. Back inside, we stopped in Eartha's room, which featured one of the bow windows, and then across the other side of the living room, the room I would stay in, which had the other.

"I love this place, Eartha, you are such a grown-ups."

"Nah," she said, putting a stack of towels on my bed.

"You have matching towels," I said. "Even the grown-ups in my life don't have those."

"My mother enjoys shopping," said Eartha. "I'm gonna shower, then you can shower, then let's go get some real food. Sound good, roomie?"

"Everything you just said sounds amazing." Eartha hugged me and kissed my cheek with a loud smack.

"Welcome home."

Dinner was fish tacos and tortilla chips dipped in spicy salsa from a tiny Mexican restaurant down the street called Cantina. Commercial Drive reminded me a bit of Kensington Market or Queen West in Toronto, with its restaurants, head shops, and used clothing stores, but it didn't really feel familiar beyond that. The people were different. There was a lot of tie-dye and Patagonia jackets and hiking boots, sometimes as part of the same outfit. Granola, we would have called it in Toronto, where the vibe was different, less self- (and health-) conscious. Then again, our skyscrapers were manmade of concrete and glass; the skyscrapers here were volcanic rock or shale and limestone. I was used to the ocean air by now, and Vancouver's felt fresher, crisper than other places I'd been to on the west coast, but the city I had seen so far felt a bit cheerless to me really, a bit grubby. I inhaled that fresh crisp air deeply and chalked my lack of enthusiasm up to the residual sadness and we had carried with us from Tacoma and the general intensity of the last few days.

You need to take the time to decompress, I told myself.

We chatted nonstop during dinner and afterwards, as Eartha showed me around the neighbourhood ("Stay away from Victoria and Hastings," she cautioned), pausing when she ran into someone she knew for a hug and a quick catch-up. We talked about lots of things and nothing important. Finally, as it was getting dark, we stopped and ordered green teas from a cafe near Eartha's apartment called The Sparrow, where a sandwich board outside read, *If You Don't Like Soy Milk, Moooooove Along!* Sitting at a metal table on the curb-side patio, cupping our mugs in our hands to absorb the comforting warmth, Eartha looked at me for a moment.

"Are you going to tell me what happened with Horizon?" her tone was gentle but it was clear she wasn't going to let me change the subject this time.

"He has a kid," I said.

Eartha's expression revealed that she didn't know this part of the story. "He has a kid?"

I held the cup to my lips, drank the fragrant warm tea, then told her everything that had happened since we last saw each other in Olympia. About Larissa, about Donovan, about the overdose and stroke. About Dov pulling me away from the scene there, the weeks I had spent with the Pilgrims, and my phone call with Horizon's mother. I told her about the fortuitous plan to reunite with her and everybody in Bertha that I was only able to make because our beloved Ernest died unexpectedly two days after Tour ended. And I told her about being with Tzvi. She prodded me for details, but reserved judgment.

"I felt so separated from the time I had spent with Horizon, like I was in a completely different reality there. It wasn't cheating on Horizon." I had said the words to myself countless times, but letting them exist out loud chipped away at the protective detachment I had coated them in. "I needed to do it, and then I wanted to do it. It was . . . confusing being there."

"You don't have to feel bad, Kait, I mean, Horizon found out he had a kid and then OD'd." We laughed at the absurdity, happy that we could.

"Yeah, but this wasn't revenge or because I was upset with Horizon; I felt terrible about abandoning him. I felt so guilty about not being with him that I would wake up having panic attacks. I had no idea what I was doing there with the Pilgrims at first. For whatever it's worth, Tzvi at least helped me feel something different." I didn't tell Eartha about the Kula necklace.

"So he totally took advantage of you. He's a pig."

"I wasn't afraid to say no to him. I didn't *want* to say no to him. It's complicated."

"I'm not judging you, Kait, but it sounds messed up."

"It's all been messed up, Eartha." Our mugs were empty by then, but I still clutched mine with both hands.

"So you're going to see Horizon?"

"Maybe. I need to figure out what I want to do first."

"You know you can stay with me as long as you want. You can stay with me forever. My mother pays the rent; we just have to pay the bills, so your half wouldn't be much. And hey, I guess I need a new plan now too. Maybe we can both go to UBC. What did you apply to university for anyway?"

"Women's studies. You?"

"International Economics."

I gaped at her. "Who are you?"

"I am your sister from another mister and the smartest damn hippie you'll ever travel in a disgusting van with." She stood up. "Let's go."

We walked the block back to the apartment and got ready right away for bed; we were both exhausted. We hugged each other tightly before heading to our own rooms.

"Sweet dreams; I love you. We'll sort out our lives in the morning."

"Love you too. Thanks for everything, Eartha."

"Don't mention it, buddy."

The mattress on the bed in the spare room was nothing fancy, but it was the most comfortable bed I think I had ever laid on in my life. Even with the noise from the street below, and the sense of the unfamiliar disorienting me, I was asleep in minutes.

22

OVER THE NEXT few days, Eartha and I tried to reacclimate to normal life. She had the slightly busy schedule of someone who didn't really have commitments but had been away from home for a little while, and needed to take care of things that had occurred or been ignored in her absence—banking, a dentist appointment, license plate renewal, and a meeting with her friend that owned the bookstore, Dog Eared, where she was looking to take on a few shifts. I had a slightly less busy schedule of reading newspapers and *The Georgia Strait* and wondering if I wanted to apply for any of the jobs I found in the classified sections that didn't require any particular skillset. But first, of course, I had to decide if I was staying in Vancouver, and as much as I wanted to make that decision independent of anything that happened when I next reached out to Horizon (assuming I would get past his mother this time), I knew that I wouldn't be able to truly say yes or no to a future in the city until I had made that phone call. There was another call I had to make but I was putting it off, which was tough when my days so far had been spent wandering the city with Eartha, drinking tea on the deck, and trying unsuccessfully to coax the plants out there back to life.

Easy, Vivi, JuJube, and Skate returned to Vancouver a few days after dropping us off, earlier than we had expected to see them, declaring that Whistler had become a "town full of wannabe assholes from Toronto and Australia with too much money and shitty weed." I interpreted this as code for, Easy owes someone money up there and can't pay them back and they haven't forgotten about it, or some such nonsense. So the gang was all back together again for a bit, taking no time at all to make a total mess of Eartha's lovely apartment.

It was fun being somewhere that had indoor plumbing with them. We had a really good time that first night they were back, laughing, talking, eating Chinese take-out straight from the paper boxes while sitting on the shag rug around the big coffee table. Later, we huddled on the back deck wrapped in blankets against the cool damp night and smoked some very lovely weed I assumed had not been brought back from Whistler. The strange reality that I was there, that I was out on the back deck of an apartment on the east side of Vancouver with my friends, began to sublimate.

"There's an ocean here, and mountains," I said, presumably out loud since Eartha nodded and said, "Yes, there are."

"And they just put a city right in the middle of it all."

"Yes, they did."

"And now you live here."

"Yes, I do."

"And there's Chinese food *and* mountain lions here." I thought this was quite a profound observation about the way man had inserted himself in this wild land, but everybody else just laughed.

"Yes there is," said Eartha.

"And I'm going to go eat it," said Easy, getting up and walking back into the kitchen.

"A mountain lion?" I asked.

"Yep," called Easy.

"Good," I said, nodding at the sky. "Devour the thing before it can devour you."

More laughing, and even though I was smiling and regarding my friends with fondness, I couldn't really understand what was so funny. My logic was sound.

The truce with Skate held. Although we were not quite back to our previous level of comfort and friendship, the animosity he had shown me in Tacoma had faded enough that when it came time to discuss sleeping arrangements, both Skate and I agreed that we would be sharing my room. We always slept next to each other when we were travelling together (unless Skate had found some other lady in some other van to sleep next to), and I didn't want to have to share a room with JuJube. What meagre possessions I still had needed to stay mine.

So Eartha would get JuJube and Easy and Vivi would sleep on the larger couch in living room, which was as worn as I had suspected under its slip cover, but also pulled out into a comfortable enough bed. ("No sex!" Eartha warned.)

I was already laying in bed facing the door when Skate came in from brushing his teeth and got under the covers. He lay on his back, his head resting in his folded hands. I was tired from smoking so much and eating so much and staying up late, but I suspected Skate was not quite ready to let me sleep. He soon proved me right.

"Are you staying in Vancouver?"

I turned onto my back as well, glad we had the darkness of the room to help diffuse any awkwardness between us.

"I'm not sure yet. Are you?"

"No. I think I'm going to go back to Calgary for a while. Go home."

"Do you think there will ever be another Tour?" I asked him.

"A Road Tour? Maybe. Probably. I mean, it won't be the same, but I bet the rest of those guys will still want to play together. Maybe in a couple of years."

"But who will they get to sing?"

"I don't know. They've done stuff with lots of people over the years. Maybe someone who's toured with them before? Tom Cochrane or somebody."

"No, he cannot sing Ernest's songs. Maybe a girl. Maybe Natalie Merchant."

"Maybe Natalie Merchant. Yeah, she would sound good. Let's go tell their manager that we've figured it all out."

"Good plan. Let's figure out world hunger next."

Skate chuckled but then paused. "Let's figure out how to be friends again next."

"It's okay. We have."

I could tell he was starting to say something else, but he stopped himself.

I dreamed that mountain lions that were walking down Commercial Drive. I watched them from the window of my bedroom, which was still the spare room in Eartha's apartment, but it looked exactly like the bedroom I had in my parents' house when I was a kid and we were all still a family.

The gang left two days later; JuJube went back to Whistler because somebody had told her they could get her a job up there for the ski season and clearly she didn't mind Torontonians or Aussies that much, and Easy and Vivi were going to her mom's place in Chilliwack. Skate was going to hang out with them there for a while, Vivi's mom being notoriously nonchalant about taking in strays, then he would take a bus to Calgary and sort things out for himself at home.

"Calgary is shit," he said, "But it's home. I miss my mother's cooking."

"I get it," I said.

But I didn't really. Even if I missed home, there would be nobody cooking for me there. I did miss the notion of home; the idea of it. I could conjure nostalgic feelings that seemed like affection for the place I grew up, but not many, and not for long. Any snapshot of idealism usually revealed itself as simply a moment's refuge from turmoil. I could remember perfectly the feeling of sitting on my bed, my room a sanctuary at age thirteen or fourteen, listening to a particularly sachharine song over and over again because it resonated in a deep, spiritual way that nearly defined my maudlin mood that year. But when I zoom out from that snapshot, I recall the moment had occurred because my mother had just screamed at me in front of visiting school friends for disturbing her with our boisterousness. My friends had quietly left and I had fled, humiliated, to the asylum of my room and my stereo and the resonant voice of a woman who wore heavy black eye makeup and sang of being misunderstood. It was hard to feel fondness for a place where happiness had almost always disintegrated into chaos.

Knowing that I would still have to deal with that chaos if I did return to Toronto quickly overrode any desire I had for home cooking.

I wasn't sure yet if this could be home, but I knew there was something I had to do before I could ever find out, and I couldn't put it off any longer. The next day, after everybody had left and Eartha went to go work her first shift back at Dog Eared, I poured a big glass of water, steeled myself, and picked up the phone.

Three rings. Four. Five, and I was about to hang up, but on the sixth ring, a distracted, curt greeting. I took a second.

"Hi, mom."

The conversation was brief, even more disorienting than I had anticipated. My mother was preoccupied. "I'm just very busy right now; you know the Gallowitz family down the street has moved out and I'm afraid the new family will be here today." She felt that she had to watch for the truck; watch for objects falling off the truck or anything they might put at the curb later. "Do you have any idea what people will throw out?" she asked.

"Garbage, mom. Garbage." I sighed. I told her where I was; gave her a loose timetable of where I had been. "Yes, yes," she kept saying. I tried to word the next part carefully.

"So, mom, were you—were you worried about where I was?"

"No, no, no; I knew you were fine and anyway, you don't care what I worry about."

That familiar bitter tone would usually have exhausted me or made me mad, but today I was just confused by it.

"I thought—I thought that maybe you wanted to get in touch with me while I was gone."

"Your father did."

I wasn't sure I heard her right. My father?

"He did? Mom, are you sure?" I wondered if this had been before or after I had left him the message and probed for more information.

"Yes, I'm sure. He wanted to know where you were when he came to get Janine."

In bits and pieces, interrupted by concerns about a broken vase and glue that might be too old to cement it back together, various pauses to look out the front door for a moving truck, and a stretch where I was put on hold while my mother answered the call waiting beep ("Wrong number," my mother casually trilled when she finally returned), I got enough of the story to figure out what had happened.

She said that when my dad was in Toronto in May, Janine had asked to live with him. He was going to be moving again, this time to a research job near Winnipeg, which I already knew from his visit. Apparently, Janine wanted to go with him. To live with him. Janine hadn't said anything to me. But when my father was back in Toronto about a month ago ("For a conference," my mother insisted, "Not to see your sister, no, no, no, he was only here for a conference."), Janine left with him. But he also wanted to know where I was, and when my mother answered, "How the hell should I know?", he got angry with her, and told her that she should have called him if I was missing. I'm sure Janine told him that I wasn't actually missing, but I had only checked in with her once, while I was still in Big Blue Bertha.

"He has no goddam right," my mother kept saying, but I wasn't sure what it was he had no goddam right to. To care about where I was? To demand information from my mother? Or to take my sister? But she didn't fight him or Janine, didn't try to stop either of them.

"I am busy too, you know." She said by way of explanation.

"Mom," I said, "Mom! Can you please let them know that I called; that I'm fine? Tell them, please? Tell Janine?" I wanted to say more, but she cut me off.

"The truck! The moving truck! Listen, I have to go. I have to go!"

I thought that calling my mother and ending my months-long avoidance of that reality would be like checking a box. Done, I could tell myself, for better or for worse, whatever the result was. I could let her know I was ok; make sure she was ok. But our phone call had only revealed an entirely new checklist of things I had to figure out, even if there was not much I could actually do about a lot of it. I had to call my dad, talk to Janine. But my nerves felt like a sprung lock, unfastened and vibrating. I thought about the timing of the call I made to my dad from the Pilgrims' and the timing of his return to Toronto. What had I actually said in the message I had left on his machine? I could only recall the grimy service station where we had stopped and the payphone on the wall near the restrooms. But the details of the call were as foggy and distant as an early morning in the Cascade mountains.

I needed to shake off my unease and refocus. Outside, the rain that had been coming down earlier had stopped, and though the sun wasn't out, the air had an inviting freshness to it. I pulled on a hoodie and decided to make my first foray onto Vancouver public transit.

I was only waiting for a few moments before a bus stopped in front of me. Stanley Park, read the block-lettered banner atop the front. I got on. From my window seat near the middle of the vehicle, I watched the city go by. Shops, restaurants, empty buildings. I tried to commit some of these to memory as landmarks, but my constant attempt at re-centreing on a map I wasn't familiar with became confusing and I gave up trying to figure out where I was. Instead, I watched the people as we drove past them. Men in suits, women in heels, groups of students, joggers, couples holding hands. The drizzle had begun again, but it didn't seem to deter people from being outside, or maybe they had no choice. I wondered not about who these people were, but what their story was; would I want it to be my story? Would I want a place to walk to in the drizzle here? Could I be one half of the couples holding hands? Would Horizon be the other? The bus stopped periodically to let riders off or pick riders up. I stood up and pulled the window open a crack despite the misty rain finding its way in with the breeze.

My thoughts wandered. *Look at it here.* Tour, and its endless road trip was surely over. This place offered me simpler highways. Did I want them?

My favourite game to play with my father was giving objects real and made-up collective nouns. They were always so much more interesting than their solitary counter-part. Who would want one caterpillar when you could have a kaleidoscope of butterflies. Why have one duck when you could have a plump of waterfowl?

Why struggle to get through this life on your own when you could be part of a family? None of us lived in isolation unless we worked very hard for that to be the case. The relationships in nature were almost all massive life-giving orgies, symbiotic and dependent on each other for survival. The nurse trees, the lichen on the rocks, the birds in the branches; nature didn't exist in a sovereign state. I thought of my mother in the basement with her things; of my sister willing to resurrect a relationship with a father she hardly knew rather than feel alone. Once when I was little, I asked my dad what we call a group of people.

There are lots of names for that group. What's your favourite, he responded.

Family, I told him.

Stanley Park came into view. It was buttressed on every side by nature—the mysterious ocean, the solid mountains, built to last, and the forests; the trees were ancient giants. Through the open window I could smell the park, earthy and damp and almost oppressively verdant. Just inside the park's boundary, the bus stopped and the doors opened with a hydraulic sigh. I made my way to the front door behind several other passengers also disembarking, and as I did I watched out the windows, surveying the area to plot my course in to the park.

"Thank you," I said to the driver, but stopped short on the bottom step. Nearby, outside a small squat building that was perhaps a block of washrooms or maybe visitor information, a group of guys were playing hacky sack. One of them had his back to me and I had almost convinced myself I was seeing things when he turned around to pluck the missed beanbag from the ground. He was wearing one of the Pilgrims' memorial t-shirts, Shoshana's design unmistakable now. Someone slammed into my back, and I gripped the handrails, almost losing my footing.

"Sorry, sorry," I said as I turned around. A woman in a straw hat with binoculars around her neck was glaring at me. "Sorry," I said again. "Wrong stop."

After the driver gave me an irritated wave of his hand that yes, that I could re-board the bus, I quickly made my way back to the seat I had just vacated.

We continued on a route I didn't recognize and it soon became clear to me that the park was not the apex of the trip. We were not going right back to Commercial Drive, to Eartha's. It didn't matter. I didn't want to go back yet. Didn't want to go back to any of it. How long could I stay on this bus? We crossed over water, False Creek, the sign on the bridge said, then continued slowly, making our way down streets whose names I didn't recognize, past people whose faces I didn't recognize. Could I recognize anybody anymore? Yellow Birds, Twinkies, Pilgrims; everybody was essentially the same, we just called them something different.

The bus turned off the city road we had been travelling and into an area that was more residential. The homes were a mix of arts-and-crafts style, with large, inviting porches and siding painted in watery, coastal colours and mid-century bungalows with low, wide windows, plus some newer, modern houses built on the footprint of tear-downs, all glass and angles. Many of the houses were set back from the street on a bit of a rise, with gates at the bottom of white-washed stairs that led to front decks. I let my thoughts drift to what it would be like to live in such an inviting house on such an inviting street, and if I would ever get the chance to find out. The bus halted at a stop sign, and I turned to the other side of the street, catching a glimpse of the street signs jutting out of the top of a post at 45-degree angles to each other. My heart leapt and my mouth went dry. I jumped up and pulled on the string to signal to the driver to stop. I pulled it again and then again in rapid succession. I grabbed my bag from where I had put it down on the seat beside me and walked quickly to the front of the bus.

"Right stop this time?" The driver pointedly asked.

I held on to an overhead rail and peered out the front window, looking for the bus stop, hoping we would approach it soon. A few blocks further and the bus stopped. I quickly exited and the bus pulled away. I stood, not moving for a moment, my breathing shallow. The street was quiet. There was nobody walking towards or away from me. I looked at the houses on both sides of the road, then dug into my bag for the pouch I used as a wallet. Scared for a minute that the thing I sought would not be there, I pushed coins out of the way until my fingers came upon the folded piece of paper.

The note was where I had put it after my phone call with Horizon's mother. I tried to ban Tzvi from my thoughts even as I re-read the words he had written. His handwriting was blocky and clear, sure of itself. The only waiver was in my own hands as I peered at the address number, then at the houses in front of me. I was on the correct side of the street, but had gone too far. I walked back in the direction the bus had come from, my heart beating faster and faster as I realized that I had already passed the house Horizon lived in. Which one, which one?

After intently tracking the numbers on the houses, walking as they tallied backwards like a ticker counting down to New Year's Eve (*or a bomb's explosion*, I couldn't help thinking), I stopped short a half a kilometre or so from where I started. The number on the house matched the number on my paper. This was it.

I walked up the stairs to the two-story Craftsman-style house. It was so pretty, with cedar-shake siding that had been painted a dark ocean blue, offset by white windows and white trim. On either side of the stairs, the slight incline was landscaped with shrubs and grasses giving way to a colourful wildflower garden that met the front porch. I didn't remember passing the house the first time.

Standing by the door, I fought the urge to turn and run, afraid that his mother would answer; afraid that he would; afraid that a stranger would have replaced him. And I was afraid to leave because despite everything that had happened, I believed that my collective noun was right beyond the door.

23

AMONG THOSE WITH medical and esoteric practices, a phenomenon called The Rumpelstiltskin Principle is widely accepted. It is the belief that we are able to better know a thing once we name it. And in this naming, we neutralize any unbalanced power structures, or, as in the eponymous fairy tale, gain power over the thing that had been plaguing us. Doctors use this principle to help patients come to terms with disease and disorder; professors use this principle to quickly build trust and repoire with students. Someone's name is usually the first thing we ask of a person, the first lesson we teach a child about herself. It is the cornerstone of our identity, and the thing that lovers whisper in the dark. What's in a name? Everything.

I knocked. Waited. Horizon answered.

"Kait," he said.

We held each other for a long time in the doorway of his house. Horizon was thinner in my arms, but the arms that held me were still strong; still true. I buried my head in his chest; he buried his head in my neck and we didn't sway, didn't dance, didn't move. Behind him, I heard footfalls coming down the stairs, but we didn't break our tableau. After a moment, more footfalls, going back up.

We got cold in the doorway, warmed each other, got cold again. Finally, the Vancouver rain began in earnest. We stepped over the threshold. Horizon tipped my head towards him and looked at me with sadness and relief in his eyes, which mirrored the very things he was seeing in mine. Tears clouded my vision for a minute, but I smiled, wiped them away.

"Kait, you're here," he nearly whispered.

"I'm here," I said. We held each other again. "Horizon," I said, "Can I ask you to do something?"

"Yes," he said, "anything."

"Please call me Ari."

ACKNOWLEDGMENTS

People say that being a writer can be a lonely profession, so I will count myself eternally lucky that there are so many who have stood beside me during this process and allowed me to feel endlessly supported—and never once alone on this wild ride.

To Rebecca Eckler, Chloe Robinson, and the RE:BOOKS team, thank you for choosing Yellow Birds and for guiding it into the world with enthusiasm, encouragement, expertise, and tenacity. Your faith in this story and this first-time novelist has been nothing less than soul-affirming. I am so happy and proud to be part of the RE:BOOKS family.

To my hilarious and talented editor, Deanna McFadden, I will never again allow a protagonist to gaze, stare, look, glance, or regard with impunity. I promise. And I still don't know where all the 'E' names came from. Thank you for helping me make it all make sense.

Thank you to my earliest readers, those who have offered feedback and those who have championed this book from the beginning. Rebecca Keenan, you are first in that line and the person that was literally there when the first lines of Yellow Bird were conjured into existence. Thanks to you and our partner in crime, Louise Gleeson, for the laughter until three in the morning, the unwavering reinforcement of many good ideas and some very bad ones, and miles and miles of group chat transcription that keep me going.

To the OG MMM—we connected because we loved and respected each others' words, and stay friends because that love and respect so easily translated to into real, and sometimes surreal, life. Emma Waverman, Nadine Araksi, and Emma Willer, thank you for the adventures, the hilarity, the advice, the unmatched championing of this project, and so much else. Where would I be without the head, the heart, and the cruise director?

To my Williams family, moving here to be closer to you all and have the space and time to write was one of the best decisions we ever made.

You constantly show up for us and for each other and it is something I cherish. Thank you for helping me find home.

My sibs, Jennifer, Jared, and Karla—when I write, it is for your ears first. We know what we share, what we've lost, what we have experienced, and what records were playing through it all. There is nobody I'd rather have all around a table together, especially as we watch that table continue to grow. And thank you to our mom, who never once told us not to embark on an adventure, not to take that chance, not to hit the road at age 16 to see Grateful Dead shows all summer. Although I'm not sure we asked.

To Mischa and Cassidy, my barnacles, my loves. Thank you for your joyous energy, enthusiasm, and for not asking to hit the road at age 16 to follow a band around two countries. You two are my everything and I am grateful and privileged to be your mama.

To Chris, who literally said yes to upending our lives a decade ago so we could live a simpler, more creative life that has led to this moment—there is truly nobody else I would rather be moving through this world beside. Your love and support is matched only by your keen sense of storytelling and problem solving, and thank you for helping to make this book better in dog-walking increments and middle of the night whispered chats. It's you I love.

And finally, to everyone who understands the magic of the shows and travelled there with me, in a crowded blue van, or a stickered up Honda Civic, or a '67 Ford Falcon with no windshield wipers, or a Greyhound Bus leaving from the parking lot of a neighbourhood school. And to the memory of our friends, Nady and Matt. May the music never stop.